Inga Simpson began her career as a professional writer for government before gaining a PhD in creative writing. In 2011, she took part in the Queensland Writers Centre Manuscript Development Program and, as a result, Hachette Australia published her first novel, *Mr Wigg*, in 2013. *Nest*, Inga's second novel, was longlisted for the Miles Franklin Literary Award and the Stella Prize, and shortlisted for the ALS Gold Medal.

Inga won the final Eric Rolls Prize for her nature writing and completed a second PhD, exploring the history of Australian nature writers. Her first book for children, *The Book Of Australian Trees*, illustrated by Alicia Rogerson, was published in 2021. While finishing the first draft of *The Last Woman In The World* she was evacuated twice as bushfires engulfed surrounding settlements. She lives near the coast among trees.

Also by Inga Simpson

Mr Wigg
Nest
Where the Trees Were

Non-Fiction

Understory: A Life With Trees

For Children

The Book of Australian Trees

INGA SIMPSON

THE
LAST
WOMAN
IN THE
WORLD

SPHERE

SPHERE

First published in Great Britain in 2022 by Sphere
This paperback edition published by Sphere in 2023

1 3 5 7 9 10 8 6 4 2

A CIP catalogue record for this book
is available from the British Library.

ISBN 978-0-7515-7856-0

Typeset in Horley Old Style by Palimpsest Book Production Ltd, Falkirk, Stirlingshire
Printed and bound in Great Britain by Clays Ltd, Elcograf S.p.A.

Papers used by Sphere are from well-managed forests
and other responsible sources.

Sphere
An imprint of
Little, Brown Book Group
Carmelite House
50 Victoria Embankment
London EC4Y 0DZ

An Hachette UK Company
www.hachette.co.uk

www.littlebrown.co.uk

For Lisa

prologue

They knocked again, louder this time. The lights were on, the fire was crackling and smoking – there was no pretending she wasn't home. It was like her worst nightmare, someone getting inside, appearing next to her bed, being unable to move or speak. But she was wide awake.

Move. This time – you have to act. Rachel reached for the poker, forced herself to her feet and across the room, socks silent on the floorboards. She waited by the door, back flat against the wall, poker by her side. *Breathe, Ray. In through your nose, and out through your mouth.*

They hadn't come through the gate, up the road. And no one could descend the cliffs behind – well, almost no one. Not without rope and kit. They could only have come from the river – *that wooden sound: oars, a boat*. In all the years, no one had ever found their way out to her property, turned up. Which was exactly as she wanted it.

They knocked again – and kept knocking. Rachel tried to breathe, to think through the noise. She wiggled her toes, clenched her hand tighter around the poker handle. The doors were locked, the windows locked, the perimeter secure. It had taken some doing, fortifying the old cottage against the world. Whoever it was would probably go away if she stayed quiet, if she could stay calm. Most of the things she worried about never came to pass.

'I know you're in there. Please – help!' It was a woman's voice. A young woman.

Then, a baby crying. It *was* real. The shrill notes, and the distress in them, shut down her thinking, her breathing. The room started to spin, the fire to roar. She slid down the wall, until she was crouching on the floor, arms around her legs, still gripping the poker. *This isn't happening.*

the river

one

Rachel pulled the molten glass from the heat, liquid bright. She closed her lips over the end of the pipe, and blew. It still took her full lung strength to force the first tiny bubble of air into the glass, beginning its transformation. Then, back for more heat. Blowing was easier now, just a steady gentle breath, and again. All the while rolling the pipe in her hands. Glass had to be kept turning, or it would stretch and blob out of shape. It was all centrifugal force, second nature to her now – moving without thinking.

More heat, then three steady strides across the polished concrete floor, pipe held level, to the chair she had made, its steel arms for supporting the pipes, rather than for comfort. She cupped the glass with the cherrywood block, shaping its surface, rolling the pipe back and forth with the palm of her hand.

Then heat again – the glory hole – resting the pipe on the trolley, pushing it forwards with her boot, her goggles reflecting orange. She stood tall and swung the pipe, dropping it out, using gravity to elongate the vessel. Heat, breath, turn, move – there was a rhythm to it. She could do it in her sleep. Indeed, her dreams often were of glass.

Outside, the unsettling wind that had hung around for days had finally stilled. The floor-to-ceiling windows gave her a clear view up the slope to the bluff. Straggly ironbarks and mahogany gums clung on. She could see only trees and rock, nothing man-made for miles. Lorikeets chirruped and squawked in the treetops, little rainbows every one of them, more beautiful than anything she could make.

She flattened off the base, pushing the wet paddle against the glass until it steamed and smoked. It was two-parts mechanical, turning out identical vessels, but some magic remained, the old alchemy of combining the elements: earth, fire, air, water. With the world changing so fast, it was grounding, something she could control. And with sand in short supply, every piece was precious.

Rachel opened up the vessel with the tip of the tweezers and teased out the shape, the glass fluting and flaring at her touch. It was the most delicate part of the process, and the most pleasurable, where she still lost herself, every time. When the spirit of each piece emerged and took its final form.

It had been love at first sight, with glass, on a school excursion. There were all sorts of artists at the studio, working wood, metal, clay, canvas and paper, but Rachel never left the hot shop. It might have had a little to do with the glass blower's tattooed biceps, the contradiction in the delicate spheres he shaped with his breath. Like the paradox of glass itself; so tough in molten form, so fragile on the shelf.

She touched a drop of water to the baseline, watched it fizz,

6

and tapped the pipe. The vessel – an oversized drinking glass – dropped safely into her hot mitt. A flash with the blowtorch to smooth the break, pressing in her stamp – and it was done. She set the finished piece next to the other five in the annealer, their colours already deepening. They needed two full days to cool. Too quick and the glass would lose its clarity, shatter too easily. It was her most popular combination, the rich blue working magic with the opacity of the white, like a swirling, cloud-flecked sky.

She tidied her tools and refreshed the timber water buckets. At the tub, she removed her goggles, splashed her face with water, and scrubbed her hands, wiping them on the front of her overalls.

Last week's batch – her 'Purple Rain' vases – were ready to send out. She wrapped each one in a sock of eco-foam, and slipped them into their individual recycled cardboard boxes. Every box was stamped with her mark – the stylised phoenix she had come up with in her art school days, refined by a highly paid designer in her exhibition and biennale days. She still thought about those big pieces. The one-offs. Months of work coming together in an exhausted birth of heat, colour and light. The wonder on people's faces when they saw the installation for the first time. It was only through fire that anything was really transformed.

Rachel packed the boxes into larger cartons, two rows of three, like eggs. The stack was growing. Her delivery woman, Mia, would take them, and then the couriers would deliver them to galleries, museums and stores – into people's homes. The glass still travelled, in a way she no longer could.

She slid open the timber door, fresh air cooling her cheeks.

She turned her face to the blue sky, to fill her lungs. Above the courtyard walls, the spotted gums were heavy with blossom, a hint of honey on the air. And something else, something unfamiliar.

She crossed the bricked space in seven strides, pausing at one of the raised vegetable beds to pluck a handful of rocket. She scraped her boots off on the step and slipped through the sliding glass doors into the sun-drenched kitchen.

It would be a meagre lunch: the last of the bread, a cracked heel of cheddar from the fridge. She was almost out of dairy. Other things, too: gas for the stove, her medication, books, supplies for the studio, her monthly *GlassWorld* magazine. Mia was overdue.

Over the years, Rachel had simplified everything: just one person coming in and out, one person to deal with. She had known Mia all her life. Her long grey hair and quiet determinedness, like the little van coming every fortnight, was one of the few things she could rely on from the human world. But they had never really figured out a backup plan.

Still, there was plenty in the pantry, the narrow galley-space between the floor-to-ceiling shelves she had built herself. Dry goods on one side, her lidded glass jars holding flour, sugar, grains, cereals, herbs and spices. The other side was all colour: preserved peaches, pears and apples, blackberry, raspberry and rosella jam, pickled vegetables, bush-tomato relish, fruit paste, chunks of honeycomb – all lit up beneath the skylight like a stained-glass window. Almost everything came from her garden, or the surrounding bush. But it was the finger lime pickle she was after, the last small jar from the top shelf.

She ate her sandwich on the back step, in the sun. The lime was sharp against the cheese, its pulp-bubbles popping against the roof of her mouth. Everything tasted better outside, when she was working her body – making things.

The feeling hit before she had finished chewing. That familiar warning, low in her belly. She used to shake it off, wait to be proven right. But that was *before*. Now she trusted herself, her body's senses, implicitly. She had to.

The lorikeets took flight all at once, an uplift of colour and noise. Rachel padded inside, placed her plate and glass on the sink, all without a sound. The row of monitors in the laundry showed nothing. The gate was locked, no one on the road. No fresh tracks. There was nothing in the driveway. The rendered brick wall that surrounded the house was clear on all sides. She counted the chickens, picking over the garden beds: all present and accounted for. The river was calm and empty but for a white-faced heron stalking the shallows, and a cormorant hanging her wings out to dry on the end of the jetty, a dark-feathered cross.

She took the stairs two at a time, up to the timber mezzanine where she slept, grabbing her binoculars and flinging open the window all in one movement. There was only undisturbed forest for miles, the town in the distance. And between them, the slow-winding river, shifting back and forth with the tide. A slight smoke haze was the only thing out of the ordinary.

Sometimes it was someone else's fear she felt, channelling it like a tuning fork. But there was no one for miles. The nearest property was a weekender, and it wasn't the weekend. 'It's nothing,' she told herself, taking the stairs down more slowly, pushing back the wave of unease. *It's never nothing.*

She lit the gas under the kettle, spooned tea leaves into the pot. Somehow her hands sent the pile of letters waiting on the bench tumbling: to her sister, her agent, her accountant, the department of revenue. *Keep it together, Ray.* It wasn't so much the clumsiness that had been creeping in – a death knell for a glass artist – but her dependency on others. She checked the monitors again while the tea steeped. Half-hoping to see Mia's van, throwing up gravel dust. But there was no one.

The spotted gum forest, under-sown with spiky cycads, was unchanged. She had a clear line of sight for miles. Nothing moved. She carried the mug of tea back to the studio, cradling its steady warmth, filling her lungs with bergamot steam, and slid the door closed. The place was a fortress. Whatever was happening out there couldn't reach her. In the studio, working the glass, Rachel wasn't afraid.

two

She closed the windows, switched off the lights, and locked the studio door for the night. Outside, Rachel was no longer able to keep separate all the worrying lines of thought. Where had all the small birds gone? She hadn't heard the heavy *thump* of a wallaby bounding away for days. And why hadn't Mia come?

But then there was the comforting *pleep pleep* of oystercatchers on the river, pelicans flying in for the evening. She went out of the tall gate, with its crazy squares of coloured glass set in the timber. The path was well worn, by her own feet. Years of ritual, walking down to the water. She passed the blackened trunks, scars from the last fire. The ghost trees from the big one before that, still sentient somehow.

She placed her hand flat on the largest spotted gum as she passed, her fingers and thumb a fit with its deep dimples. Closer to the riverbank, her feet crunched over fallen she-oak needles. She could hear and smell the river, still a touch of brine, within the sea's tidal reach. The walk was her daily meditation – but it wasn't working. The forest was too quiet. There was no hum of boats or cars in the distance, which should have pleased her. But somehow it was unnerving.

The boat shed was as she had left it, just her kayaks inside. The previous owner had been a fisher, built the jetty. She would have preferred unspoiled riverbank, but it was pleasant walking over the water, looking down through its glassy surface, into the world beneath.

The cormorant moved off at the sound of her feet on the boards. She lay on the end of the jetty, stretching out her back, loosening her worries. The river flowed beneath her much as it always had, for thousands of years, slow water over round stones, coming down from the mountains, past her little beach, on to the town, and emptying into the sea. She dipped her hands in its cool, touched her wet fingertips to her temples.

On the way back she gathered up fallen sticks and a clutch of dry leaves. The warmth was leaving with the light. A perfect night for a fire. She paused at the gate, scanned the forest for something out of place, listened. Still nothing. Nothing to match what she was feeling. She locked the gate behind her.

Rachel opened the door of the slow-combustion fire and set the kindling. She reached for the matches and shook the box – almost empty. As she held the flame to the leaves, a foreign sound echoed down the chimney. Something above the shushing of the river, the breeze in the she-oaks, the forest's evening song. Timber striking timber and . . . *a baby?* It was a long time since there had been koalas in her forest. But perhaps they were coming back. It was a classic rookie error, mistaking the wail of a female koala for a child crying. She shook her head, to clear the anxious thoughts. Those well-worn tracks.

She focused instead on the pinch of eucalyptus oil in her nostrils, the crackle and pop of the fire. No one could get in. Nothing could happen. It had taken a long time to rebuild, to believe, but she was safe in this place.

Still, she went to the monitors again. Just in case. No one on the road, nothing in the driveway, the walls that surrounded her clear and intact. She checked the solar battery levels and topped up the backup generator with fuel. In the courtyard, she tapped the poly rainwater tanks – one full, one half full – and locked the chickens in for the night.

She picked the last of the rocket, a chilli and a ripe lemon, locked all the doors and downstairs windows. The routine actions soothed her, and the knowledge that whatever happened, if the world ended tomorrow, she'd be fine.

For a while.

In the pantry, she pulled down the sourdough starter and the flour jar – rye this time, and carraway seeds. She mixed flour, water, salt, a teaspoon of honey and the yeast, working until her forearms were aching and the mixture came away from the sides of the bowl. Bread was harder than glass in some ways, more temperamental. She patted the dough into a rough loaf and placed it in the oiled tin.

As she set the loaf on the shelf above the fireplace to rise, the sick feeling returned, taking her breath, as if she had been struck in the solar plexus. Rachel heard the step on the front deck first, and then the creaking board. She froze.

How the hell?

They knocked. Four urgent raps.

three

'My child is sick,' the woman said.

The child did sound distressed. So did its mother. But it could be a trick, to get her to open the door. Anyone could be out there. Waiting. Anything could happen. They would force their way in and ruin her, the life she had built. They were ruining it now.

'Please. Open the door.'

'Go away!' It took all she had to make the words, to make the shapes with her lips and tongue, to force them out of her mouth, over the banging and crying and the woman shrieking. People inside her space.

'Please. It's nearly dark.' The woman was weeping now.

Rachel needed the noise to stop, this woman and her crying child to disappear. To wake up and find it was only one of her nightmares. Her hands were slippery on the poker, her breathing ragged. She tried to focus on the cool metal. The process of heating, striking and cooling that had made it the shape it was.

'Let us in! Don't leave us out here with *them*.'

The woman was crazy. Delusional. Somehow the thought

14

calmed Rachel; this wasn't an attack. The baby had quietened, too, whether at its mother's words, or just tired out. *It's a boy.* The thought came from nowhere, as they did when she was open like this, porous to the world. He was still mewling, but it was low and quiet, easier for her to bear.

Rachel forced herself up and forwards, to the door, and bent to squint through the peephole: a slight woman with straggly blonde hair, a bundle strapped to her chest. She couldn't see anyone else on the deck, in the garden, or the driveway. Nothing her side of the wall. The trees beyond stood still. *How did they get in?*

The woman looked up, as if she knew Rachel was watching. 'Please, my name is Hannah. This is Isaiah. We need help.'

Biblical names.

'Please,' the woman said, through sobs.

Rachel closed her eyes, as if that would block it out. They were human beings, and they were scared. It was miles to the nearest neighbour. An hour to town by car. She tried to imagine sliding the bolt, turning the deadlock, opening her door to these strangers, letting the world in.

All she could do was rest her forehead on the timber and try to manage her breathing. She was not equipped to deal with a sick child. People. Even if the woman was who she said, even if the baby *was* sick, she couldn't have them in her space. 'I just can't. I'm sorry.'

'Please. There's no one else. They're all gone.'

'What do you mean, gone?'

'Dead.' The woman shook her head. 'Haven't you seen the news?'

'No.' Rachel had shut off 'news', social media, the outside world, a long time ago.

'It started in the cities: Sydney, Melbourne, Canberra. And now it's here. In town.'

'How?'

'They don't know. But everyone is dead.'

Except these two. It made no sense. The woman reached into her pocket, pulled out her phone and touched its screen, cool blue in the almost dark. Her hands were unlined, pink with cold, nails bitten down. The bright foreign object was as unwelcome as they were.

The woman brought up a picture and held it to the peephole. Rachel squinted. There were bodies in a street, in huddles, and ones and twos. Dead dogs. It did look a bit like Church Street, but she couldn't see very well. The woman's hands were shaking – it could have been from a film, photoshopped or anything.

The screen went dark. The woman swore. 'Please. Just let me charge my phone. I'll show you.'

She bent to the peephole again. The woman's face was wracked with something – something real. And there was the sensation Rachel had picked up on during the afternoon.

Rachel stood up straight, filled her lungs with air and released it. *Something* had happened, and there were two people outside who needed her help.

She fought to control her hands. Just her hands. Forced herself to slide back the bolt and turn the deadlock. Its click made her sick to the stomach. She leaned on the wall a moment, took a deep breath, and opened the door.

four

Her house was so much smaller with them in it. The baby was coughing and crying, and the woman had traipsed in a trail of muddy sand. She was at least now slipping off the flimsy sneakers she had chosen to flee disaster in, exposing wet pink feet. The papoose arrangement strapped to the front of her body unfolded to reveal all manner of plastic items, which she placed on the floor, and finally the baby itself. It couldn't be more than three months old, face red and swollen. He was sick, that much was true.

'What's wrong with him?'

'I don't know. He has a fever and a cough.'

'Is it contagious?'

The woman shook her head. 'People weren't sick. It's . . . not like that.'

'What is it like?'

The woman's face twisted. 'Horrific.' She turned away to plug her white charger into the wall and her phone into the charger. Cords, mess, microwaves, devices – connection with the outside. It was all so intrusive.

'Do you have a landline?' The woman's movements were erratic, clumsy.

Rachel shook her head.

'But you still have power.'

'I'm on solar,' she said. 'And I don't have a phone. The grid's down?'

'What about a laptop – internet, email?'

'I don't have any of that,' she said. Rachel stood back, tried to breathe more space into the room. 'I'm Rachel.'

The woman was peering around the cottage. 'What about your husband?'

'There's no husband.'

'But the boots. Out front?'

Rachel raised one of her enormous, socked feet. 'Mine, I'm afraid.'

The corner of the woman's mouth turned down, her face softening. She moved towards the fire, picking up the baby, trying to stop him crying.

Rachel folded her arms, tried to steady herself against the noise. 'Can you just start from the beginning?'

'Isaiah was a bit off-colour the day before. But during the night he got worse. Wouldn't stop crying. I called Mum first thing, but she wasn't answering. So I made a doctor's appointment online. The system seemed to work, there was no sign that anything was wrong. But outside, there were cars and people everywhere. And when I got to the medical centre it was chaos. The waiting room was packed. Doctors hadn't shown up, were refusing to see people, hiding in their rooms. Already dead, maybe. It was all over the news, up on the TV screens. Everyone was on their phones, trying to contact people, online, reading all about it – panicking.'

If there was one thing connectivity was good for, it was spreading panic. 'But . . . what is it? Another pandemic?'

The woman closed her eyes. 'I know it sounds crazy but it's nothing you can see. No blood, or any warning. People seem to suddenly experience something terrifying. And then kind of . . . empty out. They were dying right in front of us. Everyone.'

It did sound crazy. 'Except you?'

The woman shrugged. 'All I can tell you is what I saw. I was focused on Isaiah. But then the power went out, people were screaming. I had to get out of there. On the street, cars were crashing into each other, trying to get out of town. There were bodies on the footpath. I just ran, I tell you. And it felt like something . . . like *they* were coming after me.'

Rachel had a vision of the confusion: people's contorted faces, a lurching view of the pavement, screaming, metal crashing into metal. The woman's fear. Then the baby started crying again, the sound filling the room, Rachel's senses. She tried to breathe through it. There was no blocking it out, or stopping it, it seemed.

Keep it together, Ray.

'Let's see how bad that fever is.'

She went to the laundry for the first aid kit and a facecloth. In the kitchen she filled a bowl with cold water, simplifying her movements, making them precise, keeping her breathing slow and regular.

She set the things out on the hearth and kneeled on the floor. Waited for the woman to sit down.

'Then what did you do?' Rachel said.

'I went to Mum's,' she said. 'But she was gone.'

'Not there?'

'Dead,' she said. 'Like the others. Her face . . .'

Rachel glanced at the woman. Surely she wouldn't make something like that up? She opened the first aid kit and pulled the thermometer from its velvet case. She shook it, warmed it in her hand, and gave it to the woman.

The woman unbuttoned the baby's jumpsuit and tucked the thermometer under his arm, wiping away tears with her sleeve. 'It was hard to leave there. To just *leave* her. She has a car. I thought about taking that, but cars seemed like the worst place to be. So I went down to the marina, where my brother moors his boat. I took it and headed upriver. Away from the town.'

It was just what Rachel would have done.

'I could still feel *them* on my back, but it was fading. Then the boat ran out of fuel. So *typical* of my brother, leaving it empty. I had to row. It was getting dark. One of the news reports said that it happens at night. Whole cities wiped out by morning. I was really starting to panic. And then I saw your jetty, the smoke, lights.'

'How did you get over my wall?'

'What?'

'The wall around my house.'

'There's a tree hanging over. I climbed along the branch. And lowered myself onto the wall,' she said. 'Then onto the ground. It wasn't *easy*, I can tell you. Especially with him.'

'It's not meant to be.' It wasn't meant to be possible. She would have to chainsaw that branch off in the morning.

The woman held up the thermometer, read the gauge.

'What's it say?'

'Thirty-nine.'

'Okay, that's high.'

She watched the woman sponging her son's pudgy limbs, blowing on his pale damp skin. He whimpered when his jump-suit came off and cried louder with every touch of the facecloth. His nostrils flared when he breathed, his ribs sucking in, as if it was hard work. With that cough it probably was. It was awful to watch, wracking his whole body.

'He probably feels cold. Even though he's hot.'

The woman nodded.

Rachel got to her feet and went to the kitchen. She braced her hands on the bench and breathed, trying to inhabit all of her body, the empty space in the familiar room around her, everything in its place – the distance between her and the crying. The trees, the forest. A slight breeze shifting leaves against one another, the larger world she was part of. There was a pause in the baby's wailing. Rachel ground up half a Panadol and mixed it with warm water in the bottom of a glass. Even if the woman was mad, the baby had a fever. That much was true.

She counted the ten strides back to the fire. 'See if he'll take some of this.' She rummaged in the kit for an eye-dropper, broke it free of its packaging. 'You need to bring his temperature down.'

'Are you a nurse?'

Rachel shook her head. 'My sister is a doctor. And I've done some first aid training.' It had been a prerequisite in the hot shop, when she was teaching. In case of burns, cuts, fire.

The child's mouth, probably knowing only its mother's breast, rejected the eye-dropper. The woman had to force it in, prompting

21

more screams. Rachel wanted to scream herself. Walk out the door and leave them behind. She tried to block it out, reasoning that it was only a child. A sick child. He couldn't help it.

The woman's hands were raw around the thumb and forefinger, from rowing. One of the blisters had already burst, the skin beneath red and weeping. Rachel handed her two waterproof bandaids.

'For your blisters,' she said.

'Thanks.'

Rachel backed out of the room, in part to escape the noise, clear her head. There was a medical book in the library. It might have something useful in it. The volume was on a high shelf, its spine barely broken. A gift from her sister, to reassure herself that Rachel would – could – look after herself. Monique's phone number was still written on a sticky note inside the front cover. She pulled the book down, switched on the desk lamp. The section on babies was long and confusing; a temperature and difficulty breathing could mean multiple things. Most likely it was pneumonia, and he probably needed antibiotics. Unless it was a virus. She could never have been a doctor: too many decisions. So much riding on every one of them.

Back in Nimmitabel, her sister was town doctor and vet. And still she did more, taking in refugees, lobbying their local member on no end of issues. Absorbing the trauma of so many. She was all the things that Rachel wasn't.

She leaned in the doorway of the lounge. The woman was fanning the baby with an old *GlassWorld* magazine, trying to calm him with a finger in his mouth. He was sick. And she was upset and scared. That much was clear. But surely it couldn't be as bad as the woman said. She could ring her sister, ask what to do.

'Are his fingernails blue?'

The woman examined his hands. 'A bit.'

'Do you have any signal on that phone?'

The woman went to the phone, touched its screen. It lit her anxious face with cold blue light. 'Nothing,' she said.

'What time was it when the power went out?'

'Mid-morning.'

'The mobile towers only have enough backup power for eight hours.'

The woman turned, phone still in hand. 'That's all?'

Rachel shrugged. 'That's what happened during the fires. No one could get in to replace the batteries.' It had been months until normal service was restored. 'You said you had more pictures?'

'The ones I sent Kyle should still be here.' The woman swiped her screen. 'If you don't believe me.'

There were images from around the country, the world. Cities, towns, in chaos. Bodies, cars piled up. Reporters' faces grim, as if knowing it would be their last broadcast. The bright colours swirled and came together, liquid as glass. Rachel handed back the phone. She already had that particular headache she used to get from scanning information online, staring at a screen. *Could it be true?*

Was this why Mia hadn't come? She had never been late before – not even when her mother died or when she broke her arm.

five

They sat in the darkening room, the fire warm on their backs. The baby had finally stopped crying. There was too much to take in. Rachel wished she could wind back the clock, throw these people out and have a normal night at home. A simple meal and a cup of tea, an early night. So she could get up early and go back to work in the studio as if nothing had happened.

She frowned at the child, its face an ugly red. *Saviour.* Wasn't that what the name meant? And here they were, appearing on her doorstep, with an elaborate story about being the only ones left alive.

'Why is he called Isaiah?'

The woman touched the child's cheek. 'My partner, Kyle, chose it. It was his grandfather's name.'

'You're religious?'

'Kyle was raised in a faith. But we're not part of any church.'

It wasn't a no. The religious right had a lot to answer for, derailing the country, dragging it backwards. 'And where is Kyle?'

The woman's eyes filled with tears. If she was acting, she was good. 'He was working in Canberra. I tried calling him this morning but . . .'

Rachel reached forwards to open the fireplace door and threw on another piece of wood. The bread had risen above the edges of the tin; it needed knocking back. 'You mentioned a brother? Is he in town?'

'He's working up north,' she said. 'No answer this morning.'

The baby started crying again.

'I have to feed him,' the woman said. 'He hasn't been taking much but I'd better try.' She started unbuttoning her top.

Rachel blushed. It was all too much, too personal. But the child was probably the only thing keeping the woman together.

'How long since *you've* eaten?'

'Not since breakfast.'

'Why don't I make us something? While you figure out what to do.'

In the quiet of the kitchen, Rachel kneaded the dough first, using her palms, working her forearms, until the mixture was springy and elastic. Motion, familiar movements, making – it soothed her. She rubbed oil over the top of the loaf, covered the tin and returned it to the shelf above the fireplace for its final rise, careful to keep her eyes averted from the woman breast-feeding her child.

Rachel counted her steps back to the kitchen and stared out into the dark. None of this would be happening if it wasn't real. A woman wouldn't have rowed all the way from town to turn up at her door with a sick baby.

She boiled water for the pasta, fried off onion, garlic and fresh chilli. The smells and sounds reminded her that she had been hungry. She wilted the rocket, zested the lemon, then added the juice, ground pepper, drained the pasta and stirred it through. She spooned it into deep earthenware bowls and grated the last of the parmesan over the top.

The woman put the baby down in his papoose, which, when turned inside out, was fleece-lined, like a nest.

'He might sleep a little now, at least.' She took the bowl Rachel offered. 'Thanks.'

They forked food into their mouths. A piece of wood in the fireplace collapsed into red coals. The baby was quiet. If he got better, they could go away in the morning. Leave her in peace.

The woman seemed calmer. Rachel's own mind was starting to function, questions forming. 'Do you know Mia, in town?'

'From the co-op?'

Rachel nodded. 'Did you see her?'

The woman kept her eyes on the fire. 'Only her van.'

'Crashed?'

'Up against the wall of the post office,' she said.

Not Mia. She had spent more time with her than her sister, these last years.

The woman stretched her bare feet towards the heat. 'How do you know her?'

'She brings . . . my supplies. But she's been there my whole life.'

'How long have you lived out here?'

'A while now.'

'Five years? Ten?'

Rachel nodded. She was too tired to count. Mia couldn't be gone. And what about Monique? For a moment, all her fears were close to the surface, the woman's, too. Crowding the room. The baby woke, started crying again. As if he felt it.

Rachel sighed. There was no throwing them out now. They would have to stay the night. The woman lifted the child to her chest, tried to soothe him.

'I'll clean up,' Rachel said. 'See that tin? Could you put it in the oven underneath the fire? The handle lifts up.'

She made up the spare bedroom downstairs. The sheets could be fresher, but it would have to do. Monique came down to visit once or twice a year – always with plenty of notice – but no one else. Until now. Rachel was longing for her own bed. For quiet. Space to think. It was more people contact, more information, than she'd had for years.

'I don't have a cot or anything.'

'He can sleep with me.' The woman set the baby up in the papoose-nest on the bed.

Rachel touched the outside of her little finger against his head, the way Monique would. 'He's still very hot.'

The woman unbuttoned his jumpsuit, blew on him.

'This thing. You're sure it's not a virus?'

'If it is, there are no symptoms,' the woman said.

'I'll get more water.' Rachel refilled the bowl from the jug in the fridge, crushed another chunk of Panadol in the bottom of a glass and dissolved it in warm water. She rinsed out the eye-dropper and facecloth and took it all into the bedroom.

'Give this to him during the night,' she said. 'And try to keep him quiet. I'm tired.'

The woman sponged his wrists and hands, throat and chest, legs and feet. 'What are we going to do?' she said.

We? 'Rest, for now. Hopefully he'll be better in the morning.'

She sat staring at the fire until the bread was done. The woman was singing. Not a lullaby, but something familiar. Her quavering voice might soothe the child, but in the flickering light it only added to Rachel's unease.

Rachel slipped her hands into the hot mitts to remove the bread from the oven and set it on the hob to cool. The yeasty smells filling the house were real, normal.

When Rachel climbed the steps to her loft, her legs were heavy, as if she had been walking all day. She lit a candle, cleaned her teeth and stripped off her clothes. Under the shower, she let the water pummel her, gazing up at the trees and stars through the glass. She dried herself with the towel and lay on the bed, windows wide open, with just a sheet. The forest was still out there, still the same: crickets, frogs, gliders, bats, a boobook owl in the distance. It calmed her, but she could not sleep. There was a strange woman and her baby downstairs. In her house. She could hear and feel them.

Rachel placed some calming drops under her tongue – one of Monique's concoctions – and went through her breathing routine. Twice. *Easy now, Ray.* It was her sister's voice she heard in her head. When Rachel had tried to leave the world, Monique had taught her meditation and breathing techniques, fed her, washed her clothes, as if she were a child again. Sheltering her from television, radio, papers, internet, social media – people.

Monique had created a bubble in which Rachel could come back to life.

But now, on her platform beneath the forest canopy, there was nothing that could settle her. If something had happened to her sister, wouldn't she *know*?

six

She sat on the end of the jetty as the sun came up over the treeline, the same as ever. The forest was quiet, just the subdued murmurings of birds. She couldn't pick out a single man-made sound. No distant engine or voice. On top of what the woman had told her, it was eerie. Only the river was the same.

The last time Monique had visited, they had taken the kayaks out. Downriver, that day – with the tide. To land on the heart-shaped island and swim in deep water. They had set out a picnic in the shade, eaten too much of Monique's fig and goat's cheese tart, and lain back against the bank, their wine bottle cooling in the river.

Monique had asked, as she always did, how Rachel was. And she never meant about the glass, her work, although she always took an interest. She had been careful, too, not to mention any news or developments, any further decline. They talked instead about art and books and birds and trees, and the other people in Monique's life. The town where they had grown up.

She hadn't seen it clearly at the time, but something had been different that day. Monique was unable to hide the wear and tear of caring for people, whatever was worrying her. Even after two glasses of wine, by the water. 'I hope it stays like this for you here, Ray. For ever,' she'd said.

Rachel rubbed her face. The baby was crying again, the sound carrying through the forest over the water. A sound she couldn't ignore.

She let the chickens out on her way back, collected the four eggs they had left. 'We'll be okay, girls,' she said.

The baby's temperature had gone up, not down: thirty-nine-and-a-half degrees. The woman didn't appear to have slept. None of them had, with him crying through the night, the sound echoing around the house. Rachel had heard the woman crying, too. The sort of crying you couldn't fake. She had lost her mother, seen horrible things, her partner and brother were uncontactable, probably dead, and her baby was sick.

The woman was pacing around the kitchen table, trying to settle him. 'We need to get help,' she said.

'Who from? If everyone is dead, as you say.'

'There has to be someone.'

'Well, I can't leave here,' Rachel said.

'Why not?'

'I just can't.' Her hands were gripping the kitchen bench, the timber warm and solid. 'I'm not going out there.'

'Well, you can't stay here, either. Not on your own.'

'*I can.*' But she couldn't feed two people for long. She tried to slow her thoughts, clear her head. 'If it's pneumonia, then he probably needs antibiotics.'

'Do you have any?'

Rachel shook her head. 'I would usually, but I had an ear infection in the winter.' She had swum in the river after rain, though she knew she shouldn't.

'Then we have to find a doctor.'

It wasn't clear if *we* meant her and the child, or now included Rachel. 'What about the other medical centre, in town? Are you *sure* everybody died?'

The woman closed her eyes. 'I might've seen *one* other person, a single mum I went to prenatal with.'

'Might've?'

'I was running. It was just a glimpse of her carrying her baby, near the boat ramp.'

So they mightn't be the only survivors. Everything needn't be up to her.

But the woman wouldn't give up. 'What about your sister?'

'She's in Nimmitabel, up in the high country.'

'That's tiny, right? Maybe . . .'

Rachel shook her head.

'Don't you want to know if she's okay?'

Rachel glared. They had already interrupted her life, upset all her routines, her work. 'Of course I do. But I'm not leaving here.'

'Well, I have to do *something*.'

'That's not my problem,' Rachel said. 'I don't even have a vehicle.'

'You live out here on your own, cut off from the outside world, and don't drive?'

Rachel shrugged. 'No need.'

'Well, maybe it's for the best. The roads, cars, other people – it's dangerous.'

That had always been the case, for Rachel.

'What about your boat? I have fuel in the shed.'

'And go where?'

'Upriver. You motor as far as you can, and then there's a path, right up to the top of the mountains, through the bush.'

'How long would *that* take?'

Rachel appraised the body before her. Early twenties, slight but wiry, carrying a child. Having recently given birth. Having to stop and feed him, change him, rest. Losing her way. Thin-soled shoes, ankle socks. 'Two, three days.'

'We don't have that long.'

The woman insisted on speaking as if it was Rachel's responsibility. She should never have opened the damn door. Then she wouldn't know and wouldn't care. She would be in the studio working the glass, with the trees and birds.

'It's the most direct route, as the crow flies,' Rachel said. The roads, in either direction, had to tack right around the mountains, covering twice the ground.

'We're not crows.'

'Well, what do you want to do?' It was what her sister always asked when Rachel was having a meltdown.

The woman shut her eyes. 'I don't know! It's impossible. I need to do everything I can to care for him. But we can't go back to the town. That's more dangerous. If something happens to me, he has *no* chance.'

It was hard not to take on the woman's desperation, to *feel* it. Rachel tried to focus on the green of the vegetable beds. The haze from the day before was back, diffusing the light.

'Why don't you see if he improves? If you can get the fever

down. That way you're not putting him through a whole lot of travel unnecessarily. If it's as dangerous as you say out there . . .'

'Rachel, please.'

'I need to start work.'

Rachel carried her breakfast and sketchbook into the studio and closed the door. She powered up the glory hole, and sat on the bench nursing her coffee. The smooth green glaze of her favourite mug, from the potter in the next valley, was a comfort. She had commissioned a dinner set in the same colours, only months before his studio and workshop were lost in the fires. The whole village had gone up – its historic main street, weatherboard shops and homes. The heart of the valley with it.

The light streamed in as usual, everything in its place, the forest still breathing outside. Trees didn't have to remember to harness light to process sugars, exchange carbon dioxide for oxygen. They breathed for her. Pencil on paper was another type of breathing, releasing what was inside. She'd had an idea, for a new piece, earlier in the week, but now it was blocked, behind a logjam. She sketched an outline, a more detailed panel, made some notes, before the shape slipped away. She placed her plate and cup in the tub and laid out her tools. Even through the studio's soundproofing, going through her routine, she couldn't forget the woman and her screaming baby. Or the scenes she had described.

Rachel gathered molten glass from the furnace, doused the pipe with water, cooling it enough to hold in her bare hands.

Then, three steady strides to the stainless-steel bench – the maver – where the colours were laid out. She rolled the glass, flattening and shaping it into a workable wedge.

More heat, and then back to the bench, dipping the tip into the crushed glass: blue first for this batch. It took her full arm-span to hold the pipe vertical, one of the advantages of her height. She was almost out of blue; purple, too.

Mia.

Outside thoughts, again. Rachel wiped her face on her shirt sleeve. *Trust your process, and it will come.* Hans had drummed that into them from day one of unit one, right up until his Champagne-fuelled launch speech for their graduating exhibition.

She returned the glass to the glory hole, watching the colour fizz and sparkle in the heat. More mavering to get that perfect shape, then breath – the all-important starting bubble. She was dropping it out, twirling the pipe like a fire dancer, moving with the glass, taking pleasure in her power. As she stood and turned, the outer edge of the vessel touched the arm of the chair – and shattered.

Rachel stood staring at the mess. It was as if her thoughts had done it. Mistakes happened. And, with glass, it was always dramatic. But she had almost removed them from her practice. She deliberately took her time, repeated the same movements over and over, changed nothing. Everything had its place, its order. Concentration and focus were her strengths in the studio.

But she hadn't been concentrating. If what the woman said was true, and society had come to some sort of stop, there wasn't really any point making vessels for rich people anymore. Perhaps there hadn't been any point in the first place. Even if things weren't as bad as the woman said, without Mia, there would be no more glass, and no one to take the pieces away.

When she opened the door, she could hear the baby, still crying inside her house. The sound reverberated up the valley, disrupting the forest, the river, setting her whole body on edge.

She let herself out the gate and strode uphill, away from the noise. A scrub wren scolded from a cycad. She pulled back her shoulders, filled her lungs and emptied them. The sun was warm overhead. Her boots found the right places to land, her legs and glutes moved her steadily upwards.

By the time Rachel reached the top of the bluff, she was out of breath. She sat among ferns, solid rock at her back, gazing out over the valley where she had chosen to live out the rest of her life. The ominous haze was building, clouding her view of the river. Fires were burning again somewhere.

Something rustled in the undergrowth, drawing closer. The dark snout of an echidna emerged, making her way downhill, spines flat, sniffing for ants, oblivious to Rachel.

It was a simple choice, on the face of it. To stay where she was, as long as she could, alone. Or go back out into the world – help these people. But how much help would she be? And what dangers would they face?

She should have ordered more antibiotics. She had a stack of prescriptions. *Mistake*. After the fires, Rachel had stocked up on everything and sworn she would never be caught out again. But she was rarely sick, and with her sister coming down regularly, had grown complacent about the first aid kit. Even after Monique's last visit.

Her sister had left Rachel six months' worth of anti-anxiety medication, plus another script for Mia to fill, and a whole box of her calming drops. And the envelope, full of cash. The notes were brighter and slipperier than she remembered. She hadn't handled money for years. Monique paid Mia, her accountant paid her bills and did her taxes, and her agent managed her sales and orders through Mia. It had been the two gold ingots that really pulled her up. Their father had always said gold was the only currency in a crisis.

'What's going on, Mon?'

'I mightn't be able to come down for a while. I just want to make sure you'll be okay.'

'But I'm fine.'

An expression had crossed Monique's face that Rachel couldn't read. 'I know. I might end up on your doorstep to live with *you* awhile.'

Rachel laughed. 'Stay, then.'

Monique shook her head. 'I wish I could.'

She should have asked more questions. What was wrong, what had happened. Perhaps it would have helped her to make the right decision now.

Sometimes she liked to ask the forest for an answer. When in doubt about whether she should climb the final summit of a mountain of spiritual significance to Yuin peoples, she had asked the land, the old people, the mountain itself. And a lyrebird had called, scratching up dirt right next to her, and continued up the path, uphill, his tail wafting behind. She had taken that as her answer and walked on. But today nothing came, though the forest was alive all around her and she was attuned to it with all of her being.

She brought her leg up to her body, to retie the lace, which had worked its way loose. There, next to her boot, was a lyrebird feather. A fluffy grey curl, the hint of a stripe.

Her sister would help them without question. Especially a child. 'I took an oath,' she always said. But Rachel was not her sister. She wasn't even the Rachel she used to be. People were not like glass, they couldn't be melted down, remade.

They had knocked on the wrong woman's door.

seven

When Rachel slipped back into the house, it was quiet. Everything was clean, tidy and back in its place. Perhaps they had gone, made the decision for her. Maybe the whole thing had never happened. She padded through to the spare room in her socks. It was empty, the bed neatly made.

She let out the breath she had been holding. But when she turned around, the woman was standing in the doorway, holding the baby. With the afternoon light behind them, Rachel couldn't see her face.

'There you are,' the woman said.

Rachel cleared her throat. 'How is he?'

'*Worse*.'

'Temperature?'

'Almost forty.'

Shit. The Panadol and cooling him down wasn't working. He was blotchy and miserable, skin clammy. He needed antibiotics.

The woman was packing her things into the papoose. 'I have to get help,' she said.

Rachel followed her into the kitchen. 'From where? It's too late to set out now.'

The woman's shoulders slumped. The baby started crying again. Crying that built to a howl. The woman paced around the kitchen, rocking him, but it only amplified the sound, made him more agitated.

In the small room of the small house, it was all too much. Rachel needed her sister. Even as her thoughts started shutting down, there was a moment of clarity. The woman would never make it on her own. And Rachel needed to know if Monique was alive. To do everything she could to find her.

There had been times like this, in her old life, which presented themselves when she least expected it. When it was most inconvenient. In the middle of preparing for a show, or while working on a major piece. Difficult decisions, situations – emergencies. If a friend called in the middle of the night, she had been there. Not once had she been sorry. For a time, she had been that sort of person. And Monique had *always* been that person, especially for Rachel.

She knew what she had to do. There wasn't really any choice. There never had been. Even if she was afraid – to leave the property, to go back out into the world. Rachel struck her palms on the kitchen table, made a noise from deep in her throat.

The woman stepped back.

'All right. I'll take you. We leave in the morning. If my sister is okay, then . . . good. If not, I can get in. We'll at least have access to her clinic. But that's as far as I go. Okay?'

The woman frowned. 'Can't we just leave now?'

'We have to prepare first. Pack everything we might need.

And we can't walk in the dark,' Rachel said. 'We go at dawn, we'll be in Nimmitabel the day after tomorrow.'

'But—'

'Look. If you want me to help you, we do things my way.'

'Okay.' The woman tried to grab Rachel's arm. 'Thank you.'

Rachel pulled back. 'Don't thank me yet,' she said. 'It's a long way. And a hard walk.'

Rachel fetched her pack from the laundry and started laying out gear on the kitchen table: sleeping bags, tarp, water bottles, first aid kit, cooker, map, compass, micro towels, facecloth, the last of the matches, billy, tongs, two splades, torch, multi-tool, foil, duct tape, sunburn cream, binoculars.

The woman stared at the growing pile. 'What can I do?'

'Make us something for dinner. There's not much: eggs, and the bread. Out the back you'll find spinach leaves, a few cherry tomatoes. And there's a relish in the fridge.'

The woman moved straight away, the baby strapped to the front of her. Mercifully, he was quiet, giving Rachel space to think.

She packed four small tins of tuna, four muesli bars, her last two apples, and poured the last of the rolled oats into a canvas bag. The end of a block of chocolate, coffee, tea, salt and pepper, the tube of condensed milk she kept for an emergency. It *was* an emergency, though not any of the scenarios she had imagined. She had thought only fire or flood would drive her out.

What else?

The tiny coffee press Monique had given her for her last

birthday. Her new Gore-Tex jacket, and her old one, for the woman. Two thermal tops, beanies, a T-shirt and checked shirt from the clean clothes pile, spare underwear. She went back for a thermal neck-warmer, which would fit around the baby's body.

The woman finally returned from the courtyard, her hands full of green and red. 'Quite the set-up you've got.'

And now she had to leave. Twenty-four hours ago, she had been unable to imagine even one day without working, collecting eggs, harvesting greens, walking down to the river.

The pack was lumpy and lopsided. She pulled everything out and started again, heavy items at the bottom, soft against her back, things they would need straight away at the top, or in the side and front pockets.

'Food's ready.'

The woman served up eggs and spinach on toast with grilled tomatoes. It was a bit of a mess on the plate but smelled good.

'Thanks,' Rachel said. She cut a square of toast, egg and tomato. 'What was going on, before this?'

'The pandemics, and the downturn. Another string of natural disasters, and a new wave of climate refugees. The collapse of the US leading up to the election. A crackdown on protestors, media.'

Rachel held up her hand. 'Enough.' It made her head hurt.

'What are you thinking?' the woman said.

'I don't know. My sister tried to warn me about some sort of breakdown.'

'Hopefully we can ask her.' The woman's face was open for a moment, kind even. But hope was dangerous. It only led to disappointment.

Rachel pushed her plate away and spread out the map between them. 'Taking the river will save us some time, but we're pushing against the flow, and there are rapids higher up. I figure we'll go as far as we can. Hopefully to here.' She tapped the map at the point where the river forked. 'Then it's upriver on foot. It's good going until here – the falls – then it gets pretty steep, crossing these mountains. And it can be cold, even at this time of year.'

The woman stared at the snaking river, the swirling contours of the mountains. 'Have you done this before?'

'Yeah. I used to walk up to see my sister.'

'How long did it take you?'

'Two days each way, but I didn't have the boat.' She hadn't had a town woman and sick child with her, either. And she had practically run it, especially on the way home. 'There's a hut, halfway.'

eight

It was a relief when the light finally came. Rachel had only managed a few hours' sleep, between the baby's crying and worrying about everything that could go wrong on the journey. She chose bamboo underwear, her best walking socks, khaki cargo pants, an old black T-shirt, and buttoned a flannel shirt over the top. She strapped on her father's watch, its face chipped and marked. Not so much to tell the time, but their direction.

The whipbirds were up, their cracking calls waking the forest. Then the cicadas, the rising vibration she had long become attuned to. Rachel washed and moisturised her face, applied sunscreen, tied back her hair and tucked it under an old baseball cap.

She made her bed, threw her dirty clothes in the basket, shut the windows and took a last look around her room. It was like a fire evacuation, packing for what could be overnight, a week – for ever. She wasn't sure if or when she would be back, or if her house, the studio, would be as she left them.

The woman was pale and puffy-eyed, the baby's temperature still sitting on forty. Way too high.

They scoffed their toast and coffee at the bench. The woman walked back and forth, trying to settle her baby, Rachel ran through her checklist over and over, for anything she had missed. She made two rough sandwiches and slipped them in an outside pocket of the pack, tucked the binoculars in her shirt pocket. Then wiped down the breadboard and bench, drained the sink and put everything away.

Rachel brushed her teeth and took her tablets. She added two toothbrushes, a travel toothpaste, her drops, and the last of her medication – enough for five days – to her wet pack. Hopefully Monique would have more.

She handed the woman a hat and an old ziplock bag. 'For your phone.' Not that it was any use. But Rachel had seen her slip it in her pocket, and the charger was gone from the wall socket. Her gaze lingered on the woman's white Converse. 'Got any better shoes?'

The woman shook her head. 'I wasn't exactly thinking of a long hike when I left the house.'

'You have everything you need for him? Something warm for his head?'

'Yep.' She patted the side of the papoose-sling.

At the last minute, Rachel added her sketch pad and a pencil. Her daily habits, routines, were what kept her together.

'Can you take one of the water bottles?'

'Do you want me to carry something else?' The woman gestured at the towering pack waiting by the door. 'That looks heavy.'

'I'll be fine. You just worry about him.' The pack would get lighter as they went, and she wouldn't need much for the return.

Rachel checked that the doors and windows were locked and scanned the monitors again. Somehow, part of her still hoped to see Mia's van. The jetty was clear, even of cormorants.

She crouched, backed into the pack and shrugged it onto her shoulders. The woman opened the door, Rachel locked it behind them. At the gate, she stopped to look back at the broad cedar door of her studio. The weight of leaving was far more than what she was carrying on her back.

I can't do this.

The woman touched her arm. 'What is it?'

'I just need to check on the studio.'

'Studio?' The woman followed close behind, as if worried Rachel might renege, even now.

The door was secure, of course, but she unlocked it, slid the timber across to check inside. Everything was just as she had left it. Light streaming in like a bright idea, calling her to work. All the colours of the high windows lit up like a cathedral.

The furnace stayed hot around the clock, keeping the glass liquid. It couldn't be turned off, not without emptying it out. Its glow was always with her.

Give me strength. All she wanted was to shut the door and start working, like any other day. The glass, this place – it was who she was.

How could she leave? What would she do if something had happened to her sister? And the world, more wrecked than before. Images flickered, of ravaged landscapes, starving animals, no way back. She didn't want to see it.

Rachel leaned against the wall, chest tight, the pack adding to the weight. She couldn't draw a breath.

'Please,' the woman said. 'Let's go.'

You can do it, Ray. You have to. Monique's voice. She was still with her.

Rachel strode ahead, down the path to the river. The quicker they got there, the quicker she would find Monique, be rid of the woman and her baby, and head home. She heard a robin, and caught a glimpse of his reassuring yellow belly, peering from a low branch. It was better in the forest, her body moving. All the things that worried her, worried her less outdoors.

The woman hurried to keep up, her shorter legs working in double step. They were already at the casuarinas; their breeze-song shushed her, smoothing the assault of the intrusion, her world blown apart. The world.

She paused at the river's edge, listening for human sounds. Just the usual straggle of cormorants arranged on the dead river gum. A lone pelican floating upstream, its own island. The tide was coming in.

The boat was an old timber skiff, with nice lines and immaculate detailing, sanded back and fitted with a new outboard. If she was going to set off into the unknown in a boat, she didn't mind it being this one. They stood for a moment on the jetty. 'Your brother's a boat builder?'

'It's just a hobby. He works in mining. Reforesting old sites.'

'He did a great job on her.'

The woman looked over the boat, not seeing. The baby started crying, destroying the moment. It set Rachel's teeth on edge. The noise itself, which there seemed to be no getting used to, the worry about what was wrong with him, and what might happen. And, worse, who or what might hear.

The woman knew it, too. Better than Rachel. She had seen it. *Them*, she'd said. As if someone was pursuing her. She rocked her child, turned her back on the river and crouched down over him, creating a cocoon that muffled his cries.

Rachel dumped the pack in the stern. 'I'll get fuel.' She unlocked the boat shed, filled the jerrycans with unleaded. One of the many relics from the past she was hoarding. It took a whole can to fill the tank. She stowed the other under the rear seat.

She returned the empty jerrycan to the shed and ran down the jetty. The woman had already climbed aboard, setting herself in the bow, still rocking the baby to quieten him. Now the river was rocking him, too. Rachel freed the knot the woman had tied – a perfect half-hitch – and threw it on board. Women who grew up on the coast knew how to handle boats, boards, waves and tides – to be in and on the water. The woman was going to slow her down, but perhaps she wouldn't be completely useless.

Rachel climbed on board, steadying herself with one hand on the jetty. 'I'm going to row, while we're with the tide, until we're past the houses. Just in case.'

The woman nodded.

Rachel fended off with the oars, locked them in the brass clamps, and started rowing. A little rough at first, then settling into a rhythm. It was good to work her upper body, to utilise the strength and breadth of her back and shoulders. To move across the water so effortlessly. Just the dip of the oars, the creak of timber, the gentle whoosh of the prow of the boat, carving a neat wave. *This, I can do.*

nine

The river was strong and clear, its round stones a rainbow beneath them. She-oaks leaned over the water, as if to admire their own reflections. Three yellow-tailed black cockatoos flew ahead, their mournful cries and slow wingbeats from another time. Rachel matched her oar strokes, her breathing, to their rhythm. Even the baby had calmed, just a low grizzle from the front of the boat. The woman watched the way ahead, jaw tight, glancing back every now and then. As if whatever had happened in the town might follow them upriver.

The water was still half-salt, shifting to fresh. The fires had torn right through the valley, roaring and leaping through the canopy, almost to the back of her place – and then the wind had changed. Another ten minutes and she would have lost everything. Not that any of that would have mattered, not compared to what *had* been lost. Billions of trees and animals. The pain rushed up in her chest, her heartbeat too fast, breathing too shallow. As if the land was her body. Rachel felt tears on her cheeks, but kept rowing, moving forwards, upriver.

Afterwards, when the rain finally came, floods following fires, she had understood that the earth was trying to heal itself. The bush had come back, though not the same as before. The regrowth was strange and shrubby, the understorey all vines and prickles, colonising species.

She watched the river for threats: people, boats, movement. For beauty, too. The details were somehow more pronounced, more precious – almost painful. They passed an egret close enough to see the defined muscles of his chest, his kinked neck unfolding to dip his yellow beak, white plumes flaring.

There were more structures than Rachel remembered, shelters thrown together out of scrap in small clearings. But they saw no one. Only a skinny brindle dog, making a run for cover. The old gravel road had never been sealed, slowing progress, the relentless spread of people. And the fires – the loss of lives, homes, failed insurance claims, new building codes – had scared people off.

When they rounded the next bend, Rachel couldn't stop herself from crying out. They had reached the state forest, on the other side of the river, which ran right to the water's edge. The spotted gums thinned and then disappeared into a wasteland of churned-up earth, stumps and discarded trunks. The after-char of slash burning. A few cycads coming back was the only sign of hope. *So much waste.* Acres and acres of spotted gums, hundreds of years old, torn down, chipped, pulped and traded, turned into cheap paper towel. The woman hadn't even flinched.

The first hurdle was getting past Kevin's place. She examined the cabin for movement, its slot-windows dark blanks. A survivalist through and through, if things were looking grim, he would have holed up there, fortifying himself against the world.

They had only spoken once, through the barbed-wire fence, and he had been polite enough. But his buzz cut, camouflage outfit and the hunting knife hanging from his belt had given her chills. His bearing screamed military, special forces, probably. He kept to himself, never approached her or came onto her place. But he cleared great tracts of trees and shot kangaroos. For meat, not sport, but the violence hurt her. Too many trees had fallen, too much blood had already been spilt.

They were almost at his boundary, spotted gums spreading above the barbed wire, reaching for freedom. The riverbank rose, turfed earth and tree roots obscuring their view of his cabin.

Rachel thought she caught a glint – from binoculars, or a rifle-sight. She watched without breaking her stroke, expecting the bullet, hopefully only over the bow. They were vulnerable, moving so slowly. Her heart was beating hard in her chest. To speak would only alarm the woman. To hurry only let on that they were afraid. If he wanted to shoot them, he would.

The boat moved over the water, and still the shot did not come. Rachel rowed, digging the oars deep. The water swallowed all other sounds. She looked back, half-hoping to catch a glimpse of Kevin – someone else left alive, to cast doubt on all the woman had said. But nothing moved, except them and the river.

Real fear coursed through her, more than just her own. It was tempting to fire up the motor, speed away, but she wanted to sneak past the commune. They were harmless. Or they used to be. But if what the woman described had reached them, broken through their Hare Krishna enlightenment or whatever, she wasn't taking any chances.

She shifted to the other side of the river, keeping her oar strokes minimal and clean. The baby was coughing like an old man, the woman trying to quieten him. On the water, every sound carried.

ten

The woman checked her phone again, though there had never been any signal this far up the valley, and sealed it back in the plastic bag. Her movements were slower, more measured, trying to keep the baby quiet. She seemed to have found a way to keep herself calm, to keep him calm.

They had moved into scrubby country, ironbarks and stringy barks, tall she-oaks at the water's edge, their roots deep-drinking from the river.

'There's a settlement coming up,' Rachel said.

The commune's clearing on the riverbank had expanded into a small town. Citrus trees and raised vegetable beds had been netted, a square enclosed by a ribbon of electric fence for goats. Fading caravans and a fresh row of bright tents filled the spaces in between.

They were anti-cars, anti-technology, anti-systems, anti-multi, anti-consumption. People called them flat-earthers but, as it turned out, they were the smart ones. Not caught up in the click, swipe and like frenzy that had infected the world.

Perhaps, like her, tucked away upriver, they had escaped whatever scourge had hit the rest of society.

Or they might be as addicted to social media as anyone. How else would they drum up business, raise revenue, manage their profile? Even the most hardcore alternatives had been sucked into that vortex.

She stopped rowing to look through the binoculars. Checking for life, for threats. There was no smoke from their fires, no movement that she could see. Then the colours and shapes came into focus.

There were bodies. Lots of bodies. Huddled in chaotic scenes that didn't make sense. One family – a parent and two children – was still entwined on their caravan steps, as if for comfort, but their upper bodies pulled away from each other, faces contorted. As if what they had seen at the last minute was unbearable.

Crows circled. Goats grazed on rich green river grass as if nothing had happened. Rachel lowered the binoculars, energy draining from her limbs.

'It's the same here, isn't it?'

Rachel nodded.

Hannah saw them first. Pointed without speaking. A man and two women, running down to the river's edge, waving their arms. There was no sneaking past now.

Rachel and Hannah made eye contact, for the first time, across the boat.

'Let's get out of here,' Hannah said.

Rachel stowed the oars and scrambled back to the motor. She flushed the engine, pushed the choke, pulled the starter cord. It coughed, spluttered and did not start.

Fuck.

The people dived into the water. They were swimming out. The boat was still drifting with the tide, but so were the swimmers, trying to intercept them. Apart from whatever they might bring aboard, infect them with, they couldn't risk them capsizing the boat. People panicking in the water were bad news.

She tried the motor again. It coughed and almost caught but then choked. Maybe the fuel was dirty, the jerrycans rusted. Rachel's hands were shaking, her thinking muddy.

'Help!' It was the man, dreadlocked and tattooed, out in front. The women's shaved heads held clear of the water, tie-dye robes drifting out behind them, slowing them down. He was almost on them, close enough for them to see the deep lines on his face. Too close.

Rachel tried the motor again, and again. Still it would not start.

'Please!'

Not this again. She saw his desperation, fear – felt it. They couldn't afford to have those feelings anywhere near them. She *knew* that, somehow. That's how it happened. He was big. His expression, the way he was moving, he would take the boat; he didn't care about them. The women weren't far behind, screaming for her to stop. But they were tiring. The water was deep and cold.

At sea you were obliged to help someone in distress. But they were not at sea, and all the usual rules had gone overboard. *You have to be the calm one.* But there were too many things going on, too much movement, noise, too many decisions to make. Should she go for the oars, hit him over the head?

'Rachel!' Hannah's hair was streaming out around her. 'Hold down the choke, then pull.'

The motor roared. She full-throttled it, swishing hard to port, churning up the water. They were away. When she turned back, though she knew she shouldn't, the man's face shifted from fear to panic. Then he was thrashing, turning in circles, fighting something they couldn't see. He opened his mouth to scream, but it only filled with water. Rachel thought he would drown, but his face seemed to crumple and collapse, all the life suddenly taken from his body, and then he was still. Half-floating on the river.

The women called after the boat, screaming at them to stop. One swam towards the man with short, choppy strokes. And then she was thrashing, too, her head slipping under the water. Rachel was thankful she could no longer see her face.

The presence was stronger now, her heart hammering hard in her chest. As if someone had appeared out of the dark and placed a hand over her mouth. The other woman headed to shore, her arms beating at the water, but making little progress. Rachel forced herself to turn her back on them, rather than watch what she knew was coming.

They sped upriver, leaving those desperate people in their wake. The engine roared in her ears. Hannah was holding the baby close to her, as if she would never let him go. Her lips were moving, as if she was singing. Or praying.

When the eastern seaboard was burning – firestorms closing in on multiple fronts, joining together, like a creature intent on consuming every last bit of forest – all the roads were cut, the power out, whole towns evacuated. Just on dark, at the height of the chaos, with so many people displaced, firefighters cut off, the network went down. No one could contact their loved ones, no information was coming through. Not even the emergency alerts.

They had been blind, except to what they could see and feel in front of them: the sky a terrible deep orange, black leaves raining down, white ash, so much smoke. It had been days before survivors could find out whether they had lost their homes. Five long days before she had heard from Mia and Monique.

Rachel shook her head to stop the rush of memory. Things she had worked hard to forget had been dragged to the surface. They were blind now, too, vulnerable – exposed to something they didn't know or understand. On the run. It was just as Hannah had said – as if something was pursuing them, trying to move into the dark space left by not helping those poor people.

eleven

Their grip on her was easing, like getting her breath back after running, but she couldn't unsee what she had seen, or free herself from the feeling. Its residue somehow accentuated all of her self-doubts. Her mind retreated from images of the man's face, but kept circling back, not able to let it go.

Hannah stared ahead, holding her baby tight. Alone with her own fears. There wouldn't be much room for anything other than her choices, his survival.

'Okay?'

Hannah turned. 'You believe me now?'

'I do,' Rachel said. 'I felt it.'

'It was like they grew stronger with each person they took.'

Rachel's stomach lurched. *Like something feeding.*

Eventually the wind in her face, the briny water, cleared her head. Freed from rowing, she could focus on the riverbanks, but it was harder to take in the details at speed. They had passed the river's upper tidal reaches. Properties stretched further and further apart, fence lines in various states of disrepair, neglected orchards, falling-down horse yards. Original cottages made from stone, timber and tin, clinging on. Shacks and studios hinted at modest lives lived in private. Only the house near the old bridge was still grand, the domed crown of a bunya tree towering above. It had been built in more prosperous times, when there had been settlements, towns. When rivers and alluvial plains offered up the country's riches: gold and good growing land. For the white settlers lured to the area it must have seemed like the centre of the world.

There was a new mine. An open scar in the riverbank, massive machinery lining a fresh-cut road, tree trunks pushed into piles either side. Tailings clouded the water.

They saw no one, alive or dead. Rachel sped past.

The baby had fallen quiet – asleep, hopefully. With any luck, the fever had broken. The river, too, was beginning to break into pools and rapids. They threaded through rocks and around a floating log. A kingfisher swooped ahead of them, skimming low over the water, bright as a jewel.

Hannah looked back over her shoulder.

'I saw. Beautiful, right?' There was still beauty in the world.

Hannah was feeding her baby. Discreetly, but Rachel kept her eyes elsewhere. They'd had a pregnant woman as their life model once. Rachel had found her feminine curves, another life inside her, deeply moving, but baulked at expressing any of that on the page. Their teacher, still Hipwell in those days, had made clear her disappointment: pausing in front of Rachel's easel, shaking her head and moving on. The teachers all had their ways of getting the best out of them.

The fail rate had been 29 per cent. When she made it through, to honours, graduation, first exhibition, she'd thought she had passed her toughest tests, that life would continue on that upward trajectory.

The riverbed turned and turned again, shallower now. Rachel eased the throttle, keeping to the deepest channel. The water was clear, fish darting off into the shadows.

'How much further in the boat?'

'Half an hour.'

The river burbled over stones, diluting the images from the commune. Rachel reached for her flask and drank deeply. For the moment, there was calm, beauty and plenty of fresh water.

'You're an artist?'

'Yeah,' she said. 'What do you do, Hannah?'

'I'm just a librarian,' she said.

'At the school?'

'The public library, in town. The Hub, they call it now.'

'Do they still have real books?'

'Some,' she said. She dangled one hand in the water, wet the child's face and wrists. 'We had no choice, you know. Those people. We did well to get away.'

Rachel nodded. They'd been lucky. But that didn't make her feel any better. Or stop the recurring thought – more like a feeling. *It's only a matter of time.*

twelve

They were running out of river. Twice Rachel had to pull up the motor, push past a shallow spot with an oar, into another pool. It was hard work for the little boat against the force of water rushing to get away, down to the ocean. But they were making progress, moving steadily closer to Monique.

Her last letter had been full of news about the clinic, and the musician and retired dentist from Sydney who had taken over the antique store. Monique had them over for one of her dinner parties, to introduce them to the other interesting people of the town. Nimmitabel was full of characters; it had been that way since they were children – their own parents among them.

The year Rachel stayed, Monique had rarely left Rachel alone overnight or brought home strangers. But towards the end there had been a small dinner. Good food and conversation with artists and writers, which she realised she had missed. When she woke the next morning, her hunger for making had returned.

In the roar of water as they approached a moderate set of rapids, Rachel didn't see the submerged tree. The current swirled the boat around, jamming the hull hard up against the trunk. Timber ground on timber. The pressure of the river rushing beneath the tree sucked the side of the boat under, trapped them. Water was pouring in.

Fuck. The last thing they needed was to capsize, lose all their gear, end up with soaking wet clothes. How would Hannah hang onto the baby, keep his head above water?

Hannah shifted to the other side of the boat and leaned back. Rachel pushed hard against the log with one hand, revving the motor with the other. Water already covered Rachel's boots. They were trying to fight the river. She cut the engine and used an oar to push backwards instead, with the flow. It was enough to right the boat, to fend off properly, and spin away from the log. The jerrycan had worked loose, floating over the side and away, down-river. Hannah dragged the pack up out of the water and onto the seat. Rachel rowed towards a narrow beach.

They had taken the boat as far as they could. When she dropped the oars, her hands were trembling. Hannah hopped out, shoes tied around her neck, the child still strapped to her front, and pulled the boat onto the sand. Rachel grabbed the pack and leapt ashore, her boots plunging deep in the coarse sand. Together they dragged the boat above the high-tide mark, tipped out as much water as they could, and hid it beneath casuarina branches. She wasn't sure who they were hiding it from, but she wanted it to be there when she returned.

The baby's crying brought an end to the quiet.

'I have to change him again,' Hannah said.

Rachel nodded, fished a bag from the front of the pack. 'Just leave it in the boat.'

Rachel slipped off behind the trees to empty her bladder. She washed her hands and climbed onto an outcrop of water-worn rocks, like giant molars. Dragonflies flitted over the water. Wherever they touched the surface, tiny ripples flowed outwards. Even the tiniest creatures had an impact.

She was staring at coloured river stones, bright beneath the clear water, wondering how to achieve that effect with glass, when she noticed the pale insides of two halves of a shell. She scrambled down to the rockpool to examine it more closely. When she searched the sandy bottom, there was another, intact, poking up from the sand. Once she had her eye in, she found more and more, stuffing her pockets.

Hannah came down to the water to wash her hands. 'I'll just feed him, and then I'm ready.'

'Look.' She held up a handful of the dark shells.

'What are they?

'River mussels,' she said. 'We'll eat now, then press on.'

'Stop already?'

'They'll be ready before you're done.'

Rachel's stomach was already growling. Pasta, chilli, garlic and white wine would have been perfect. But warrigal greens would have to do. It would be a good nutrient boost. Who knew when they would eat well again?

Once the food supply was interrupted it only took a few days for the system to collapse. During the fires, with no power and no network, all the service stations, ATMs and supermarkets had closed: no money, no fuel, no food. One small local store with a generator opened for cash only. The owners worked the tills themselves, even though they had just lost their home. Milk, bread and toilet paper were the first to go. Then long-life milk, batteries, water. Wild-haired people with bare, sooty feet counted out coins in exchange for tinned food, cereal, potatoes. They moved with the fragility of newborn kittens, helping strangers, taking modest amounts, but for one woman, in full make-up, somehow untouched by fire or the scale of the disaster, who asked, too loud, why there weren't any bananas.

Rachel lit the gas, scooped an inch of river water into the billy and sat it on the burner. While she waited for it to come to the boil, she picked handfuls of warrigal greens from a shady spot, and hunted around until she found river mint, and a few handfuls of cress.

Hannah lay out the tarp on the flat rocks and sat cross-legged to feed Isaiah. Rachel dropped the mussels into the billy, with the warrigal on top. She popped the lid on for two minutes, drained the water, added oil, salt and pepper and the mint. She served up Hannah's mussels on the lid and ate her own straight from the billy.

'Thank you,' Hannah said.

They watched she-oak needles raining down on the pool's calm surface. The occasional bubble. Fish down below, in their own worlds. Platypus, perhaps. Whenever she sat a moment, all the details came into focus. Rachel's heart rate had dropped, her senses keening again.

Hannah fastened her shirt and shifted Isaiah to her other arm. 'Do you think it's passed from person to person?'

'Like something needing a host?'

Hannah nodded.

'Why not us, then?'

64

'We were moving away, and they had those other people,' Hannah said.

Rachel shut her eyes. 'I'm sorry about your mother,' she said.

'It's a lot to process, with everything else.'

'Your father still around?'

Hannah washed her hands in the river. 'I spent time with him when I was a kid,' she said. 'In the holidays. But it was never that comfortable. He was a drinker.'

'He's passed away?'

'Just before we fell pregnant. Liver cancer.'

It was funny how often things worked out like that. One life ends, another begins.

'What about your parents?' Hannah asked.

'They died when I was a child.'

Rachel squatted on the rock to pack coffee grounds into the basket of the press. She filled its tank with boiling water, screwed it shut and pumped the piston until a steaming espresso filled the machine's lid. She handed it to Hannah and repeated the process, using the cap of her aluminium drink bottle. By the rushing water, coffee had never tasted better. Monique always had managed to find just the right gift.

Then the baby stirred, started to whimper and cough. It was taking hold, wracking his little body.

Rachel rummaged for the first aid kit, handed Hannah the thermometer. They waited, watching his unhappy face. His breaths were small and shallow.

'Forty – a bit higher, maybe,' Hannah said.

'God. Should we bathe him again?' Rachel said. 'I'll mix some more Panadol.'

Hannah held him while Rachel ran cool water over his little hands and feet, sponged his face, neck and chest. Fairy wrens flitted in the spiky undergrowth. The ritual seemed to calm him. He made a half-hearted grab for her ponytail. His eyes were blue, like Hannah's.

'Hang in there, Isaiah,' Rachel said.

Hannah stared up at the steep cliffs. 'Where's the path?'

'We'll follow the river up to the falls, and then I can find the trail.' Hopefully *they* couldn't follow.

thirteen

Rachel leapt from rock to rock, planning her way several moves ahead. Her boots gripped stone, her legs strong, body balanced, despite the extra weight. Water rushed underneath. The air was fresh, the sun high overhead, warm on her back. The breeze in the casuarinas was like the sea, wild and constant. Whenever she looked over her shoulder, checking her pace, making sure Hannah could follow the same path, she was right behind, Isaiah bundled in front of her.

Rachel's parents had been rockhoppers. Family walking expeditions more often than not involved a river. The Snowy River was the first thing she really remembered. In November the water was still icy and, in the beginning, no one had wanted to get wet. But they were hot by the end, making their way down from Blue Lake at speed, the slopes unfolding around them. Monique and Rachel had stripped off and taken the plunge into a deep pool, their squeals echoing up the valley. Their parents had smiled indulgently, lounging on a flat rock, her mother's head resting on her father's thigh.

Monique had said since that it was a tradition that pre-dated them, something their parents had done as a couple. As a child, Rachel had been oblivious to them as individuals, without children. Her mother called her father Rockwarbler in correspondence, notes left on the fridge, and in moments of tenderness. He climbed, he leapt, and when he was happy, he sang. When they finally saw his namesake, the russet robin-like bird, when climbing in the Budawangs, Rachel imagined she could see the likeness. Rockwarblers were gone now, too, the last pairs lost during the fires.

Her parents had taught her how to read the landscape – to *feel* it. That gift was one of the reasons she had chosen to stay in the world, but also why it was so painful to see what was happening to it.

Rachel unzipped her fleece. Hannah had loosened Isaiah's top, and the papoose, trying to keep him cool, but he was crying, coughing and wheezing. Being shaken and jolted wasn't helping.

Then she heard a splash. Hannah swore. Rachel turned in time to see Hannah falling forwards, Isaiah half out of the papoose. Rachel lunged towards them but couldn't bridge the distance. Hannah landed hard on her forearms, Isaiah's soft head stopping only millimetres from the rock.

Rachel let out her breath. Hannah slowly got to her feet, pulling her wet shoe out of a rockpool. The strain of the journey, and so much worry, was beginning to show on her face.

'Okay?'

She shook her head but did not stop or complain, only kissed the top of Isaiah's head.

They kept going. It was all they could do. Rachel settled into a rhythm once again, leading the way steadily upriver. Like working in the studio, when her head was clear and she got into a flow, as if connecting with something larger than herself.

A shadow passed over the water. When Rachel looked up, a wedgetail eagle soared overhead, fingered wingtips upturned, following their progress. The river was a short cut, the most direct route across the land.

Rachel could hear the falls. She raced around the bend, leaping higher and further, until she reached the rock shelf. The river had opened up, white ribbons cascading into the deep blue pool. At its edge, the water spilled over smooth rocks, calm again after so much turbulence. She tilted her face into the rainbow of spray.

Hannah stopped beside her, out of breath.

Rachel had always thought that if something happened to her place, or if she had to live in the wild, this would be her spot.

'Rest here. We're going to leave the river after this, head up into the mountains. I just need to poke around a bit, find the trailhead.'

Isaiah was crying again, red in the face, clenching his little fists. Struggling just to breathe.

'I'll feed and change him,' Hannah said.

'You should bathe him again, too, cool him down while we have the water.'

Hannah nodded, started making her way over the mossy boulders, down to the pool's edge.

Rachel went in the other direction, using her hands to lower herself. The rocks were slippery from the spray. She made her way around the edge of the pool to the base of the falls and leaned the pack against the furred trunk of tree fern. She stared up at the rock face, searching for the path she knew was there.

After a couple of false starts, she retraced her steps and found the hand- and footholds between mosses and ferns and orchids. In some trick of the path, the carefully placed flat rocks were as obvious now as they had been hidden before.

Just before the top, she ducked under the side of the falls, cold droplets running down the back of her neck, edging across the hidden rock shelf to look out through the curtain of water. She acknowledged those who had gone before, worn the paths, stood in the same spot. The roaring was so loud she couldn't hear Hannah, Isaiah or any of her thoughts. It might be a portal to another world, if only she was brave enough to take the plunge, freefalling into the pool below.

Uncle Leon had shown her how to walk softly, with fox-feet, to feed herself from the land. When he saw the thunderstorm coming, he led the way into the cave to wait it out. There in the gloom, he had told tales of other galleries, in the mountains, of which he and his brothers were custodians. Though not necessarily all the same ones. They would head out for a walk together, but each sneak off at various points, to tend to their own respective sites, keeping the location secret even from each other.

Rachel felt her way to the back of the cavern. Even she had to stand on her toes to reach for the tin she had left in the high rock alcove. The money Monique had given her was still sealed in the beeswax wraps. Rachel hadn't wanted it in the house. She still didn't see a use for it. But it seemed that she was now in the situation Monique had been planning for. She packed the notes flat in the leg pocket of her cargoes, the ingots in the chest pocket of her shirt.

She left the cave through the tunnel at the back, emerging on the other side of the river, behind three belly-round boulders. It was the perfect place to evade pursuers. But what pursued them didn't seem to move over the ground or rely on sight. For a moment, Rachel considered slipping away. But she had led these two people into the wilderness, now she had to lead them out.

Hannah was waiting, staring in the opposite direction, dribbling cold river water over Isaiah's bare feet. Rachel coughed to announce her return, deliberately scuffed a boot. A startled water dragon skittered over the rocks, moving so fast that he ran over the water's surface.

Hannah turned, frowning. 'Found it?'

'Yeah.' She made her way around the pool's edge, focusing on her feet, rather than the drop below.

She drank from her water bottle and squatted down to refill it, put her hand out for Hannah's. 'It will be a while until we see water again.'

Rachel led the way to the base of the path and hauled on the pack. It was more a climb than a walk, using the rocks to lift themselves. Hannah's once-white shoes had taken on the colour of river dirt. At first she kept the pace Rachel set, without any visible sign of fatigue. Perhaps she ran normally, went to the gym. Or maybe being a mother gave her superpowers. It did look like hard work.

Then Isaiah started crying again, cutting the quiet, his distress echoing up the valley. Rachel closed her eyes, tried to control her breathing, her heart rate. They had entered the national park, but the falls were accessible by road and a public walking track. They were announcing their presence to everyone – anyone left alive.

'Wait.'

Rachel turned. Hannah couldn't reach the next handhold, not with Isaiah strapped in front of her.

Rachel wedged herself into the ledge. 'Can you give him to me?'

'I don't think I can unstrap him.'

'Grab my hand. You can push off that rock there,' she said. 'It's a bit of a stretch.'

'Looked a whole lot easier when you did it.'

Isaiah was coughing and wailing, made more uncomfortable by the irregular movements, fern fronds scratching his tender face. Hannah gripped the strappy leaves of a lomandra with her free hand. But its roots gave way in the loose soil. Rachel held tight to Hannah's wrist, and leaned back, to stop them falling. 'Got you.'

Hannah shut her eyes a moment and tried again.

'One, two, *three*.' This time Rachel pulled as Hannah pushed up and everyone was safe on the ledge. They stopped to catch their breath, looking back over the river, the way they had come. Until now, Rachel had been held by the valley. The country ahead didn't give her that same feeling.

'Okay?'

'Yeah,' Hannah said, getting to her feet.

Rachel took one last look towards home.

'Were you happy living out there, all alone?'

'I *am*,' Rachel said, over her shoulder. She led the way along the path ahead, deliberately lengthening her strides.

Above the falls, the track was flat and easy to follow, threading between lomandra and lichen-covered rocks. Rachel pushed ahead, long-striding across the country.

She took the lesser path, veering away from the main track, which led to a public car park and camping area. The thought of tents brought on images of a couple waking in fright, scrabbling for the torch. A brother and sister screaming for their parents. An overturned esky, the campfire kicked up, the open door of a burned-out car. Faces melting.

When Rachel turned to Hannah, she was breathing fast, hand on Isaiah's back. 'I feel them, too.'

'There's a campground near here,' Rachel said.

'*They* are there. And now they know we have a child.'

They walked as fast as they could without running. As if *they* were only feral dogs, and to run would be to show fear, give in.

Hannah was humming, rubbing Isaiah's back. Rachel focused on trying to pick the tune, remember the lyrics. Until they were deep in the national park, with nothing but trees for miles around.

fourteen

Each time they topped one crest, another, even steeper, loomed ahead of them. So far from home, so far to go. But the path was clear and even through trees, allowing them to keep up a good pace.

Walking among unburned trees, solid trunks as far as she could see – yellow box, forest red gum, silvertop ash on the ridgelines – it was almost possible to forget. But the trees weren't giving her the peace they had. The people on the river, at the campsite. Their fear. The money her sister had left her was weighing heavy in Rachel's pockets. What had Monique been carrying while Rachel hid away, blowing glass?

They startled a swamp wallaby and stopped to watch her thump away, crashing down the steep slope, her rufous ears and belly bright against the dull green foliage.

When they reached the bare limestone outcrop, the sun was beginning its descent, dropping right into her eyeline. It was giving Rachel a headache. Hannah had stopped yet again, to feed and change Isaiah.

Rachel slipped off the pack, removed her water bottle, the waxed parcels, and the first aid kit. They sat on a fallen log, eating their half-squashed sandwiches. They tasted ordinary after the mussels, but she needed the fuel. Rachel could no longer see the river, her valley. There was just the haze hanging over the coast, a strange stillness. She gauged the rugged mountains they had passed, the state forest and mountain range to the north, and the sheer rock faces and claw-like spurs of the range to the south-west – where they were headed.

'It's like the end of the world.'

'It's beautiful,' Rachel said. She had looked at the mountains nearly every day of her life. They were part of who she was – or who she wanted to be.

'This was a kind of highway, from the coast up to the high country in summer. For thousands of years, tens of thousands. Long before our soft white feet.'

Hannah stared a moment, patting Isaiah's back while he coughed. It had got a hold of him. Every step was wearing him out, even though he wasn't taking them.

Rachel made a line with her hand. 'Local creation stories say it was a platypus who travelled through here, up to the escarpment, and made all the tunnels and galleries.'

'We had a Yuin elder at the library every week, to tell a story or read a book to the school groups. The kids loved that one the most,' Hannah said.

Rachel pictured Uncle Leon's long white beard, his measured gestures, hoping he was okay somehow.

Hannah held her water bottle against Isaiah's temples. Rachel stuffed the last of the sandwich in her mouth and handed over the thermometer. She tucked the waxed wrapper in the front pocket of the pack, waiting for the thermometer reading. It was one of the ways they were measuring their journey.

'Still forty,' Hannah said.

Isaiah coughed, this time bringing up a wad of yellow phlegm. His face was miserable, as if shocked that there could be so much pain in the world. It seemed too much for such a little body to bear.

'God.' Rachel shook her head. She was no doctor, but she knew it wasn't good. And it was her fault. They could have been at Monique's by now. If she hadn't delayed leaving.

Hannah wiped away tears. 'He's so sick. What if he dies out here?'

'Come on,' Rachel said. 'All we can do is keep going.'

The path narrowed, until it was barely distinguishable from a wallaby track. Rachel stood a moment on the crest. She could almost see the line where dry eucalypt forest gave way to heath. They were up into the tablelands. She ran her hands over the scrubby wattles and dwarf she-oaks growing back after the fires. They were waist high on her, but she could see only Hannah's head and shoulders. The pale trunks of jilliga ash bent in the breeze. Small birds called all around but kept themselves hidden. Rachel sensed movement: a peregrine falcon soaring on an updraft, high overhead.

It was a relief to walk downhill again, to use different muscles, though more mountains loomed ahead. It had been spring when Rachel had last enjoyed the same view, brilliant with wildflowers: yellow, pink and white. This time, the flowers were gone. It was still beautiful, but tinder dry. They were in a deep dish in the landscape. It was hot. The air so dry it almost crackled, as if the height of summer. There were trees, scrub, as far as she could see. No clearings or structures. If a fire started, there would be nowhere to hide.

Hannah swore. 'What makes square shits, and why always on the steps?'

'Wombats. They like to get their butts up high, in a clear spot. I don't know why.'

The wind was picking up, moving the heath in waves. Hannah's hair swirled around her face. Clouds tore up the sky, skimming low over the treeline, their shadows moving fast over the ground. A clap of thunder was the only warning. The sky darkened, and large drops, set wide apart, started to fall.

'Where did that come from?' Hannah said.

The moisture was a relief at first. But they were exposed, and Rachel couldn't read the conditions or pick what would happen next. They hurried downhill, two steps at a time, back below the treeline. It was mainly wind. Only sticks and leaves rained down.

No lightning, please.

There was no shelter. The trees were as much of a threat, the wind roaring in their crowns, bending them low. A limb creaked, cracked and crashed to the ground not far from the path. Ribbons of bark tore at their skin, flew through the air. Hannah was trying to run with her hand over Isaiah's head.

They squatted behind two boulders, out of the worst of the wind. Isaiah's crying competed with the howling all around. He was giving voice to the fear they each felt. More thunder, low overhead, and then lightning, cracking – striking something close.

77

Rachel tensed. A tree or large limb came down, crashing to earth. And then the smell of burning eucalyptus. The incendiary of the bush. When she peeked around the boulder, she saw that a tree had been struck, its trunk splintering. Flames spread out into the heath, fanned by the wind. Not towards them, but not away from them, either.

'We need to get out of here,' Rachel said. 'We cross another river, the Shoalhaven, about a kilometre away.'

They ran down the path, Rachel slowed by the pack, Hannah by carrying Isaiah. The smell of smoke drove them on. When they looked back, the fire was sweeping uphill, with the wind, the way they had come. They slowed to a jog, but it was still too close for comfort, everything so unpredictable.

She had planned to cross the river further west, where it was easier to ford. Now they would have to swim or wade across. But hopefully it would stop the fire behind them.

When they reached the river, they did not have to wade or swim – or even remove their shoes. It had shrunk to a shallow creek. They stepped across on slimy rocks. The riverbed was cool, tall trees reflected on the water, wet stones beneath, but it couldn't offer them much protection.

'This is it?' Hannah said.

'Yeah.' Last time, Rachel had had to strip off and wade naked, holding her pack above her head, towelling herself dry on the other side. The winter rain hadn't come. It hadn't come for a long time.

Isaiah balled his hands into fists and coughed. A horrible

rattling cough. Hannah rocked and shushed him but he couldn't stop. The smoke wasn't helping.

Hannah bathed his legs in river water while Rachel leaned on a tree trunk, to try to get a read on the landscape. The current wind direction would take the fire away from them. They could only hope it didn't change.

She spread out the map. It was already mid-afternoon; they had a lot of ground to cover if they were going to make the hut before dark.

'We can stick to the waterway for a while, and then get back on the path, head over the next range,' she said.

'Okay.' Hannah's face was pale and without expression as she bundled Isaiah away again. Still he coughed and cried. Smoke was filling the valley, scratching at their lungs. Even Rachel had started to think it was hopeless. But then a crimson rosella flew right between them, a burst of blue and red leading them on.

fifteen

The river rocks were small and mossy – not made for hopping. The banks were too steep for any consistent path. After they had each slipped and got their shoes wet, they just splashed through the shallow water. The cloud of smoke was building, but not pursuing them. Rachel slowed her breathing without slowing her pace, taking in everything around them, using all of her senses. In the studio, fire was her companion, not something to be feared. Still, her heart was heavy with the suffering of the land, its depletion. It should not be burning this early in the season.

The lorikeets and parrots were aware of them, chattering with each other, at least as social as humans. Not for the first time, Rachel wished she could understand, ask questions.

Hannah refilled their water bottles and they took advantage of a low point in the riverbank to scramble up into more open forest, rising towards the next ridgeline. They followed an old bridle trail between ironbarks and stunted mallees.

Flies were hanging around their faces, covering their backs. Hannah swatted at them, waved them away from Isaiah's mouth and eyes. Rachel's shoulders were chafing under the pack straps. Should she have made a different choice: stolen a vehicle, gone by road? They could probably have been there in four, five hours. And she wouldn't have put Hannah, or Isaiah, through all this. Taken such risks. But then, the roads, other people, were risks, too.

Breathe, Ray.

By agreeing to help, she had made herself responsible for both of them, forgotten her resolve to be responsible only for herself.

'Ray,' Hannah said.

Rachel frowned and turned around.

'Sorry. I hear you talking to yourself, you know.'

'You can call me Ray,' she said. 'And just tell me to stop muttering.'

'It doesn't bother me. At least I know what you're thinking.'

Rachel snorted.

'We haven't seen any houses yet?'

'We're on private land now, so we'll start to pass some properties,' Rachel said.

'Do you think *they* are already out here?'

'Hopefully not, if they need people to move,' she said. 'Can you whistle?'

Hannah pursed her lips and imitated the *hey, baby* call of a male crimson rosella. 'My brother taught me that,' she said. 'He has like a million animals, all wildlife rescues: blue-tongue lizards, possums, a galah.'

Rachel gave the answering whistle, of a female crimson rosella. 'Perfect. That's our alert signal, okay?'

*

Hannah had stopped again, complaining about the flies, the heat. Isaiah's wailing was a constant. Even Rachel found herself tripping on the tussocky grasses, stumbling into wombat holes. She had started to watch her feet, not the landscape, and lost the path again somehow.

It was more open country: power lines, paddocks, cattle and sheep. She caught the red streak of a fox, running for the safety of trees. He kept stopping to look back, caught between caution and curiosity, shaggy tail on alert.

She held the fence wires apart for Hannah, handed the pack over, then snagged her cargoes when she slipped through herself. She freed the fabric, but it was torn, and the rusty barb had nicked her skin. 'Crap.' It wasn't much but she stopped to disinfect the wound and cover it with a bandaid.

Rachel counted every step until they were back beneath the cover of ironbarks and yellow box. Limestone boulders huddled like trolls set solid by a sudden dawn, eons ago. Rachel unfolded the map and spread it over a lichenous boulder-top, checking their direction with the compass.

Hannah put her water bottle away, half empty already, and leaned over Rachel's shoulder. 'Show me how to read it?'

'Haven't you ever used GPS?'

'Yes – but it just tells you where to go.'

'Well, you can see the river we crossed, here. And these lines show the hills and mountains. Their shape. The closer together the lines, the steeper it is. North is set on the map, at the top – and the compass tells us which way is north, here on the ground. Using the landmarks, we can figure out which way to go. If you didn't have a compass, or a map, you could also use your watch.

In the southern hemisphere, you point twelve o'clock in the direction of the sun. North is always halfway between the hour hand and twelve o'clock.'

Hannah blinked. 'But the path isn't actually on the map?'

'No. It was always easy to follow. But I lost it this time, somehow,' Rachel said. 'I think we're here.' She touched the map. 'That's the hill ahead. And I know the path runs between that hill and this one – so we just need to go this way to find it again.'

'How far to the hut? I'm so tired.'

Rachel hesitated, then unfolded the next two sections of the map. 'Here,' she said. 'That symbol.'

Hannah shook her head as she assessed the distance. 'Isn't there anything closer? A town?'

'No towns.'

'Will we even make it before dark? We can't be out in the middle of nowhere at night.'

'This is what *you* wanted,' Rachel said. 'We have no choice now. Except to keep going.' She folded the map, stowed it away, and heaved the pack onto her tired back.

Hannah's eyes filled with tears, she sniffed, and adjusted Isaiah's collar.

'We'll make it, Hannah. We have to.' Rachel turned and started walking, listening until she heard Hannah's steps behind her.

sixteen

The farmhouse itself was small, a fibro shack dwarfed by an untidy tangle of corrugated-iron outbuildings and abandoned cars, trucks and utes, stretching back at least three generations. A shiny new satellite dish pointed north. Despite its size, the neglected air, the place gave the sense of having once accommodated many people, an extended family, perhaps.

Rachel trained the binoculars on the bare front yard. Toy trucks and tractors were paused in the middle of moving sand from one pile to another, an echo of the life-sized machinery outside the fence. A faded cap lay in the dirt. The windows were dark, no shoes or coats by the front door. A barbecue gas bottle had been left out the back, as if preparing for a fire evacuation.

A shed door swung in the breeze, with an empty-sounding screech. Rachel half-expected someone to walk out, but no one appeared. They might have left yesterday, or last year.

Hannah's breathing was loud beside her, Isaiah's wheeze building. He was about to cough.

Rachel had the urge to cover his mouth. 'It feels really bad here,' she said.

They broke from the cover of the trees at a jog, not wanting to show fear but desperate to cross the clearing in the shortest possible time. The property owner's name was burned into a piece of packing case: *Thompson*. If it was a natural disaster, in any other circumstances, they would check on the Thompsons, see if they were okay.

Rachel had trained as a volunteer firefighter the winter after buying her place. It was in her interests, living remotely, surrounded by forest. During Black Summer, they had worked around the clock, leaving their own homes unattended. But, as they began to understand, they weren't the sort of fires they could really fight. They didn't behave as fires should, as the modelling predicted, but joined together, creating their own weather, firestorms, exceeding worst-case scenarios. The best they could do was evacuate people, try to save homes. On properties, the outbuildings would go up. If they were lucky, the helicopter would drop a load of water, or pink fire retardant, on the house, and it would be left standing amid the black.

When there was a lull, a brief easing of conditions, they would work around the clock again, building containment lines: bulldozing great tracts of forest in the hope that the fire would not cross. All the while, the fire fronts crept forwards. When temperatures rose, if the winds were right, it leapt over those lines like they were nothing; over roads and rivers, taking everything in its path.

It was as if it had been someone else trying to defend the potter's village, burning embers raining down like meteors.

Holding a high-powered hose, pointing it at the wall of fire, only to have it blow the water back – mixed with flame. As if it was laughing at her. The birds trying to flee the forest, their wings and tails on fire, burning alive, falling from the sky: parrots, lorikeets, black cockatoos. Screaming in pain. Helicopters *whoof-whoofing*, low overhead, trying to drop water, pitching in the wind the fire made.

Houses, the whole street, going up faster than anyone had thought possible. The heat melting their equipment, trees falling on the truck, the terrible roaring in her ears that had burned out part of her mind.

'Ray!'

Rachel blinked away tears. Hannah and Isaiah were in front. Whatever had happened at the Thompsons' was trying to get to her, somehow, inside her head. Worming into the shadows, blacking everything else out. Until it was real.

She ran. Something in the backpack was clunking against her drink bottle. But she did not stop until they were among trees again, out of sight of the house, puffing and heaving to get their breath.

Hannah tucked her hair behind her ears. 'You can't freeze like that. That's how it happens.'

'They were inside my head. Dragging up my memories,' Rachel said. She felt in her pocket for her drops, tipped her head back to place them under her tongue.

'They're trying to take Isaiah.'

'Is that what you're most afraid of?'

'Of course,' she said. 'You?'

'I was in a fire. Maybe it's different for everyone?'

'Maybe.'

Rachel watched Isaiah's face. Did he feel fear? Was this something they could even protect him from?

'How did *they* get all the way out here?' Hannah said.

'I don't know.'

seventeen

By the time they reached the top of the last hill, the light was fading, and she still couldn't see the hut. Hannah was starting to stumble, humming to Isaiah, herself. Rachel had been grateful for the quiet, but now she worried he might never wake up.

A cockatoo, bright white, wheeled against the dark green canopy below. The fires had swept through the area again the summer after she last did the walk. An original slab hut, with a post and rail fence, surrounded by forested hilltops – it was vulnerable. She had slept rough, under the stars, plenty of times. But the night air, the cold that would come, wouldn't be good for Isaiah's cough. Or Hannah. The dark had never really bothered Rachel, but without sight, without a firm grip on the real world, it was easier for shadows to move in, fears to take hold.

She was working on a backup plan, perhaps sheltering in a shed, when she spotted the hut's roof, the one straight angle among curves. Only now did Rachel consider the possibility that it might not be a safe space. That there might be other people inside – or might have been.

She held up her hand. Hannah paused, close enough behind that Rachel could feel her body's warmth. The humming stopped. She crouched, searching the cabin, the valley, for movement. Kookaburras called up a pink dusk, their song reverberating up the valley. The pale tail of a rabbit disappeared down a burrow.

She lifted the binoculars. The cabin was dark, no smoke. The doors and windows were closed, but the curtains were not drawn.

They walked on, more quickly now. There were no tracks on the path ahead of them. Still, her skin was tingling, her body on high alert. She slipped out of the pack. Hannah took it, leaned it against her body, rocking a little with the weight.

'Wait here.'

Rachel ran, crouched over, down the track, senses keened. At the door, she stopped, listened, but there was nothing from within. Just crickets, a yellow robin somewhere, having the last word on the day as usual.

She had brought no weapon. If there was someone, something, inside. If *they* were in there, she would just have to shut her mind to them.

Keep moving. Rachel gripped the handle, turned it and pushed through the doorway all in one movement. Ready for whatever waited.

The room was empty. It had been empty for some time. Dust covered the table and chairs, bunks and lamps, cobwebs softened the corners. She didn't feel any other presence. Rachel let out her breath. They had made it. They would be safe and warm for the night. And, somehow, in the moment, she had forgotten to be afraid. Her body, her instincts, had taken over – remembered how they used to operate together.

Rachel gathered an armful of kindling. Hannah swept out the hut's dirt floor with an old straw broom. The stone fireplace was big enough to climb into. Rachel lit a tepee of sticks and leaves and, once it was away, fed in cut branches from the basket on the hearth. There was enough wood stacked outside against the wall of the cabin to last several weeks. She closed the curtains, lit the lamp on the table and another in the kitchen, turned them to low.

While Rachel ferried in armloads of wood, Hannah wiped down the table, shook out and flipped the bunk mattresses. Pulled the sleeping bags from their covers and rolled them out. The place already felt warmer, homier. Safe.

When Hannah tried to feed Isaiah, he wouldn't drink. His little body was floppy.

Rachel handed Hannah the thermometer, leaning on the back of a chair, waiting for the verdict.

'Still forty,' Hannah said.

It wasn't good. But at least it was no higher. Rachel unloaded the pack, dug around for the facecloth, found a bowl and went outside to fill it with tank water. It was already cool outside, the breeze carrying a scent she didn't recognise. Hannah took the facecloth with her free hand, put it to Isaiah's forehead. Rachel sponged his wrists and ankles, tried to will him better.

Hannah watched her. 'You didn't have children?'

'No,' Rachel said. People were always so quick to judge women choosing to live without children or a partner.

'Did you want them?'

'Not really.'

'Smart.'

Rachel glanced up. 'You didn't?'

'He wasn't planned,' she said. 'No one tells you how hard it is.'

'It's not exactly normal circumstances.'

'Before this, even.'

Rachel dissolved half a Panadol in water. *Should we even be giving him Panadol?* In adults it was better to let the fever take its course, kill the bug. It was part of the body's defence system. How exhausting it must be, the responsibility for another human life. One you had created. Rachel tortured herself over every mistake, double-guessed every decision, and she only had herself to worry about.

'How long has Kyle been away?'

'He was there for the birth,' Hannah said. 'And he's home most weekends. But he'd just started the new contract, with Defence. And could only take a few days off. It was a decision we made, to take the extra money.'

'Makes sense.'

'It did,' she said. 'But now – what does a couple of thousand dollars matter? I mean, I'd rather have my husband. Or have been with him when . . .'

'You couldn't have known.'

The air was cooling fast. The new moon was just a fingernail, enough to offer hope, but dark enough to conceal them for the night. There were no human sounds: no voices, vehicles, not even the background buzz of power lines. Nimmitabel felt further away than when they had set out.

Rachel peeled off her clothes, folded them on the timber bench, and stood beneath the stream of water. It was cold, but invigorating, every cell of her being absolutely alive. Some of the weight of the day washed away.

She and Monique had still gone camping and walking together while Rachel lived in Canberra. When Rachel moved down the coast, they had always said they'd meet in the middle – here at the cabin – but somehow it had never happened. As she chammied herself dry, she could still hear Isaiah inside, the exhalation in the sound as Hannah rocked him.

It helped keep things in perspective. She was fit, healthy, alive. They had shelter, food, water. She pulled on her thermals, clean socks and stepped into her boots without lacing them, clomping back inside. The cabin was already warm. She left her boots at the door, hung the towel by the fire to dry and sat at the table with the first aid kit to apply fresh bandaids to the cuts on her finger and leg. 'What's that?'

Hannah was slicing vegetables with Isaiah swinging between her arms.

'I found an old potato and an onion in the cupboard,' she said.

'Cool.' They were scavengers now, like the foxes. Rachel wiped out the pan, fired up the little gas stovetop. She fried off the vegetables, ground salt and pepper over the top, and took it off the heat to stir through a tin of tuna.

They ate at the table. Isaiah's eyes were closed, but his face was a little less tortured.

'What is this place?' Hannah said.

'National Parks owns it. It's a shelter for walkers.' In the high country, everything could change so quickly: a storm, a sudden drop in temperature, even snow. The flames had settled into coals, the evening into night. It was only a little more than forty-eight hours since Hannah had knocked on her door. Since the world had split open. It already felt like months ago.

Hannah changed Isaiah again, tried to settle him. Washed out his nappy and hung it by the fire to dry. Rachel boiled water and made cups of sweet tea. She divided the chocolate in two, offering one half to Hannah.

'Thanks.'

They sat in the deep chairs beside the fire, hand crafted from sticks and branches, long ago. They would have heard some stories, in their time.

Rachel's muscles were stiffening, her body beginning to register fatigue. Some of the thoughts that came, in the stillness, were unwelcome. What would they find in Nimmitabel, at her sister's house? How long could they keep whatever it was from happening to them, to Isaiah? Her mind had started filling the gaps with new horrors. The imagination had no limits, it seemed, once unleashed. Maybe that was all fear was.

Hannah started at every creak of the hut, every sound outside, her head turning to the locked windows and bolted door. As if *they* had followed them there. Maybe they had. She couldn't seem to shake the stain of them from her body.

'Are we safe?'

'Yeah,' Rachel said. The cabin, with the bush around them, felt as safe a place as any.

'What if *they* come in the night?' Hannah said. 'While we're asleep.'

Rachel put her cup on the floor. 'At the campground, they tried to reach us but couldn't. We got away. And they couldn't follow,' Rachel said. 'Or they would have, surely. Same at the house.'

Hannah nodded.

Rachel stood and took their cups to the sink. 'We should probably get some rest, while Isaiah is sleeping.'

Hannah went to the door but hesitated. 'Will you shine a light for me while I go to the toilet?'

Rachel leaned in the doorway, making a path with the torch, while Hannah ran to the little outhouse. Cold air cooled her cheeks. The stars were bright but far away. Hannah's pale face appeared out of the dark, running back to the cabin. Back to Isaiah. When Rachel stepped outside, she heard Hannah bolt the door behind her.

Rachel took the headtorch but switched it off, letting her eyes adjust to the dark. The black plastic seat was cold, only the stars gazing down. She took her time, trying to ease her mind around new information, the new reality. She just had to get them to Nimmitabel. When she started to shiver, she headed back to the cabin and knocked on the door.

Hannah didn't respond and, for a moment, Rachel worried that something had happened, that she would be shut out. But then the door opened, and Hannah was there, relieved to see her, too.

Rachel waited while Hannah untied her shoes and removed her outer layers, taking the lower bunk. She snuggled into the sleeping bag, Isaiah against her. Rachel turned out the lamp in the kitchen but left the one on the table on the lowest flame, to ease Hannah's fears.

She climbed up to the top bunk. The first few minutes trapped inside a sleeping bag were always a battle. It was too tight, confined. She struggled to get comfortable. Her hips were sore, her back, her heels. And it was hard to settle, with two people beneath her. It was a very long time since she had shared a room with anyone.

Let alone a bed. She flinched from the thought, envious of Hannah and Isaiah's intimacy. The body heat of another, skin against skin, was something she worked hard at not remembering, but even she had to admit it would be welcome against the cold wall of the cabin.

eighteen

Rachel woke with a jolt. She had been holding the man in the river underwater, with the oar. It was still dark in the cabin. Isaiah was wailing. It was awful to hear. Not just the noise, at the worst possible pitch, like a knife scraping over her skin, but the pain and fear in it. He had coughed right through the night. Hearing him struggling to breathe was impossible to shut out. She wriggled out of her sleeping bag and climbed down from her bunk.

'Morning.'

'Morning, Ray.' Hannah had dark rings under her eyes. 'Could you take him, while I go to the toilet?' Hannah handed Isaiah over without waiting for an answer.

It was as if he could sense her discomfort, wriggling and squirming in her hands. She remembered to hold his head up. But nothing she did, silly faces, calming words, humming, could quieten him. She was going out of her mind after a few minutes; how did Hannah manage twenty-four-seven?

'Let's see what your temperature is, then.' She carried him to the table, shook out the thermometer, warmed it in her mouth.

Hannah came back inside as she was reading it. 'What is it?'

'Still a solid forty.'

'Shit.' Hannah massaged her forehead. 'He's not really feeding, either.'

Rachel was glad to hand him back. But she could no longer hand over the worry as easily. A temperature that high for that long could damage his brain, his development.

'We should be able to start him on the antibiotics tonight,' Rachel said. But they had to get there first – and it might be too late. She revived the fire with her breath and fresh kindling, put the oats on to cook, and slipped out the door into the quiet.

Dawn had come, and they were alive. Her breath made fog in front of her face. The forest behind them was shrouded in mist, their path ahead obscured. But it would be a clear day.

She used the toilet, stopped at the tank to wash her hands and face, tied back her hair. A pink glow rose from the first pale blue, the sun still out of sight, behind the mountains ahead of them. She wandered out to the fence, leaning on the weathered timber. Pastels were the hardest to achieve in glass, giving her a particular appreciation for the world's more delicate shades. She took a moment to breathe in the wildness of the place, the stillness. In less than eight hours she would know if her sister was alive or dead.

When she opened the rough door of the cabin, Isaiah had stopped crying. Hannah was serving up porridge.

They ate by the fire. Hannah cleaned up and got Isaiah ready. Rachel warmed his tiny beanie and socks, dug out her neck warmer. 'You could put this around him. It will be cold for the first few hours.'

'Thanks.'

Rachel compressed their sleeping bags into stuff sacks and stowed them in the pack, found a place for everything else. It was lighter, but not much. She cleaned her teeth, took her tablets, tied on her boots. Wherever she was, whatever happened, mornings were much the same. A body-memory.

'Ready?'

Hannah nodded, her face half obscured by beanie and scarf, Isaiah rugged up in front of her. Rachel took one last look around the cabin for anything they had missed and closed the door.

Their noses ran in the cold air. Mist clung to the gullies, gums dragged it thin. Rachel pulled her beanie down over her ears, tucked her hair out of the way, and pulled up the hood of her fleece. A new day, a new start. It was almost possible to believe the world had been restored to normal.

'No freezing up today,' Hannah said. 'Let's keep talking to each other.'

'Got it,' Rachel said.

The path had broadened again. Other than the winding track of a large goanna, claw marks either side of a tail, there was no sign of anything travelling ahead of them.

Everything ached: her feet, her back, her calves, her right knee and hip. But she soon loosened up, got back into rhythm. 'The worst is behind us,' Rachel said. 'No more scrambling.' Still, it was relentlessly uphill. Rachel set the pace at steady, rather than flat out, not pushing as hard as she had the day before.

The sun soon burned off the mist and melted the last of the frost. The tree-covered hills shifted from mauve to green. The sky was so clear, so blue and, at that altitude, there seemed to be so much of it. It was hard not to keep looking up.

Hannah stopped. 'You know what's missing?'

Rachel shook her head.

'Planes. I haven't seen a *single* aeroplane or contrail.'

It was part of the wrongness to the quiet, the constant hum of the human-made actions that even she had taken for granted every day. Planes full of people travelling from city to city, from country to country, crossing seas and continents, mountain ranges and war zones. For work, for holidays, for love, for weddings, funerals. Rachel pushed away images of aircraft crashing into the ground, buildings, cities, forests. The terror of those trapped on board.

'I mean, it was weird, during the pandemics, but there were still aircraft, drones. This . . . it's not like there are helicopters out searching for survivors,' Hannah said.

After the fires, helicopters had *chop-chop-chopped* overhead for weeks, alongside the spotter planes, filling up with river water, until they seemed part of the red skies themselves. Whenever they had flown over since, it had triggered something in her body, taken her right back to that time. But it would have been hopeless without them, the fires on their doorstep the entire summer. And the silence was so lonely.

Hannah and Rachel stood side by side, staring up into the empty sky.

They stopped at the edge of a clearing, where the valley sloped away, mountains piling over each other in the distance. Mountains they had yet to cross. Rachel reached into the side pocket of the pack for the muesli bars and handed one to Hannah.

'Thanks.' Hannah had removed the wrapper and bitten the bar in half before Rachel rezipped the pocket.

The ground started to shake beneath their feet. A sound like thunder, but there were no clouds, the sun bright above them. Perhaps it was an earthquake, the earth itself finally moving in anger. Hannah moved closer, so that their arms were touching.

The air was electric.

Then they saw them. A mob of brumbies, moving fast – the feral descendants of domestic horses that had come to dominate the alps. They were magnificent: lean and proud, shaggy mains and tails, coats in all colours and combinations, powerful muscles moving. They spread uphill as one animal, galloping full speed, hoof to hoof, flank to flank, heads held high. Something had spooked them; they wheeled and turned, running for the trees. Their whinnies carried up the valley, untethered.

Rachel had never warmed to horses but in that landscape, the sound was wild. They were majestic, magical even. A glossy black mare and her new roan foal clung to the edge of the group, protected, but avoiding the crush.

There was nothing driving them. Nothing they could see. Hannah and Rachel held their breath, half expecting the animals to fall, one by one, but they scattered among the snow gums and disappeared from view.

There was life, yet. Beauty.

'So, dogs, but not horses?' Hannah said.

'Maybe because they're wild?'

'Or dogs are closer to us.' Hannah shook her head. 'I hope we didn't do this, unleash something terrible on the world.'

nineteen

Rachel heard a crimson rosella's call. It took a moment to register the off note. She had been in a different landscape altogether, walking without seeing. An exhibition opening in the city with Hans. Wearing a suit jacket, T-shirt and skinny jeans, holding a glass of Champagne in some city, a lifetime ago, among admiring art aficionados. It had been her second or third show, but Hans was there, commanding the audience. She had been grateful to find pride on his face – even if it was for his part in her success. Monique had been there, too, of course. In a green dress, and glamorous silk scarf. She had never liked Hans, suspicious that he was preying on vulnerable students. But she was always polite, charming even. It was only the slight narrowing of her eyes whenever Hans spoke, or touched Rachel, that gave her sister away.

Rachel turned, on high alert, scanning the landscape for threats. Hannah wasn't behind her. She strode back down the path, only now seeing the farmhouse huddled up the back of cleared paddocks.

'Sorry,' Hannah said.

'What's up?'

'I need to change Isaiah. And I have a blister.' Her shoe was lying on its side in the dirt. She hopped to a rock beside the path, its surface pale green with lichen. Rachel pulled out the first aid kit and took hold of Hannah's heel. She peeled off the grubby sock, cleaned the wound and dried it, stuck a padded plaster over the top, and a waterproof dressing over that. 'There you go,' she said. It wasn't ideal. Once you had a blister, walking was uncomfortable.

Rachel went back for Hannah's discarded shoe, so small she checked to be sure it was an adult size. The fabric had turned a dirty grey and torn away from the sole, not designed for real walking, let alone rocks, mountains and river-crossings. She rummaged through the pack for the duct tape, ripped off a strip and wrapped it around and around the shoe.

She waited while Hannah changed Isaiah, but watched this time, to see how it was done. In case she ever had to do it.

The feeding she definitely couldn't help with. Rachel packed away the duct tape and first aid kit, and drank from her water bottle, staring out over the farm. The fences were well maintained, the stock healthy. Cattle and horses, by the look of it. It was hard country – exposed. They were right on the snow line but the paddocks still carried a tinge of green.

Rachel wandered back to the rock, offered the duct-taped shoe. Hannah started to laugh.

'What's so funny?'

'So. Many. Things.' She was holding her stomach.

And then Rachel was laughing, too. 'There's a hole.'

'I know,' she said. 'But . . .'

'Not the look you were going for?'

'Who even carries duct tape? Except serial killers.'

'Well, you knocked on my door.'

A rooster crowed, reminding them that they were in full view of the farmhouse.

Rachel raised the binoculars. It was a brick colonial with a corrugated-iron roof. A new satellite dish pointed towards the city. The windows were heavily curtained, doors closed, the broad verandas neat and tidy. An ashtray on the arm of an old lounge facing north was the only sign of human life.

'What does a white flag mean?' Hannah asked.

'Surrender? Peace?' she said. 'Why?'

'In front of the house. Maybe they need help.'

'Huh.' A flagpole. Normally flying the Australian flag, perhaps, one of those aggressively nationalistic households she knew to avoid. Flags could be a welcome – or a warning.

Chooks roamed free, scratching in the dirt. The bush had been cleared in a wide circle around the house. The ornamentals planted instead were dead or dying. Except an evergreen deodar out the front, which would look like a giant Christmas tree when it snowed.

'Should we go down?'

Rachel shook her head. 'No way.' Not after what she had felt at the Thompsons'.

'I'm almost out of water,' Hannah said. 'With changing Isaiah, cooling him down. There's a tank there.'

'Take mine.' Rachel held out her water bottle, still two-thirds full.

'You'll need that.'

'I'll be fine.'

'You make it seem effortless. But your back is soaked,' Hannah said. 'You need to keep drinking. And I need to wet him down.'

Rachel frowned. She did like to make it look easy. But the pack was heavy, dragging on her shoulders. And now she was frozen on the ridge, in plain view. If there was a next life, it wouldn't have any complex moral decisions in it.

Rachel fiddled around with the pack, her bootlaces, not wanting to leave the path or add a single unnecessary step to the journey. They needed to minimise risks. But they also needed water. Perhaps the people did need help. They might even have antibiotics in their bathroom cabinet. For a moment, she saw a mirrored door, opening. Packets of medication inside.

She had to stretch to full stride to catch up with Hannah. The black Angus cattle stopped chewing and stared as Hannah and Rachel crossed the paddock. The horses – two mares – took note of the intrusion and tossed their heads, but returned to their feed bins. It was a small, bare paddock, and the feed bins would soon be empty.

There were boot prints in the dust around the flagpole. The metal cleat clanged against the mast, the flag fluttered overhead. The sick feeling in Rachel's stomach intensified so quickly she couldn't speak. *This was a mistake.*

Hannah went to the water tank. The tap was tight, and then squealed when it released. *Too loud.* Hannah filled her bottle and put her hand out for Rachel's flask. Rachel passed it over, ears strained, watching the front door. There were clothes on the line behind the house: once-white sheets and pillow slips, a mattress protector. The back door swung open.

While Hannah's back was turned, Rachel forced herself to move, one foot in front of the other, up the steps. It was better to know than to be surprised. And better her than Hannah. The final step creaked. Rachel froze, waited. There was a blue plastic dog bowl next to the couch on the veranda. Empty. *Where's the dog?*

No one showed themselves. The curtains hung still. She heard the soft ting as Hannah put one of the water bottles down on the tank stand. The sharp scent of deodar burned her nostrils.

Don't freeze.

She strode to the front door, and turned the handle without knocking, in case someone was inside, waiting. They would expect that. Politeness; rules from the old world. There was no hallway or entrance. She was in the darkened living room before her eyes could focus.

Oh no.

It was an older couple, on the couch in front of a screen. They were holding hands, as if they had known it was coming. Their faces were stricken, mouths pulled back from their teeth and gums. In their last moments, they had each been alone with their worst nightmares.

She hadn't felt *them*, outside, but they were in the room. As if they had kept themselves hidden somehow, drawn her in. Now they were swirling all around. So much stronger than at the Thompsons', like a *pressure* – a high-pitched noise. The sort of noise that shut down her thinking.

They were reaching into her mind, linking memories and fears, drowning her with images, a rapid-fire feed of logging, mining, fracking, extinction, still no treaty. Her whole country on fire.

The ice caps melting, seas rising, as if trying to extinguish the flames. The leaders of the world arguing with each other about irrelevancies, substituting the word *economy* for society, making excuses why they shouldn't act. People posting pictures of their cats, while wild animals went extinct, one species after another.

She should have shut it down sooner. The constant stream of information, feeding her anxieties. In the end it had shut *her* down. Her mind stopped functioning, then her body, alone inside that locked apartment.

And now *they* were trying to do it all over again. To feed on *her*. She forced herself to move, to try to make it out. One boot, then the other. She backed away from the staring eyes, awful open mouths. There was something else, in her peripheral vision, something rearing up in the corner. With all the noise inside her head, it was just shifting shadow, intensity of noise and feeling. Her heel caught on the stoop. She grabbed at the door frame to stop herself falling.

'Hannah!' So much for the discreet whistle.

'I'm here,' Hannah said. She put her hand on Rachel's arm, spun her around. Rachel held her gaze, though it was uncomfortable. As if Hannah could see into her, too. But together they were stronger, shielding Isaiah between them. She focused on his little hand against Hannah's breast, Hannah's humming, as if nothing was wrong. She slowed her breathing to match Hannah's, until she remembered her own techniques. Three deep breaths in and out.

Fear is what they want.

Hannah nodded, mirrored her. They mirrored each other. It was a matter of forcing fear from her mind. Shutting it out.

106

Focusing on the sick child who needed them. Isaiah. Hannah's eyes were flecked with brown. She hadn't noticed that. As if there was a fire in the blue. Rachel was present, in her body, with this person. These people. They needed her. And she needed them.

When they were calmer, when she had control again, Hannah tipped her head towards the track. Rachel nodded.

They walked from the house without looking back. Rachel stopped to open the gate, freeing the horses. Then they ran. Back up the hill to the path, and onward, into the mountains.

Rachel kept checking over her shoulder, to see if Hannah was behind her.

'Just keep going, Ray.'

Hannah was singing. An old pop song Rachel recognised, about getting away in a car. Remembering the tune, the beat, lifted her. She found an extra length in her stride. Moving over the landscape at speed was something she was good at. For now, they *had* got away, survived some sort of test. Though she wasn't sure how long they could outrun them, or what they were running to.

the high country

twenty

They didn't stop until the next ridge. Doubled over, hands on their thighs to recover their breath from the climb, pump oxygen into their burning muscles. Hannah passed over Rachel's flask. She swallowed two mouthfuls, then two more. Tank water not river water, but it was wet.

'Thought you'd left that behind,' Rachel said.

'As if,' Hannah said. 'Even if you did slip off, trying to be the hero.'

Rachel half smiled. 'As if.'

'Why did you go in without me?'

'I didn't feel *them*. It was like they hid. And then suddenly they were stronger than ever.'

Hannah wet Isaiah's face and chest. 'There was the flag. And I was so focused on the water tank, being thirsty, keeping Isaiah cool. It's like I wasn't thinking straight. And then I saw you were gone – I was freaking out. Thought you'd left us there.'

'What if they can influence us, somehow?'

'We really have to stick together from now on. Check in on each other. We're stronger that way.'

Rachel nodded. 'Let's keep moving.'

They had left the forests for the open country of the Monaro. The topsoil had been stripped away, decades of farming exposing it to the elements. The path was more worn, used by native animals, grazing stock and people. There had been plenty of fox tracks – their back footprints layering over the front, from their swinging gait – but now Rachel was seeing dog tracks as well, and not just in ones and twos. They weren't pets or working dogs. Rachel's own hackles were up, expecting danger. Sensing it.

The town was the last place they should be headed. But it was where they had to go. They followed a four-wheel drive track through a valley, a short cut through properties to the road leading to Nimmitabel. Orange poly pipes ran along one side, to guide the way in snow.

Granite boulders had claimed the hilltops, like standing stones, speaking from the past. The snow gums grew around them, white trunks nursing sparse green crowns. Crows cawed, far too many for Rachel's liking. Waving away flies, the marker of stock and grazing country, kept their hands fully occupied.

Rachel walked on, trying to push the pace. The shadows were lengthening, reaching down the valley. She would have been at Monique's hours ago, on her own. But then, she wouldn't necessarily want to be there on her own.

Her eye was drawn to the out-of-place object against the fence line: round wheels, green paint. A quad bike, on its side. The driver lay where she had been thrown, in jeans and a blue home-knitted jumper, Blundstone boots. Rachel hesitated only for a moment.

'We could take it?'

Hannah nodded. 'I'm exhausted. And he's so weak he can't even cry anymore.'

They were thieves, scavengers. What other niceties would they have to let go of?

Rachel approached the woman side on, wary after *they* had tricked her back at the house. She was face down. Flies buzzed all around, settling on the body. She had been there several days. Someone's partner, mother, sister, daughter. Rachel did not feel the same threat as she had at the houses. Only stillness, a kind of *emptiness*. The lack of life.

Hannah chewed her lip. '*They*'re not here.'

'Perhaps it was just an accident.' They could still hope *they* hadn't come that far. Yet.

'Should we do something?'

'We don't have time to bury her.'

'Cover her, at least?'

A crow had followed them, calling from the branch above. Rachel shuddered. She pushed the bike back onto its wheels, wincing at the crash it made, hitting the ground. She opened the storage box on the back of the bike and rolled aside a cold thermos to remove a long Driza-Bone. She spread it over the woman. Hannah weighed it down with rocks.

They stood beside the body. Isaiah's eyes were closed, his face pale.

It was Hannah who spoke. 'Thank you for this gift. When we're in need. May you rest in peace.' The tears she shed weren't really for the woman.

Rachel removed her pack, clipped it to the back of the bike, climbed on and turned the ignition. It started. Too loud in that sad valley.

Hannah settled behind her, gripping Rachel's shirt, Isaiah between them. Rachel accelerated gently, heading uphill. A white-necked heron watched their progress, hunched in the crown of a dead tree.

They had to navigate two rusty gates and a fallen snow gum before picking up speed. The creek bank was holey with wombat burrows. They were like bulldozers, only furry. They followed the track around the ridgeline, closer than they would have liked to a log cabin with a ragged stone chimney, a sprawling shed behind. There was no smoke. No movement. A newish tractor and farm ute were parked out the front of another long building that may have been a poultry shed. Rachel didn't slow down for a closer look.

The tyres slipped on loose stones, lurched sideways. She gave it more throttle to climb the steep slope to the road. The sound and vibration of the unbaffled muffler had Rachel on edge.

She started to imagine the machine throwing them off, too. Hannah and Isaiah in the dirt. *Them* pushing. But she told herself that moving so quickly, they weren't as vulnerable.

She had hoped to ride to the edge of town, or until the bike ran out of fuel. But when they reached the gate, they found it padlocked – keeping them in, rather than intruders out

'We'll have to walk the rest of the way,' Rachel said.

'Ray, I don't think I can. I don't think Isaiah's going to make it.'

'C'mon. We're almost there. This road leads right to town.'

Rachel threw the pack over the gate and climbed after it. She took Isaiah while Hannah climbed over, supporting the back of his head. He was quiet. Too quiet. The noise of the bike should have woken him. It had also been enough to alert anyone – anything – for miles around.

twenty-one

They were still climbing, the road winding through rocky hilltops, trees sprouting where they were able, where they hadn't been cleared. Boulders had grown into giants, heads atop misshapen bodies. When she was a child, out of the corner of her eye, they had seemed to move, as if making a run for the mountains. The mailboxes were giant-sized, too, in bright-painted timber. Designed to cope with extreme weather conditions, and store much more than letters: parcels, machine parts, cases of wine, bottles of milk.

Rachel was running on reserve, her hip flexor and knee paining. She picked up a smooth stick from the roadside, just the right height to walk with. The line of billboards had started, faded timber replaced by blank electronic screens. They had reached the outskirts of town.

A rush of energy, adrenaline, gave Rachel the boost she needed. The journey was almost over, the end in sight.

'How long since you've seen your sister?'

'Six months.'

'She visits you?'

'She comes to stay a couple of times a year. And we write letters every month.'

They kept talking in the present tense, as if nothing had changed. *Like when someone first dies.* She still spoke to Monique in her head. She answered, too, always sensible – and a little bossy.

'I always wanted a sister.' Hannah pulled out her phone, turned it on and stared at the screen.

'If there is any signal, it won't be until the town. We're still behind the range here,' Rachel said.

They saw only one vehicle, heading away from Nimmitabel, trying to get home, perhaps, to one of the houses they had passed. A white four-wheel drive, red dirt sprayed up its rear, crashed nose-first into a culvert. There was no sign of the driver. It wasn't an unusual sight on a country road in itself, but it extinguished any remaining hopes that they might somehow find the town untouched.

Nimmitabel had always seemed like that to her, as a child: immune to the larger workings of the world. But change had accelerated, found a way to reach even the most tucked-away places. This was not a homecoming.

Rachel leaned on her stick, concentrated on her breathing. White corellas wheeled around the treetops, their blue eye make-up and raucous calls breaking the silence.

At last, they reached the final rise. They were standing atop the Great Dividing Range, the east coast's curving spine. And ahead, in the distance, the backbone of the continent itself, the Snowy Mountains, still topped with white. The first touches of pink in the sky.

'Snow?'

'Yeah.'

They could see Nimmitabel ahead, tucked into the valley. Its name meant 'the dividing of waters', a spot where the rivers, rainwater, fell away in all directions – from one of the highest altitude towns in the country. Where her sister had lived most of her life. Rachel's stomach was churning, her body keening.

The road had shifted from gravel to bitumen. Power lines, telephone lines and white guideposts led the way back to civilisation. Or what had been civilisation.

Hannah checked Isaiah again, lowered her face to his.

'Breathing?' Rachel said.

Hannah nodded.

She heard their barking before they saw them. They had reached a crossroads; a gravel lane connecting the small-acreage sub-divisions with a sprawl of new developments at the back of town. The dogs were by a rag-tag row of mailboxes, white letters and parcels still protruding from their slots. For a moment Rachel was stuck inside thoughts of her own mail, what had gone missing, what would not be sent. Postal centres around the country, the world, full of undelivered news, apologies, declarations of love – things that would never be known.

The dogs snarled and advanced, as if under attack. But there was no one there. Not that Rachel could see, anyway. To go on, they had to cross the road or follow it. But three dogs barred the way, backs to the culvert, hackles up and growling. Their attention on something – or someone – else.

Rachel shrugged out of her pack as quietly as she could. But not quietly enough. They turned, eyes bright. She held up the stick, just a weather-worn limb. Dogs were so much more straightforward than people; you had to establish authority and keep it.

'Careful,' Hannah said. 'There's something wrong with those dogs.' She covered Isaiah as best she could, held his limp body close to her own.

Rachel stood up to her full height, raised the stick above her head, and stepped forwards. The dogs bared their teeth but did not advance. She held her pack in front of her, like a shield, the stick in her left hand. 'Go on, get!'

They only growled, but were watching her rather than Hannah, at least. Rachel was the diversion, like the mother duck feigning a broken wing. 'I'll try and lead them off,' she said.

'I'm not leaving you here.'

'You need to get Isaiah past these monsters. I'll catch up.'

They were monsters. They hadn't always been. But she did not like the look in their eyes. She walked forwards with as much authority as she could muster, pushing back her fears – there really wasn't any choice. If they ran . . . she was pretty sure the dogs would go for them. If she was afraid, they would sense it.

Instead, she channelled anger. They had come so far. And now these dogs were between her and her sister. 'Right, you lot. Let us pass!'

The lead dog leapt first. Rachel swung the stick hard, connecting with his skull, bringing him down with a wet crunch. She swivelled, blocking the next dog's attack with her pack, and driving the stick end-on into the third dog's chest. They were angry, too, but also a little scared. *They* were there, too. And, now that she thought of it, *they* behaved a lot like dogs – trying to frighten her, just waiting for her to give in and run. But she wasn't ready to give in.

Rachel roared, swung the stick around her. The dogs backed off. But two more came rushing out of the culvert. Perhaps they had pups in there. Or it was a tunnel to Hades itself, full of feral beasts.

'Go on. *Get!*' She bared her own teeth, shook the stick – but the instruction was for Hannah, who still had not moved. Finally she broke for it, crunching across the gravel in her sneakers. For a moment the dogs were torn between two targets. Then one darted up behind Rachel, latching on to her calf.

'Bitch!'

Rachel charged, swinging pack and stick simultaneously, roaring like a monster herself. The two front dogs hesitated, and in that moment, it was as if something entered them, embodied their fear. At first, they were more terrible, snarling and baring their teeth, eyes bulging, but then one stopped, yelped, and emptied out before her eyes – just a corpse. The other dogs tried to run, but that was the worst thing to do. One by one, they snarled and bit, lips curled – a ferocity designed to cover fear – and then slumped, as if eaten out from the inside, skin and meat left on the road.

As she turned, a black shadow slinked away, a dark dog she had missed. But when she looked back, it was gone.

Rachel hoisted the pack on her back, and limped up the road, after Hannah and Isaiah. Not thinking, or feeling – only moving.

twenty-two

Nimmitabel's wide main street, the highway linking the far south coast to Canberra, was a disaster zone. A logging truck had jackknifed and overturned, sending logs slewing over the road. Cars had piled into logs, into each other, crashed into buildings, shopfronts. Every vehicle had at least one corpse sealed inside. There were bodies in the street: human and canine. Some of those bodies had been food for other animals.

After the forests, slopes and valleys, it was an assault on all her senses. Rachel turned away, tried to focus, get her bearings. This had been her town, once – her childhood.

Being in a town at all had been challenging for years, though her fears now seemed small in the face of the scene before them. Only the Indian elephant statue next to the bakery gazed over the chaos, unmoved. It had always been incongruous, absurd even. But now Rachel found it comforting, something unchanged. For a moment her mouth watered for the bakery's vanilla slice, thick and sweet. A body memory.

The windows of the leather store, with its twin Southern Cross flags – code for rebels and bikers the country over – had been smashed inwards. The general store on the corner had been made over, painted white. A change of owners, Monique had said, from the city. Its doors were smashed open. There were bodies inside.

The familiar peeling yellow weatherboards of the antique store loomed over them. An orchestra of musical instruments hung in the window: viola, violin, ukulele, cello, double bass, their fine polished timbers glowing. Rachel had an image of the owners around Monique's dinner table, warm and alive. Then, the scene ruined, the house torn apart in a storm of black fury. Rachel shook her head. *It's not real.*

'*They*'ve been waiting for us,' Hannah said. 'For Isaiah.'

They were so much more powerful. More than at the commune, the campsite, the houses, the dogs all combined. Rachel held Hannah's gaze for a moment. She had to work harder to keep *them* from her mind. But their attention didn't seem as focused, somehow, or as desperate.

It was better to stay close, move fast. Rachel pointed uphill. 'That's the surgery. The stone building in front of the mill. The house is on the other side, a quieter street. We can take this back lane, stay out of sight.' Away from the bodies and cars.

It was 300 metres but felt like three miles. She was spent. Her calf was throbbing. Isaiah's eyes were still closed, his body floppy and unmoving. To think that she had resented him crying, coughing. She would have the noise back, in an instant, if it meant he would live.

Rachel couldn't process all she was seeing – hearing, smelling, feeling. And then there was what they were about to find. *I'm*

122

not ready. As soon as she had the thought, she felt *them* pushing into the space, throwing it open, encouraging her to imagine Monique's body, like the others, all the ways she might have died. Her fear and suffering. Leaving Rachel alone in the world.

'It's not true.'

Hannah took hold of her arm. 'Keep going. Nearly there.'

Rachel focused on the warmth on her skin, the sure ground beneath her boots. They passed the back of looted shops and cafes, fast-food wrappers tumbled through the laneway. A postal worker fallen from her moped, phone still in hand. Her face frozen in disbelief. The wind, always carrying a chill, seemed colder than ever, as if right off the snow. They hurried on. It was all they could do.

A man had fallen face down in the doorway of the bottle shop. Something had chewed away his fingers. House windows were closed and dark. A pink child's bike lay abandoned in the gutter by the park. Rachel looked back, at the wheel turning in the wind, but Hannah dragged her forwards. Yellow weatherboard houses sat silent, their iron roofs curling up like dead leaves.

At last they reached her sister's house – what had been their parents' house, their childhood home. On a double block, it joined the surgery at the rear. The front garden was still well tended: herbs and flowers between trimmed shrubs. A row of lavender crowded against the white picket fence, like something out of *Country Homes*. It took a lot of effort, Rachel knew, with such a short growing season. She had seen snow on the ground around the daffodils more than once.

It had never looked more beautiful. Rachel opened the gate and walked up the path, Hannah following.

The house was dark, like all the others. Rachel was on high alert for noise, for a shadow in the hall through the stained-glass panels. But this time, she hoped desperately that there *was* someone inside. Alive. Her sister. She leaned the stick against the wall, removed her beanie, and knocked.

twenty-three

There was no answer. Rachel removed the pack and leaned it against the wall, next to the stick. The sun had dropped behind the mountains. Hope was fading, darkness flooding in. She leaned down to lift the cushion on the day bed, felt underneath for the spare key. The metal was cold on her fingers. She slid it into the lock and turned it clockwise. She waited for Hannah and Isaiah to enter, lifted the pack and followed them inside, locking the door behind them.

The house was dark, everything neat and tidy. Nothing out of the ordinary, nothing out of place – nothing destroyed. As if Monique had just walked out. Up to the store, perhaps, to get milk or bread. Rachel moved quickly, checking every room, the toilet, laundry, garage – the Beast still parked inside, motor cold. When she stepped out the back door, into the paved courtyard down the side of the house with its potted fruit trees and vegetable patch, everything was a little overgrown, and no Mon.

Hannah had not moved beyond the kitchen. 'Nothing?'

'Wait here,' Rachel said.

She unlocked the security door through to the clinic. The surgery was empty. Only the dusk's low light coming in through the open blinds. The chaos on the street faded out of view. There were signs that someone had been up on the bed, the coverlet crumpled. Monique's notebook and script pad were on her desk, next to the blank-screened computer, someone's file lying open: *Duncan White*. The medical supplies cupboard was unlocked. Everything seemed calm but Rachel felt a sudden rush of movement, confusion, noise – fear. Not her own. Her sister, fighting for control.

She checked the kitchenette, storeroom and toilet, the garden out front, the path, the chaotic street. *She's not here.*

The waiting room was a different story. Magazines had been flung on the floor, paper cups, a chair upturned. Rachel tensed. There were three bodies. They had been covered with surgical sheets.

The door to the street had been locked from the inside. There were bars across the windows that hadn't been there before. Monique was effectively the town's chemist as well as vet and doctor. The medical supplies had been a target for thieves before. But Mon had always resisted altering the front of the heritage building. What had happened to make her change her mind?

Rachel lowered the blinds, felt around to switch on the battery-powered lanterns Monique used to soften the space. The surgery and house ran on solar, but she was still connected to the grid. When the power went down, her system only lasted until the batteries ran out.

They were there. Circling, strong, wanting to become stronger.

In her peripheral vision, pressing in, waiting for the scene to overwhelm her. But one detail kept her thoughts clear, logical, her movements measured, as if she were in the studio, moulding glass to any shape she envisaged.

Someone had covered the bodies.

Either Monique or her assistant had been there, afterwards. She stood for a moment, appraising the shrouded shapes in the gloom. One was too big, probably a man. The other two could be women. One of those had slipped from the waiting room couch. A patient. The other was lying on the floor in the middle of the room. She moved her feet forwards. *Keep breathing, Ray.*

Rachel let herself fill with love for her sister and her sister's love for her – even though it hurt. She crouched, steadied herself, and lifted the corner of the cloth.

The young man was on his back, hands clutching his face. The name badge on his pocket said Callum. He had worked for Monique the last three months. A replacement for Alice, who was on maternity leave.

Rachel dropped the sheet. He had seen what was happening, seen it happen to others, and known they were coming for him. The corner of his phone poked out from beneath the sheet. Rachel slid it towards her with one finger and touched the screen. It was locked, almost out of battery. No signal. There were notifications: all from the same person. His partner. More and more urgent. Two days ago. And nothing since.

Again, the images of her sister, alone and afraid, all the variations of what might have happened – in jarring stop motion. Shadows swirling in the corners of the room, in the dark places of her mind. The chasm of Rachel's solitary life, drawing her in. She dropped the phone and waited until her head stopped spinning. Until she had shut *them* out. *My sister did not die here.*

Someone was banging on the door from the house. *Hannah, Isaiah.* She had forgotten them.

twenty-four

Rachel closed the door to the waiting room and took a breath to steady herself. When she opened the door into the cottage, Hannah was in the hallway, small and pale, Isaiah just a bundle.

'I thought something happened to you.'

'She was here. Afterwards.' But she wasn't there now to tell them what was wrong with Isaiah – or how to fix it.

Hannah lay Isaiah on the surgery bed. 'Ray, we made it all the way here, and now he's going to die.'

Rachel glanced at the closed door to the waiting room. 'Hey, that's *them* talking. Don't listen.'

'There are more of them here.

Rachel nodded. 'But we're together, we're safe. Let's focus on getting him better.'

Hannah drew a shaky breath.

What would Mon do?

'We should listen to his chest. But I don't really know what to listen for. He's had a high fever for days, I think we have no choice but to give him antibiotics. He's probably dehydrated.

I'm not game to try putting in a drip with a baby. The book said lots of small feeds. And rest. At least he *can* rest now. We can control his temperature more easily.'

The medical cupboard was only half full. As if Monique had been awaiting supplies or there had been some sudden demand. The antibiotics were on the second shelf. 'Are there special ones for babies?'

'I think so,' Hannah said.

Rachel squinted at the labels. 'Got it.' There was a single box of amoxicillin for infants. 'It's oral,' she said, reading the label. 'You can mix it with milk or water. But we have to work out the dosage. Do you know how much he weighs?'

'About five kilos.'

'It says fifteen to thirty milligrams per kilogram of body weight per day, divided and given every eight hours.' It also said the calculation must be done by a doctor.

Hannah's shoulders fell.

'There are scales,' Rachel said. 'Under the eye chart.'

The scales were for adults. But Hannah sat Isaiah on the glass square, trying to hold him up without adding to his weight. 'Four point five,' she said.

'Okay. That means about a hundred and thirty-five millilitres, divided by three for each dose.'

'It's only a rough measure.'

Rachel pushed the glass measuring vial towards Hannah.

Hannah's hands were shaking, but she opened the ampoule and measured out the day's dosage. 'Is there an express kit in that cupboard?'

Rachel blinked.

'A breast pump,' Hannah said. 'I think he'd be more likely to take it with milk. If I can express some milk, I can mix it in.'

'What's it look like?'

'What's that box, bottom right?'

Rachel reached for it, a strange cup contraption and bottle. 'Bingo.'

'Okay. I'll get started.'

'There should still be hot water, and the stove is gas.'

'Wait. Are you bleeding?' Hannah said, pointing to the red splotches on the white tiles.

'One of those dogs bit me.'

'Why didn't you say something?'

Rachel unlaced her boots, removed her sock and rolled up her cargoes. The puncture marks were deep, and one had torn. She turned away, never comfortable with seeing the workings of her insides. The white room was starting to spin. She could smell the blood, hear the dogs, their dripping saliva. The floor slanted. Why wasn't Monique there?

'Are you okay?'

Rachel leaned on the bed.

'I will be,' she said. 'You look after Isaiah. The sooner he starts taking those antibiotics the better. I'll clean this up.'

'It needs stitching, Ray.'

'I can do it.' She'd had to, when she dropped a piece of broken sheet glass onto her bent knee, a few years before. 'There's a spare room, with the pink linen, and you can use the bathroom opposite. There are lamps everywhere. They should work for now. And I guess you could borrow some of Mon's clothes.'

'Are you sure you'll be okay?'

'Yeah.'

Rachel hopped back to the cabinet, found antiseptic, a surgical needle and thread, a waterproof bandage. There didn't seem to be any local anaesthetic needles, just a tube of gel.

She washed her hands up to the elbows the way her sister, and her father before her, had done. As a child she was forever coming home with cuts, scrapes and breaks. With a doctor in the house, she had taken for granted that her body, at least, could always be patched up. Now she was on her own.

She laid everything out on the bed, kneeled with her calf behind her. It was awkward. She disinfected the wound, wincing at the sting of it, and rubbed the gel around the site to numb the skin. She pushed the needle from its wrapping, already threaded, and tied a knot – trying to think of it as just sewing. But it was hard to pierce her own flesh, and it hurt, despite the gel. Her stitches were not neat like Monique's, nor her fingers as comforting.

She focused on the pain, to shut out the memories of her sister, self-doubt. *They* were trying to find a way in, as if through the broken skin. Like an infection.

Antibiotics.

She took the last packet of penicillin from the cabinet and closed the doors. Hopefully they wouldn't need anything else; there wasn't much left. She pushed two capsules from the blister pack and put them in her mouth, washing them down with half a glass of water.

And then Monique was there, in the room. *You're forgetting something, Ray. Tetanus, rabies.* She hopped back to the cabinet and rifled through the injection packs. She hated needles, but it was years since she'd had a tetanus shot. It wasn't worth the risk.

She opened both packs, lay them on the bed. While Rachel was staying, Monique had been bitten on the forearm by a dog she was treating on her assistant's day off. She had called Rachel in to help, talking her through injecting her in the buttock. 'It works better,' she said. They had giggled their way through it, like sisters, still children.

It wasn't funny now. And much harder injecting herself, forcing in the anti-rabies serum while she was contorted. Then the tetanus, an even bigger needle. She could feel the liquid, the foreign substance pushing into her body. Her head was fuzzy, the white room fading out of focus. She imagined her studio, warm and colourful, gathering glass. But then the studio was on fire, her house. *It's not true.*

She shut her eyes until the nausea had passed, imagining herself a sealed vessel, hard as glass. She pulled up her pants; slipping the buttons back through the fabric was a challenge, her hands clumsy.

Keep moving. She picked up her boots and carried them through into Monique's house, locking the surgery door behind her. Whether real or imagined, it felt safer inside. She didn't have to fight as hard.

The shower was running in the main bathroom. Rachel fetched her pack from the hallway, carried it to her old room and shut the door. In her own space at last. Everything was as she left it: her books, boxes, clothes, keepsakes. The same botanical doona cover, in soft greens.

She stripped off her dirty clothes, dropped them in the corner of the en suite and stepped into the shower. It was warm rather than hot, but it felt good to have water rushing over her. The solar hot water system was independent; it wouldn't run out, as long as the sun kept shining.

She scrubbed her body, careful to keep her calf out of the water. Then washed her matted hair, forcing her fingers through it until the knots were gone.

She leaned her forehead on the white tiles and closed her eyes, to stop the jumble of images from the journey. She had made some mistakes. But she had brought Hannah and Isaiah to safety, as agreed. To antibiotics. Her job was done. She could go home in the morning, get out of the town and away from *them*.

Except that would leave Hannah and Isaiah alone, and she still didn't know what had happened to Monique. And her leg was sore – she should stay off it for a day or two. There were no good choices. There hadn't been, since Hannah had knocked on her front door.

She shut off the taps and dried herself with the clean towel, which seemed, in that moment, the most luxurious item in the world. It *was* a luxury, to have a flushing toilet and running water, to be warm and clean, back in her sister's house. To be alive. But it was not the same without her there.

Rachel towel-dried her hair, ran the wide-toothed comb through it, and tied it back. Her pile of clothes was as she had left them, ironed and folded. She pulled out track pants, a faded T-shirt and an old hoodie. When she sat down on the bed to pull on warm socks, she registered something out of place in the dim light. She turned slowly, as if it were a small bird that might take flight.

There was an envelope on her pillow. Her name written on the outside, in Monique's untidy doctor's handwriting.

twenty-five

Dear Ray,

If you're reading this, you've come looking for me. And you're alive! I'm so glad.

I'm sorry I'm not there. I waited two days, in case you walked up. But I didn't know if or when you would find out what has happened. How to reach you. I've gone to Canberra to find Bill. To see if there is something I can do to stop this.

I've left your medication on the kitchen bench. It's all I have left. There was a lot going on here, before this happened. I've made up a batch of your drops, too. It's really important that you take them. I've listed the ingredients, in case I'm not around when they run out.

We've taken the hospital car. It's a silver Prius. JYK-196. The Beast is there waiting, if you need her. She's yours, after all.

I'll be back, Ray. But I'm not sure when.

Love always,

Mon x

The date on the letter was the same as on Callum's mobile. Monique had only written the note *today* – probably this morning. They had only just missed her.

Rachel put her head in her hands. If she hadn't delayed leaving, wasted time deliberating about what she should never have even hesitated to do, Monique would still have been there. What if that mistake meant she never saw her sister again?

When Rachel had stopped answering her phone, Monique and Bill had driven up to find her. It hadn't helped that she had stopped eating or drinking. As if she hadn't wanted to live. In hospital, they gave her body nutrients and sedated her mind. Monique had fought with the staff, intervened.

Monique had sat in the chair next to her bed, day after day, and read poetry. Mary Oliver mostly. Simple phrases of great beauty, celebrating the wonders of the natural world. It had brought Rachel back, first, to her sister's voice, the forest and, finally, to the bright white room.

Rachel wiped her face, filled her diaphragm with three deep breaths, used her drops. Before Hannah turned up, she had only used them at night, to help her sleep. Now the bottle was nearly empty.

There was still a book of Oliver's poems on the shelf. A graduation gift from her sister. Rachel ran her fingers along the spines until she found the slim hardcover. She eased it out, read the inscription, and sat it on the bed for later.

She upturned her pack, separating out items for the bin, the kitchen, the laundry. She emptied her pockets and threw her dirty clothes on the pile on the en suite floor. The antibiotics could go in the bathroom. The money, gold, could stay in her bedside table for now. She slipped the torch in her pocket and gathered up the dirty clothes.

Hannah was moving around out in the kitchen. Monique's kitchen. Rachel padded down the hall and dropped the dirty clothes in the laundry tub.

She opened the door to the courtyard, listened for a moment, and stepped outside. The town was silent, just the yip of a fox in the distance. The streetlights were out, all the houses dark. The glow above the larger town of Cooma in the distance was gone. Blackness, night, was total.

She hung their sleeping bags and her pack over the clothes line running down the side of the house to air. The rounded fruit trees were the only presence, branches outstretched. There were salad greens in the vegetable patch: rocket going to seed, baby spinach and kale. She gathered up a few handfuls and tucked them in the pocket of her hoodie.

Then she switched off her torch and waited for her eyes to adjust. Emptied of people, of light, it was no longer a town, but a collection of vacant buildings – a morgue.

Only the stars were bright, brighter than ever, and so many. The Southern Cross and its two pointers hung low in the sky. The great drift of the Milky Way holding the universe together, like a vast web.

A satellite winked its way across the sky, stuck in unending orbit. Just another piece of human junk. She could imagine the silence in space, the overwhelming magnitude of time and distance – the loneliness. The astronauts still out there, unable to get home, gazing back at the quiet earth.

Rachel's heart was full of tears, but she could not cry. She felt her way back inside and locked the door.

Hannah was in the kitchen, her hair still damp. Monique's old track pants hung from her hips, rolled up at the cuffs. A red jumper swam on her, pink shirt tails hanging out behind. She had lit candles and laid out food items on the bench.

'How'd you go?' Rachel said.

'He didn't like the bottle much. But I think he drank enough. I'll try again later.'

'Fingers crossed.'

'I was able to bathe him properly and his temperature is no worse.'

Rachel set the salad leaves on the breadboard and assessed the items on the bench. Sweet potato, eggs, the goat's cheese Monique liked. She sniffed, rubbed her face.

'Mon was here this morning.' Rachel placed the note on the bench.

'Oh, Ray.' Hannah put her hand on Rachel's arm, and leaned over to read Monique's words.

'Who's Bill?'

'Her partner. He's a big-deal scientist. Just set up the new medical research centre at the university.'

'She went out there on her own?'

'I think she had someone with her. The note says "we". It's the doctor thing. She thinks she has to *serve*.'

'What do you want to do?'

'I think we're safe in the house, for the moment. We need to give the antibiotics at least forty-eight hours – Isaiah needs to rest. And I won't be able to walk far on this leg for a while.'

'So we wait,' Hannah said. 'The fridge is still cold, but there isn't much food. A few things in the pantry.'

Living in town, with the shop up the road, Monique never had been good at keeping the place stocked, instead shopping day by day. 'We can make something with this. Worry about the rest in the morning.'

twenty-six

Rachel woke before dawn but did not get out of bed. She had dreamed about the people on the river again, their faces, their calls for help. A rooster crowed somewhere far away, a pigeon took flight with its whirring uplift. The town itself was deathly quiet. No trucks hauling up and down the highway, jake brakes juddering. No delivery vans reversing up the lane, with their annoying *beep beep beep*. No buses unloading people in front of the bakery. No one walking down to the showground with their dog, to throw around a ball or a stick to be fetched. No one speaking to each other over the fence, exchanging vegetables and gossip. No children laughing on their way to school. There would be no Monique cooking breakfast in the kitchen or sitting by the window drinking tea.

Instead, there were three bodies lying in the waiting room. They couldn't just leave them there. Eventually the smell would seep into the house. And bodies seemed to bring *them*, to give them a way in.

When she could no longer ignore her full bladder, she sat up and swung her legs out of bed, touched her calf. It was hot and tight, sore to touch – but mending. She limped to the en suite, sat on the toilet seat. She had only heard Isaiah once during the night. Perhaps he was getting better, or she was so tired that the sound had stopped disturbing her.

She washed and moisturised her face, avoiding her reflection in the mirror. Morning light lit the spines of the books she had left behind. The science fiction novels she had devoured as a teenager, a tattered edition of *The History of Glass*. The novels she had studied in school: *To Kill a Mockingbird*, *Day of the Triffids*, *Z for Zachariah*. Books she'd never forget, even if she suffered them at the time. The presents from her parents: the complete works of Shakespeare, world mythology, classical art, the great galleries of the world. Books that kept a little of her parents alive in the house.

The framed photograph was of her and Monique in their early teens, grinning by a great stone fireplace – the resort lodge of family friends. They had been skiing that day, in crisp powder and perfect sunshine. The sort of day you only had once or twice a season. Their cheeks were red, and Rachel had a smear of hot chocolate on her top lip. She could still taste it, and the sticky marshmallows. Still feel her body moving over the snow, swooshing one way, then the other, speeding downhill. The innocence in their faces reached a hurt deep in her chest. It had been their last holiday with their parents. When they were still just children, without any understanding of what life could, and would, bring.

She put the photo back in its place and dressed, carefully pulling up a pair of jeans over her calf.

Hannah was already in the kitchen, adding antibiotics to her breast milk. Rachel tried not to stare. 'How is he?'

'He fed well during the night, less coughing, and his temperature is down to thirty-nine.'

Rachel's shoulders relaxed a little. 'The antibiotics are working.'

'I hope so,' Hannah said. 'Did you sleep? How's your leg?'

'It's a bit uncomfortable is all.' Rachel swallowed her tablets with half a glass of water.

'What are they that you take?'

'For anxiety.'

'You think they help?'

'They definitely helped me recover. And the couple of times I tried to go off them weren't great.'

'I mean with *them*.'

'I didn't think of that,' Rachel said. 'But I wouldn't have been the only person in the world taking them.'

'True.'

'Do *you* want to try them?'

Hannah screwed the lid on the milk bottle. 'I don't think I can while I'm breastfeeding.'

'Of course.'

'But say that's why *you're* still alive. And maybe your isolation. Why me?' Hannah said.

'I think it's something to do with Isaiah.'

Hannah looked down at him, her forehead wrinkled. 'Maybe. I was going to make oats for breakfast. There's only almond milk.'

'I can do it,' Rachel said. Fresh milk was only one of many

things they had taken for granted. A few days was all it took for supply to dry up. And this time, supply would not be restored. Who would bring in the cows, milk them, bottle the milk, truck it to depots and stores? Without power, once fuel for generators ran out, there would be no refrigerators, even if there were people to run the stores.

Rachel checked the street and raised the blinds. The sun had come up again, revealing a world unchanged since yesterday. The trees, houses, roads were where they had always been, but nothing fitted together the way it had.

'You said that at home everyone died at once?'

'It seemed to happen within a few hours,' Hannah said. 'Why?'

'The looting,' Rachel said. 'I wonder if there are other survivors.'

'Maybe they knew what was coming,' Hannah said. 'And tried to close the shops. Or maybe some people survived initially . . . I mean *they* seem to hang around, searching for anyone left.'

Rachel shut her eyes on images of people running down side streets, through parks, the hallways of their homes. Men, women, children, already alone and afraid, picked off one by one. Images that came and went so fast but left her exhausted.

She focused on setting the oats over a low heat, filling the stove-top coffee machine with water and grounds – measured morning movements around the kitchen she had once shared with her sister.

Hannah watched her opening and shutting doors, drawers. 'You used to live here?'

'I stayed with my sister before I bought my place,' she said. 'And we lived here with our parents, when we were little. My father was a GP, too. And town vet.'

'In the same house?'

Rachel nodded. 'She's done it up since then. Extended into the space between and joined the buildings.'

While the oats were cooking, Rachel opened the box of drops Monique had left. The homeopathic remedy came from a colleague in Cooma who had become a friend over the years. Six new bottles, the same brown glass vials with pink dropper lids. Monique had handwritten the ingredients on the box: silica, stramonium, phosphorus, ignatia, gelsemium, aconite, rock rose, impatiens, clematis, star of Bethlehem, cherry plum, oxytocin, grape alcohol solution. Oxytocin was underlined. The drops did help, and she trusted her sister, but herbs and essential oils weren't any defence against *them*.

They ate by the window, Hannah in her sister's seat, nursing Isaiah. With honey and the almond milk, the oats were tasty enough, comforting. They drank their coffee black.

Monique had changed the paintings around, hung one of their mother's landscapes on the feature wall of the living area. It captured the pink light of the high country, which, in some trick of colour refraction and altitude, lasted all day during winter. The view was down the valley, the great mountains leading the viewer's eye to the space beyond and out of the frame. Into the unknown.

'I was going to do some washing this morning,' Hannah said.

'We'll have to do it by hand. There's a generator but it's noisy. I'd rather not use it until we know it's safe.'

'I figured.'

'I'll do mine,' Rachel said.

'I may as well just do it all together.'

Rachel sipped her coffee. *Let it go.* It didn't really matter in the scheme of things that Hannah handled her underwear. 'There's a clothes line outside the laundry door.'

'Okay. Thanks.'

There was no good time to say it. 'There are three bodies in the waiting room of the practice.'

'Not Monique?'

Rachel shook her head.

'You looked?'

'I did.'

'How did you . . .?'

'I don't know. I was thinking about Mon, and was able to shut *them* out,' Rachel said.

'Well, we have to get the bodies out of the building. But we'll do it together, and really focus, like at the farm.'

twenty-seven

They put on masks and gloves, as if for an operation, and opened the door to the waiting room. They decided to leave Isaiah sleeping inside. It wasn't ideal to leave him alone, but it wasn't safe for him to be present, either. And he'd slow them down. Rachel blocked the images of *them* sneaking into the house and snatching him from the spare room, Isaiah being afraid. She knew from Hannah's face that they were her thoughts, too.

'We just have to do this,' Rachel said.

Hannah placed Callum's phone and wallet on the reception desk. Between them they could almost lift him. He didn't seem like a person anymore, just a body. A body that was releasing fluids, smells.

They maintained eye contact, conscious of each other's every movement. Even then, Rachel struggled to keep her thoughts on what had to be done. And what had to be done was difficult. She had to stop, put Callum down, while Hannah threw up in the gutter.

They carried him to the laneway and laid him beneath a

liquidambar. Its leaves were green now, but come autumn it would be glorious, in all shades of red.

Hannah was humming, as if the noise in her ears would keep them out of her head. Rachel focused on trying to pick the song, the name of the band, to push aside images of the town in autumn, her mother throwing handfuls of leaves, laughing, her face upturned. The past, the future – she couldn't afford to look in either direction. Only now, the task right in front of them. It was like meditation, clearing thoughts from her mind, existing only in each moment.

They went back for the others. The woman was heavier. They had to roll her onto the surgical sheet, giving them a long look at her bulging eyes, scored cheeks. Her nails, on carefully manicured hands, were enough to have done the damage. The woman's pink-cased phone was on the ground next to her handbag, jammed so full of items it wouldn't close. Hannah held them out in front of her, as if they were poison, and placed them next to Callum's things.

They half-carried, half-dragged her out the door and down the steps. Stains spread over the white sheet. They were awful to look at, hard to look away from. Like hands, hair, shoes – the details that had made them who they were. Rachel moved backwards, using her whole body to drag the woman along the lane. They lay her next to Callum and stopped to get their breath.

Rachel scanned the street for movement, for threats, for others. She saw nothing but the twitching tail of a watching cat. Despite the eye contact, their proximity, she could only guess at Hannah's worries: for Isaiah, her partner.

They walked slowly back to the surgery for the last body. Rachel felt into his pockets, removed keys and wallet. Hannah sat them next to the other people's things. Again, they rolled him in the sheet, though it wasn't quite big enough. His mouth, unlike the rest, was closed in a grim line, as if life had delivered just what he expected. But his staring eyes seemed to follow them – until Rachel turned him over. His phone tumbled out, screen blank. Hannah kicked it behind the reception desk.

Rachel struggled to grip enough material. The muscles in her leg were straining against the stitches. This time they could only drag him, down the steps, over the gutter, along the dirty, pitted laneway, to the tree.

Rachel was walking through a ruined landscape, hill after hill of black sticks and still-smoking stumps. But it wasn't a memory. Not yet. She could no longer tell which were her own thoughts, the difference between memories and fears. If *they* came when she was afraid or if they made her afraid.

They stood close, next to the shrouded bodies, resisting the urge to turn and run. To lock themselves inside before their fears got hold of them, the reality of what they were doing, what was all around them. Before *they* overwhelmed them, one at a time. Hannah produced three sprigs of rosemary from Monique's garden, laid one on each body.

All of the usual words for death, burial, burning, were inadequate.

'Forgive us,' Hannah said.

They hurried back to the surgery, heavy limbed and nauseous. Rachel locked the door behind them and leaned against it.

'I'd better check on Isaiah,' Hannah said. She peeled off her gloves and mask, dropped them in Monique's bin. 'I need a shower before I can touch him. I feel so unclean.'

'I know,' Rachel said.

Rachel pushed back the chairs, couch and coffee table in the waiting room and rolled up the rug. She dragged it through the kitchen to the back door, and threw it out, next to the bins. The same ginger cat ran off, pouring herself over the laneway fence.

Rachel shut the door on the scene and found a mop and bucket, disinfectant. Everyday movements were somehow exhausting, the pressure of keeping *them* from her thoughts. Soon, the waiting room smelled of eucalyptus and the old linoleum floor shone. Rachel emptied the dirty water down the sink, rinsed the bucket, and put everything away. Being neat and tidy, taking proper care, wasn't necessary anymore. But somehow it was, restoring normality, keeping *them* back. It was her way of coping, always had been.

The dead people's things were sitting on the reception desk, as if they might be back for them. Rachel bent to pick up the man's phone and placed it next to the others. She touched the screens, blank now, batteries dead, and left them where they were. They were more secure inside. It would be some sort of record of who they had been. If someone ever came to do that – account for the dead.

She threw her gloves and mask in the bin, tied off the liner and carried it outside to the hoppers. The bins hadn't been emptied for at least a week. Soon all the bodies, the rubbish, would begin to create a whole new health hazard. The shadow between the medical waste bin and the fence was from the power pole, that's what she told herself. But it hadn't been there before.

twenty-eight

The generator almost filled the utilities room, the narrow compartment running between the kitchen and the garage. The tank was full of fuel but didn't appear to have been run recently. Had Monique been afraid it might bring *them*? She would have wanted to help other survivors – unless they were a threat.

As long as there was hot water and gas for cooking, the lack of power wasn't so hard to get used to. Rachel had done it for weeks after the fires. She had thought she was well prepared. Her studio met all the highest bushfire regulations. With the en suite and kitchenette she had put in, she could live in it if she had to. But it took a lot of energy to run the furnace and glory hole. When the power went out, they already hadn't seen the sun for weeks because of the smoke. And, that day, the skies were dark as night. The batteries ran flat. She had been out fighting the fires for the fifth day straight and hadn't had a chance to power down the furnace, empty it out. The glass had expanded as it cooled, cracked the casing, and run out all over the floor.

It was weeks till the thousands of power poles were replaced, substations repaired, lines restrung. People were charging their phones in their cars, driving around wide-eyed among the destruction, searching for a high point with a bar of reception. It had been easy to pick out the occupied houses from the drone of their generators. Rachel had bought one, too – at an exorbitant price – but until the furnace was repaired, she had been unable to work. The shops and post office were closed, Mia hadn't been able to deliver. Life was on pause for months.

It had taken the last of her savings, but as soon as she could order the equipment and organise a tradesman – the friend of Mia's she had used when doing up the house – she had gone completely off grid. The power line to her property had never been replaced.

There was a square grey object on a trolley next to the generator, the power bank Monique had said she was going to buy. Rachel slid open the door – concealed in the living room wall – with her back and wheeled it into the kitchen. She had to move the fridge out a few inches to unplug it. When she connected it to the AC socket on the power bank, the fridge motor started, loud and intrusive after the quiet.

Hannah was sterilising Isaiah's bottle at the sink. 'Power?'

'We can recharge it in the sun. Like the lamps.'

'My brother has one of those. He was always getting blacked out in the storms up north. Never going without cold beer again, he said.'

Hannah's face shifted. They had no way of knowing whether it was the same up north, if her brother was alive.

'How was Isaiah?'

'Still sleeping,' Hannah said. 'Oblivious. While I was losing my mind, imagining the worst. That was the hardest so far. Touching the bodies. *Them* getting between him and me. I nearly lost it there a few times.'

She was stronger with him. Or weaker without. 'Let's not leave him again,' Rachel said. 'I thought I'd go out for supplies this afternoon. The sooner the better.'

'We stay together, remember?'

'Isaiah needs to rest,' Rachel said. 'I can do it.'

'Are you sure?'

'I know my way around town. And I'm learning how to deal with *them*. I'll be fine.'

twenty-nine

Rachel lifted the keys from the hook, pulled on her beanie and checked the street before opening the front door. She slung the empty pack over her shoulder, grabbed the stick to take some of the weight from her bitten leg, and set off up the wide street. There were only two bodies to walk around. She was learning how not to look, not to linger on the wrong details. Magpies warbled from the power line: black and white on black. Could they tell that the power had stopped flowing? One flew down, picked at the spilled pie in the dead man's hand. Rachel walked on. She passed quiet house after quiet house. Their gardens empty, lawns littered with leaves.

A splash of red on a bare branch caught her eye. A flame robin, his red breast fading into a white belly between black wings. He threw back his head and sang, his piping voice an ill match for a bird on fire. And then he was gone, leaving Rachel a little more lonely.

Their mother had tried to paint birds on and off over the years. A flame robin had been her most successful, a glow around him, like the heart of the piece, and it had sold the minute it was hung, but it was the big landscapes she was known for.

At art school, Rachel could feel the teachers' disappointment when she performed poorly in the painting units. Monique had escaped that expectation, living in the shadow of their father instead.

In school, they had both been good at art. One of her sister's pencil drawings had won a first at the Nimmitabel show the year Rachel went into high school. But after their parents died, Monique had focused on getting the grades for medicine. And, although Monique had mentioned enrolling in night classes over the years, Rachel had never seen any of her work.

Rachel stopped at the back door of the outdoor store. She broke a window with the base of the stick, knocked out all the glass and threw the doormat over the sill. It was a squeeze, with her shoulders and long limbs, but she was through, landing on the floor on the other side with a thump. The dog bite was sore, and her butt bruised, where the needles had gone in.

There were no bodies inside. No signs of disturbance or panic. As if the store had been closed when it happened. Old Brett Miller hadn't changed things much since Monique had kidded him to give Rachel a job in her teens. Everything was still laid out the same way, the children's section still in the same spot.

But baby sizes were so confounding – all zeros. In the end she ignored the numbers and picked out a fleece body suit she judged would fit Isaiah, and a beanie with a pompom. She chose a quality fleece for Hannah from the women's section. She was an eight; that much was easy. There was only one pair of decent walking boots in a thirty-six, but they would be a vast improvement on the Converse. She grabbed a new pair of walking socks for each of them, three old-fashioned emergency flares, a map of the Monaro, and jammed the items into the bottom of the pack.

She propped a sheet of cardboard against the window, secured it with packing tape, and let herself out through the back door. On the steps, she took the new bottle from her pocket and placed four drops under her tongue. It was like learning to blow glass; learning by doing, gathering confidence to try the next thing, do it better next time. Except that now, mistakes could be fatal.

Rachel headed towards the supermarket. After the fires, when the power came back on, the supermarkets reopened. But their shelves emptied in hours. With the roads closed in all directions, the fires still burning, supplies couldn't get through. A state of emergency was declared, the army cleared the roads. Convoys of trucks came down the mountain, through the flames, all through the night, accompanied by a police escort.

Still, as fast as they could fill the shelves, they emptied. When Rachel finally went into town, the less impacted were piling up their trolleys with tinned food and toilet paper, snatching things from the hands of those who had lost everything. It was the last time she ever set foot in a supermarket.

The Nimmitabel store had already been worked over, its front doors shattered, shelves raided, registers prised open, the cigarette and alcohol cages emptied. Some had not made it out. The bodies of two older men at the head of the queue blocked the checkout, their trolleys piled high with tinned food, water and toilet paper. The way people were always clustered together was unnerving. Their faces made her want to run.

Rachel checked every aisle as she entered, watched for movement in her peripheral vision, mapped two possible exits from every point. Her body screamed in alarm. But there was no one left alive. She threw the pack and stick in an empty trolley and swung through the aisles. She moved fast, every sense keened, her rubber soles silent on the lino. Muesli, oats, nuts, dried fruit, muesli bars. Rice, lentils, chickpeas, pasta, flour, yeast. Spices, oil, vinegar, capers, tuna, eggs. Toilet paper, wipes, tissues, nappies, toothpaste and toothbrushes, washing liquid. Vitamins B, C, A and D, calcium, stress, multi. She reached to the back of the pallet for the last casks of bottled water.

Every step made her more anxious. What she was doing – looting – was to face what had happened, to admit that all the rules were off. They had to plan not only for the next few days, but beyond. Supplies seemed bountiful now, but were finite. They would have to go further and further to find food. Take more risks. Having everything they needed on hand was the most basic requisite for survival.

The frozen chickens, jammed in together, were just beginning to thaw. She took the largest organic one and placed it in a bag on its own. The dairy compartments were still cool. She took two blocks of cheddar, three blocks of parmesan and two tubs of yoghurt. The milk section was half empty, only skim and light milk left. She reached in for two cartons from the back.

The fresh food was in the window of the store: oranges, green apples, potatoes, sweet potatoes, a few handfuls of green beans, onions, leeks, ginger, lemons and limes.

A single bunch of bananas, just ripe, called to her over the browning iceberg lettuce heads. She pushed the trolley over, peeled a banana and stuffed it in her mouth right there, and sat the rest at the top of one of the bags, for the household. Then, that sick feeling in her stomach.

He was watching her from the street. Young, dressed in dark clothes and beanie.

thirty

Rachel stood up to her full height and reached for the stick. When he did not move, did not attack, she pushed the trolley over shattered glass, through the space where the automatic glass doors used to be, towards him.

There was no fear on his face. But then, she had never been good at reading faces. Perhaps he was as surprised to see anyone as she was.

'Are you okay?' she said.

He bolted down the lane, towards the car park.

She stopped herself going after him. The hair on her arms was standing on end. It could be a trap; a gang of them waiting. For what reason, she couldn't imagine. They could take whatever they wanted from the whole town. But he was headed back to others, that was her feeling. And, if she was wrong, he would come back, come looking for her again.

Rachel pushed the trolley back to her sister's house, but took the long way, heading south at first, as if to the government housing on the edge of town. In case he was following her.

If there were survivors here, they would be everywhere, every town. Coming together, breaking apart. Trying to survive. The landscape they had to navigate had changed again.

The avenue of closely planted poplars gave her some shelter from anyone watching, but also from the bodies. A couple lay entwined on a pink and grey checked rug, their picnic things still laid out. A bottle of fizz and the same-coloured aluminium cups Monique still had from their parents' picnic set. At least they had been together. Rachel was glad she couldn't see their faces.

She focused on placing one boot in front of the other, her hands on the trolley handle. The pain in her calf. Walk forwards. It was all she could do. But she felt *them* swirling, forcing her backwards. Her mother handing around bright linen serviettes, her father pouring cider chilled in the river, her sister lying back on the grass, hands behind her head. The easygoing young woman Monique had been before she'd had to suddenly become an adult.

There was someone moving on the showground, by the stands. When she looked through the binoculars, there was nothing. She was jumping at shadows. But the shadows were *them*. Rachel tried Hannah's trick of humming, to stay with her own thoughts, the now. To block out their sound, like a high-frequency power tool or storm wind. She cut around the showground and up the lane to home. It had not been her home for more than a decade, but it was a safe place. Her sister was a safe place. The only person she truly trusted. And she had never needed her more.

Hannah opened the door as Rachel reached the top of the path. 'Thank goodness.'

'There's a boy,' she said.

'What happened?'

'Let me get off the street first.'

Rachel pushed the trolley into the hallway and locked the door. She hurried through the house closing the blinds, while Hannah ferried the bags into the kitchen.

Rachel ripped their washing from the line. Their bright clothes drying in the breeze only flagged their presence. She dumped her things in her room, folded Hannah's and placed them on the end of her bed.

They unloaded the supplies on the table, sorting them into piles for the fridge, pantry, laundry, bathroom and surgery. Hannah examined the hiking boots, shook her head, and put them on the floor. 'I should have gone with you. Where was he?'

'Outside the store. And I don't think he was alone,' Rachel said.

'Why do you say that?'

'Just a feeling. He seemed to have somewhere to go. And the amount of food missing. The soft drink and junk food aisles have been hit hard.'

'How old?

'Sixteen, seventeen.'

'And he saw you?'

'Yes. But once I'd seen him, he turned and ran.'

Hannah assessed the sea of items on the table. 'Ray, how long are you planning on staying?'

'I don't know. It just feels better to have plenty on hand.'

Hannah started putting the dairy items and fresh food in the fridge. Rachel carried the tins and packages into the pantry, placing them on the shelves according to Monique's system.

Hannah removed the tags from Isaiah's clothes. 'Thanks for getting all this.'

She shrugged.

'What was it like?'

'A *lot* of bodies. The smell . . .'

'And *them*?'

Rachel nodded. 'I saw them, close by. But I managed.'

'Saw them?'

'If you don't look right at them, they're there. Shadows. Kind of.'

'Maybe we can do this. Survive. Beat them, somehow.' Hannah peeled a banana and took a bite, closed her eyes.

When Hannah carried Isaiah into the kitchen that afternoon, he was much brighter, eyes alert, colour in his face. Hannah was smiling. A proper smile that lit up her face. 'His temperature has come down almost to normal. He's hardly coughing.'

'That's great.' Rachel took her glass to the sink, rinsed and placed it upside down to drain. It *was* a relief. She could think about going home, heading back down the mountains to the river, the boat, her own place. Back to the studio. This time she would take a wide berth around all the properties.

'Ray.' Hannah grabbed her forearm. 'Thank you. For getting us here. Helping us. I don't know what I would have done.'

Rachel pulled away. 'I'm just glad he's okay.'

'I was working out the antibiotics,' Hannah said. 'There's only enough for a few more days. It doesn't seem like a full prescription.'

'Perhaps you're supposed to go back to the doctor. Check the dose, progress, reactions.'

'You're sure there isn't any more?'

'Yeah.'

'Where's the nearest chemist?'

'Cooma. But the hospital might be better.' Though just thinking of that building was enough to start to shut down her whole body.

'We need to get more. He's improving, but we'll have to finish a full course to be sure.'

'Right.' Rachel leaned on the bench.

'And then, I want to go to Canberra. To see what happened to Kyle. If there are survivors here, there will be more there. I have to at least try.'

'Shouldn't you wait until Isaiah is a bit stronger?'

'Monique's note said there's a car? It wouldn't be as hard on him.'

Rachel frowned. 'It's a ute.' *Her* ute.

'I thought you'd come with us.'

'I can't do that.'

'Why?'

'It's too dangerous. If *they*'re this strong here, imagine what it will be like in Cooma, on the roads, Canberra. And I'm not ever setting foot in that fucking city again.'

'Don't you want to find Monique?'

Rachel turned to face Hannah. 'You think I don't miss my sister? That I don't care?' Rachel slapped her hand hard on the bench. 'She's *all* I have. But I don't know if she even made it that far. She wouldn't *expect* me to go after her. And, at the end of the day, she chose the world, *Bill* – not me!'

'Hey,' Hannah said. 'Why don't we sit down?'

Rachel wiped tears from her cheeks. 'I don't want to sit down.'

'Well, what *do* you want to do?'

'I want to go home!'

'Ray. How would you live?'

'I'll take some things from here. Grow what I can. I have eggs, salad, vegetables, fruit. Enough in the pantry for months.'

'And then what?'

'I don't know. I'll figure it out.'

'We have a better chance together,' Hannah said. 'All of us. Just think about it, okay?'

thirty-one

Rachel sat on her bed with her sketchbook, but nothing much was coming. Nothing new. Half an idea from an image travelling on the river, bubbles cascading over stones, down one side of a tall vessel. But that image was tumbled up with so many others. Images she didn't want to reproduce on paper. Her mind was awash.

She tried reading a book – a classic space opera she had once loved – in the chair, and then lying on the bed, but she couldn't concentrate. Their own planet had been made so strange. She settled into Oliver's poems, like walking in a familiar forest – but then she could hear Hannah and Isaiah moving around the house. She should go out and apologise, for yelling.

Instead, she padded across the hall, to her sister's room, and stood in the doorway. The old timber sleigh bed, with its matching bedside tables, had been their parents'. One of their mother's last landscapes filled the opposite wall. It was the view from the escarpment, on the other side of town, where she had grown up. The twisted snow gums, their bark in rainbow colours against white snow, was probably her best work. Even as children they had vetoed it being sold at the exhibition, putting a red spot on it themselves.

Monique had left clothes draped over the chair, the classic lines in subdued colours and natural fabrics that she preferred. As if she expected to come back or decided that it wouldn't matter either way. The photograph wall was a mix of sizes, shapes, frames – different eras. Their parents' wedding photo, capturing their goofiest grins. Somehow it made it harder that they had been so happy, still in love, even if it had seemed sickening when she and Monique were children. There were a few pictures of Monique and Bill: at dinner parties and work functions in Canberra, at an outdoor table near a body of water somewhere in Europe. Her graduations, from medical and vet science, with the trio of grinning brainiac friends she'd made along the way.

Her sister had always been better at school, better at everything: friends, love, work, life. The picture of her and Monique had been taken on a cross-country skiing trip, the winter before Rachel left for art school. Then Rachel's graduation, her first exhibition, her first installation.

Where there should have been children, there was Rachel. She didn't know if Monique and Bill had ever wanted children – if it just hadn't happened, or if there wasn't room.

The one picture of her and Tom, in sepia, drinking Champagne at some opening in Venice. Her work had been dwarfed by his in the Australian pavilion, and he had been beautiful and charming. When she stayed on, to work at the Murano factory for six months, he stayed, too.

Hannah had left the wardrobe door ajar. Rachel intended to

push it closed, but found herself opening it, touching the formal dresses, jackets, scarves, smelling leather and wool – her sister. Almost a whole life lived in the house. Rachel caught a glimpse of herself in the full-length mirror inside the wardrobe door. Her face was more gaunt and lined than she remembered, her hair threaded with grey. She looked a lot like her sister, her mother. There were whole years missing from her memory, decades had flown by. She was already older than her parents had been when they died.

Her sister's shoes were still in their boxes, on the high shelf, more shoes than it seemed possible to wear. But one of the boxes, black and more solid than the others, was labelled 'Ray'. Rachel slid it out and lifted the lid. It was all her letters and cards, everything she had ever written and drawn, neatly stacked and grouped, organised by date, like an archive. Telling one half of the story of their correspondence, one half of Rachel's life.

At her own house, Rachel had a similar box, full of Monique's letters and cards and postcards. But hers were all out of order; she just lifted the lid and dropped things in. Together they did make an archive of sorts, a history. Only there was no library, museum or gallery to store them in. In whatever future there would be, past achievements were irrelevant. Only relationships – with other people, the earth.

She sat on the end of her sister's bed and, this time, she could not stop the tears.

thirty-two

Rachel kneaded the dough with the heels of her hands on the floured bench. When it was smooth and elastic, springing back, she patted it into a round, oiled the top, and placed it in a tin to rise. With no open fire, she had set Monique's gas oven to a low heat.

It had been in the same oven that she had taught herself to bake bread. She had needed to do something with her hands and, with Monique working such long hours, wanted to find ways to help out. She had made a biscuity pizza dough first, and then improved on it, understanding that there was chemistry at work. It was a matter of finding the right timing, texture – elasticity, not entirely unlike glass.

'Hey,' Hannah said, from the doorway.

'I was going to make chicken soup for dinner.'

'Perfect,' Hannah said. 'I'm sorry, Ray. I'm just worried about Isaiah, Kyle. Everything's been so hard.'

'I know. I'm sorry, too,' Rachel said.

'What can I do?'

'Cut up the vegetables? I thought we should have a good meal before we go.'

'You're coming with us?'

Rachel nodded. 'We need to make sure Isaiah gets better. You need to find Kyle. And I need to go to the medical research centre. If Bill and Mon survived, they will be there – trying to save the world.'

Hannah smiled. 'Thanks, Ray.' She started on the onions. 'I'm starving,' Hannah said. Even though they were not. This was survival; how they went on living.

'You're still eating for two. And we walked a long way.'

'That was further than I have walked in my whole life.'

'I wasn't sure you'd make it. In the beginning.'

'Didn't have much choice,' she said.

'Isaiah's still sleeping?'

'He seems much more comfortable. It's the most he's slept since he was *born*,' Hannah said.

Rachel lit the gas under the pot and splashed in olive oil. She fried off chicken pieces with the onion. Hannah scraped in the rest of the vegetables from the board with the back of the knife. Then Rachel added the stock, herbs, fresh bay leaves from the courtyard. Monique was still caring for Rachel even though she wasn't there. Even though she had left without her.

She ran her hands over the wine bottles in the back of the pantry. Monique had given up drinking decades ago, after a surgeon told her that his hands shook too much the next day, even after one glass of wine, to work with the precision he needed. She still kept wine for guests and had written in her last letter that she had started having the occasional glass again.

Though she hadn't said why. Rachel had barely had a drop for a decade. It wasn't good for her head space, and shaky hands were definitely not good for a glass blower. But she wasn't blowing glass now. Who knew when she would again.

She chose a Cabernet Sauvignon from the Coonawarra, with a label she recognised, and opened it at the kitchen bench.

'Wine?'

Hannah was still peeling the potatoes. 'Just a splash. But let me feed Isaiah first.'

Rachel opened the cupboard, chose some of her own early goblets: clear glass flecked with golden bubbles, a technique she had played with using bicarb and gold leaf. They seemed gaudy now, though the shape of them was still pleasing in her hand. Glass was so malleable in the furnace, so fixed in time once on the shelf.

She half-filled a glass for Hannah, poured a fullish one for herself. The flavours and smell were more intense than she remembered. Like the banana. It was only once something became a finite resource, perhaps, that they appreciated its value. She switched on the lamps and lit the candles. She didn't want to make it too Last Supperish, but why not have a nice dinner at the table while they could?

The wine was relaxing her limbs, its warmth moving down into her belly. She set the bottle on the sideboard. Monique had arranged a collection of Rachel's vessels, from earliest to most recent, in a kind of retrospective. She held one from the middle, when she was still sharing a studio, still out in the world. Though she had refined her techniques since then, simplified her style, the tree vase had been a high point in terms of stretching what was possible. It was almost as if someone else had done it. She turned it to the best angle, with a candle behind it, the flames casting strange green flickers about the room.

Monique had hung their mother's only self-portrait above the sideboard, as if for company. It was almost an abstract piece, except for her eyes, which were just how Rachel remembered them, always containing a sparkle, as if she had a secret. The background was dark, a twisted forest. The piece always made her wonder if there had been a different side to their mother. If she, too, had ever felt anxious and overwhelmed.

The timer went off in the kitchen, reminding her of the bread, the meal. She put her wine glass down on the bench and opened the oven. When she tapped the top of the loaf, it sounded hollow, like a drum. She slid it gently from the shelf and set it on the rack to cool. Then she turned the heat down on the soup.

Hannah came back with Isaiah strapped to her. His eyes seemed to focus on Rachel more often, his hands grabbing hold of anything that came within his reach. She could tell, now, when he had just been fed. His face took on a different expression, what could only be described as contentment.

'Cheers,' Hannah said, clinking her glass to Rachel's.

Hannah ladled soup into wide white bowls while Rachel cut the bread in thick slices. They carried everything into the dining room and sat down opposite each other.

'This reminds me of lockdowns.'

'Huh?' Rachel said.

'During the pandemics. Confined to the house. All the emphasis on food and cooking,' Hannah said. 'Finding comfort in the uncertainty.'

Rachel nodded. Mia and Monique had both tried to explain what it was like. But while galleries stopped buying for a while, and deliveries slowed, it hadn't changed Rachel's day-to-day life particularly.

'I like the lightshades,' Hannah said. 'Retro.'

'I made those when I was living here,' Rachel said.

After the dinner party Monique had organised, Rachel had started doing a little leadlighting in the garage. Without breath or fire, just the cutting tool, solder and soldering iron, on Monique's old reception desk. She replaced the store-bought exterior lights first, then her bedroom, then the whole house. By the time she finished, she had started visualising a future. Her own world of forest and glass.

'Except this one, it's blown glass – that was a gift, later. The curve is modelled on a fern frond. Mon loves ferns.' It looked better when the lights were on. Glass needed light.

'Monique raised you?'

'She's only a few years older. We went to live with Mia and Karen. They were close friends of our parents.' But it had been a very different household. 'When Monique left school, she took a gap year. Two. So we could move back here, and I could finish school.'

Hannah's spoon had paused, halfway to her mouth.

Rachel put down her wine. She was talking too much. And, for the first time, it occurred to her that Monique might not have felt she had any choice.

'When you were a kid, were you . . .?'

'You can say it.'

'Anxious.'

'More so after our parents died,' she said. 'I needed routines. Wasn't good with change.'

'What happened. To your parents?'

Rachel swallowed a mouthful of soup. 'Car accident,' she said. Her father had been on a call-out, driving back from Cooma. They didn't ever find out why her mother was with him. But she was. They had never tired of spending time together, especially in open country.

'I'm sorry,' Hannah said.

'It was a long time ago,' Rachel said.

Hannah was facing the portrait of Rachel's mother. 'Monique didn't have any children either?'

'What?'

'I haven't seen any pictures. And you haven't mentioned nieces or nephews.'

'You're right. She didn't.'

'I mean lots of people decided not to.'

'It would have been hard, with her career. And with Bill, well, it was complicated.' He had been Chief Scientist then, and still married to someone else. During the window when it might have happened, Monique was caring for Rachel.

Hannah reached for another piece of bread. 'I didn't mean to question it.'

'She already cares for a lot of people, I guess.'

'True,' Hannah said.

'What about you? Were you close to your mother?'

'I saw her nearly every day. But I don't know that we ever had a real conversation.'

'A generational thing?'

'She got along better with my brother. He who could do no wrong.'

'I can't imagine you being too much trouble.'

'I wasn't that easy when I was younger,' Hannah said. 'We just weren't on the same wavelength. Her starting position for everything was "No". But then the next time I'd come over she would have done whatever it was she argued against!'

Rachel smiled; a lot of older people were like that. Young people, too.

'And she used to set Kyle off, with her talk-show rubbish. But she was really great with Isaiah. It brought us closer. She drove me *nuts*. But I miss her so much. She was my *mother*.'

Rachel's throat was tight. 'Of course.'

Hannah wiped tears from her face. 'I took so much for granted, you know.'

'We all did.'

'It's so hard to accept that she's not going to see Isaiah grow up.'

They froze, at the sound of running footsteps. More than one person. And then the sound of shattering glass.

thirty-three

Rachel switched off the lamp and blew out the candles. 'It's the surgery. They're probably just looting.'

'Do they know we're here?'

Rachel looked towards the kitchen, lit by lamplight. Light that would be seeping out around the blinds, down the hallway, and under the door. 'Why don't you get Isaiah and come back here.'

Rachel pushed her chair back from the table and padded into the kitchen to turn off the lights. She felt her way into the hall, past the shopping trolley, to take an aluminium walking pole from the old copper bucket by the door.

They wouldn't find much in the surgery – the remaining veterinary and medical supplies, medications and bandages. There was no till, no cash, no valuables. Only what might have been in the wallets of the bodies they removed and three flat phones. In the house, there was the generator, power, alcohol, cash, gold. But they didn't know that.

They stood in the dining-room doorway in the dark, Hannah holding Isaiah to her, Rachel holding the walking pole like a sword. They heard voices, the opening and shutting cupboards, something crashing to the floor. Rachel tensed, waiting for the men to force the door, to come inside, into her sister's house. To ruin everything. For the nightmare to continue until its inevitable end. The end of her, then Hannah – and then Isaiah. *Stop*.

Why weren't *they* in the heads of the looters?

Hannah was trembling, sniffing back tears.

Rachel put her hand on Hannah's shoulder and left it there.

Then the noises faded, stopped. Footsteps and low voices passed along the laneway. Two or three people. They were male, Rachel was sure of it. The footsteps paused, outside the window, as if seeing or sensing something. Rachel held her breath, gripped Hannah's shoulder to stop her from crying out. And then he walked on.

Rachel dropped her arms. 'God.'

'Do you think they'll come back?'

'Probably,' Rachel said.

'We've got to get out of here.'

'I'm not driving in the dark,' Rachel said. 'We won't know what's around us, ahead of us. They'll follow our lights. Let's pack the ute and leave at dawn.'

The old EH Holden utility had been her father's, the pale green duco an original colour remade in a custom gloss enamel. She unhooked the tarp, flicked it back. The tray's oak boards were like a warm hug. 'This will be yours one day, kiddo,' her father had said, when she was still only waist high on him. He probably imagined teaching her to drive in it, the years ahead they had together.

'Does that even work?' Hannah said.

'*That* is a classic. And Mon keeps it running,' Rachel said.

Rachel loaded water canisters, the camp cooker, tinned and dried food, fruit, what was left of the bread and soup. Sleeping bags, woollen blankets, a change of clothes, first aid kit, her medication, drops, nappies and an empty duffel bag.

Hannah handed over a single shopping bag – her and Isaiah's things. All she had left in the world.

'How will we get fuel?'

'I had it converted to gas. Hopefully we can still get that at service stations. Try to get some rest.' Rachel said. 'I'll wake you at five.'

Rachel cleaned up as quietly as she could, her ears strained for noise, her body on high alert. She unplugged the power bank and wheeled it back to the utilities room. Something scrambled along the roof – probably a possum. She stowed the map, binoculars, compass, torch, water bottles, facecloth and food for the drive in the cab's compartments and slipped the keys in her pocket. She put on her thickest fleece and patted her pockets: cash, gold, multi-tool, drops. She was ready.

It was bright moonlight outside, but the haze was building – she could smell the smoke. She paced around the house, checking windows, doors, the time. It wasn't safe to leave; it wasn't safe to stay. But she was helping Hannah and Isaiah and heading towards her sister. *It feels right after all.*

The luminous arms of Rachel's father's watch crept towards dawn. She stared at the new plastic storage tub she had been tripping over, full of sketchbooks and notepads. It was so like something she would see at her own place that it hadn't registered. She lifted the lid and opened the black, spiral-bound sketch pad on top. Every page was covered with detailed pencil drawings: the boulder-strewn landscapes, dead gumtrees, a rushing rocky river. They were intricate, accurate, but there was something whimsical about them, too. A side of her sister she didn't know.

She was writing a note for Monique by candlelight in the kitchen when she heard them. Footsteps, low voices, then the front door handle turning. Rachel stood still. It was deadlocked, but they could just break a glass panel and reach in. The key was still in the lock on the back of the door.

But they moved away, around the side of the house. Rachel went to the front door, took the key from the lock, grabbed her boots, and ran to the spare room. Hannah was asleep on the bed, fully dressed.

'Hannah,' Rachel whispered. 'Get up. They're back.'

Rachel lifted Isaiah in his papoose with her free arm, holding him against her chest. Hannah gripped Rachel's fleece and followed her down the hall, back to the kitchen. They could hear them outside the laundry, the splintering of wood.

Rachel slid open the door of the utilities room, waited until Hannah and Isaiah were inside and closed it behind them. The men were inside, moving through the house.

Rachel followed Hannah into the garage, heart hammering. They opened the ute's heavy doors as quietly as they could.

Hannah slid into the passenger seat, hunched over Isaiah. The roller door rattled open, too slow, too loud. Rachel put the key in the ignition and turned it. The engine was much noisier than she remembered, a deep rumble amplified in the garage. There was no sneaking now.

She closed her door and roared down the sloped driveway, the bull bar sending the timber gates flying. Only the crows were up, watching from the bare branches of a dead gum across the road.

They sped along the street as the wide sky lightened, shifting to pink, revealing a fresh coating of snow on the mountains. In the rear-vision mirror, there were two shadows standing in front of her sister's house, watching them leave.

thirty-four

Hannah sat up on the edge of the seat, watching the road in front of them. Rachel had to work her way around three cars, a van and more dead bodies. They were blurry in the half-light, but the shapes were all wrong – bloated, parts missing. Disappearing from the edges, like Nimmitabel itself.

When they were clear at last, she put her foot down. The engine responded, taking them onto the highway, the open road. Away from *them*.

Hannah checked on Isaiah and sat back.

Although Rachel had not slept, there was more space to think, without the noise of *them* in her head. She settled into the old leather bench seat, hands on the wheel again. The simplicity of the dash, a full tank, dial speedo and oil temperature, even the curved thickness of the toughened glass windscreen, was a comfort.

She had driven the Beast while at art school, unable to afford anything of her own. It had been useful for picking up materials, transporting installations and shifting her meagre collection of things, from one group house to another. Or someone else's things – as became a regular weekend ritual. She not only had a ute but could lift heavy items. Life had seemed infinite then, the glass making anything possible. As if she could shape herself in the flames.

'If those men can survive, so can we,' Hannah said.

'I was thinking that, too.'

They were driving along the top of the world, Mount Kosciuszko and the Snowy Mountains on one side, the Great Dividing Range on the other, the sky so close they could almost touch it. There were few places that offered such a long view.

But, in the light of day, that long view was confronting: raw eroded slopes, the car-coffins they had to weave around and, worse, the bodies not contained inside their cars. Pieces torn from them, swelling and seething with maggots. Hannah had shut her eyes.

They passed a pine plantation, bright green against the duller gums and brown paddocks. The black ribbon of road unfurled before them. The old stone sign, half overgrown with weeds, just the letter 'C' over '30': 30 kilometres to Cooma.

Images flashed by. It had been an age since she had driven a vehicle, let alone moved her body over the earth at speed. After the forests, even the gardens of the town, the escarpment was a moonscape. Worn paddocks delineated by fence lines, power poles, cattle yards, tin sheds and silos. Tired houses squatting in the dirt. Bare slope after bare slope broken only by an occasional cluster of bleached gums. A plastic bag had snagged on a fence, flapping in the wind. Red topsoil lifted and swirled, moved in waves. A few clumps of tussocky grass were all that held the world together.

Her mother's heart would have broken to see what had happened to her landscapes. To their community, to people everywhere. Maybe that explained the ache in Rachel's own chest. As if she was picking up the pain of the land itself. The tipping point, when it came, had been so quick.

For the decade Rachel had been hidden away, she had minimised her footprint – done no harm – but she had not helped, either. And now it was too late. Isaiah, if he survived, would never see half the things she had seen, taken for granted, gulped down.

She watched the centreline, the white guideposts flicking by. There were fewer and fewer cars, most pointing towards Cooma. One of those was a minibus, carrying older people back to their nursing home after an excursion to the movies, museum or markets. They slumped in their seats, still neat and orderly, in cardigans and scarves, even the driver, as if they had simply pulled over to the side of the road and fallen asleep. As if not one of them had put up any resistance.

She checked every Prius to see if it was Monique's. In case it was her body inside.

Hannah pulled out her phone, freshly charged on the power bank, checking again for signal, a message, a miracle.

'It's not going to be any different,' Rachel said.

Hannah switched on the radio, pushing hard at the tabs with one finger. There was only static. She turned the dial, scanning manually through the whole frequency spectrum. Even the emergency station, used to broadcast information in fires, floods, cyclones – every other kind of emergency – was silent.

'Shit,' Hannah said.

'Try AM,' Rachel said.

Hannah repeated the process, dialling slowly across the band-width. 'Still nothing.'

It was a world gone silent. *Silenced*. There was no news. No help. No advice. No solution.

Rachel tried not to think about empty radio and TV booths, recording studios, all the bands that were no more. She still had her record collection, her parents' old records, their turntable. If she ever made it home, she would treasure every one of those vinyl discs. Play one a day, for the rest of her life.

A kestrel hovered by the side of the road, pale underneath with rufous shoulders, waiting to see what the car might scare up.

They passed another roadside marker. Twenty kilometres to go. Poplars clung to creeks and gullies. Thinning pines huddled around farmhouses. The old railway line still ran parallel to the road, a memory of more prosperous times. Her parents would have hated to see their world this way – all the things they fought so hard for.

Hannah stared out the window, holding Isaiah's tiny hand in hers. 'It's like the Badlands.'

'This used to be one of the most beautiful drives in the country,' Rachel said.

Her parents always treated the trip to Canberra and back like an adventure. The last time they had done it as a family had been for a circus from Russia – for Rachel's birthday. It had all been performed on ice: bears playing ice-hockey, trapeze artists swinging on snowflakes. The clowns scored their laughs on skates, while they turned figure eights.

They had sat in the front row, their mother pulling treat after treat out of the picnic basket – ham and cheese twists, mini-quiches, butterfly cakes, Smarties, cider. It was winter, the big top was full of people, rugged up in coats, as if they were Russians, too.

Rachel had lain across the back seat on the way home, her head on Monique's thighs. As they crossed the Monaro, the moon was full and low, the boulders casting long shadows. Their mother's socked feet were crossed on the dash, while their father told some story about the Russian steppes: Siberia, tundra, mink, arctic fox – words Rachel thought he had made up.

Sometimes, to get to sleep, she still imagined herself lying there, safe, on the back seat.

thirty-five

When they rounded the bend, Rachel had to slam on the brakes. A delivery truck had collided with a car and spun it around, blocking the road. The verge was narrow, falling away in deep gutters, too deep for the ute to drive through. The truck cab was empty. The couple in the car were flopped over the dash, the bonnet sheared off. A pair of crows, glossy black, watched from the power lines. *Waiting*.

'We'll have to move it,' Rachel said.

'Drive it?'

'Push it off the road.' Rachel took a breath, pulled her drops from her pocket, placed three under her tongue. She opened the door and swung her legs out.

Rachel assessed the arrangement of vehicles, bodies, angles and distances, trying not to feel anything. Trying not to feel *them*, circling, like crows. She had gone her whole life without seeing a dead body and now so many. When would it end? With her own, her sister's? Was her sister already dead?

'I'm right here,' Hannah said.

Rachel strode to the driver's door, as if she wasn't afraid, planning each of her movements carefully. It had been a woman driving: mid-sixties, her glasses broken by the blown airbag. There was a cut on the bridge of her nose but no blood. It wasn't the accident that had killed her.

She glanced through the window, at Hannah and Isaiah.

Rachel turned the key. The power came on but the engine didn't start, didn't even turn over. She used her multi-tool to puncture the airbag and squashed it down to give her more room.

She reached over the woman's swollen belly to release the handbrake, put the car in neutral. Rachel stopped, distracted by the bright glow of the dash, the messages flashing across the screen. The smell of two dead people in that small space. Her face so close to the woman's waxy face, bulging eyes, distorted by fear.

Fears had once been hidden, private. Only revealed in glimpses, a momentary loss of control or within the safety of intimacy. Now they had all escaped onto the surface.

Rachel tried not to look at the couple, or the driver of the truck, whose body lay face up on the road, his eyes missing – only Hannah and Isaiah. She braced both hands in the doorway, straining her legs, using her whole body to try to move the car backwards. It didn't shift.

Fuck. What was she against this tide of obstacles? *Them* everywhere, never giving up. The endless dead. The constant stream of emotions and images. Her parents' bodies by the side of the same road. The other driver had been an older man, Allan Mophett, someone who probably shouldn't have had his licence. It had been her father who ticked the box to allow him to keep driving, close to home, out of compassion. Only for him to plough into the hospital vehicle with Rachel's parents inside.

Hannah walked around to the front of the car, cradling Isaiah, and leaned her tiny backside against the crushed bonnet. 'Try now.'

Rachel nodded. 'One, two, and *push*.'

The car started to move. Slowly at first, and then picking up momentum. Rachel stepped back, watching it plunge into the culvert with a scrape and crash, its owners inside. *Sorry*. They wouldn't know or feel anything, but it still felt disrespectful, callous. They had to be. And she and Hannah had to live with the consequences.

When she turned, Hannah was frozen in the middle of the road, transfixed by the eye-less truck driver. 'They're going to take his eyes,' she said. 'Then his heart.'

'Hannah.' Rachel edged towards her. 'The crows did that.'

But *they* were gathered around, dark and shifting, like crows. Moving in. Hannah was hyperventilating. Rachel grabbed her shoulders. 'I'm here. Keep Isaiah calm.'

Isaiah started to cry, bringing Hannah back. She rocked him, sang to him, as she hurried back to the Beast. They closed its heavy doors against everything that was outside.

Rachel started the Beast and edged forwards, past the truck, around the driver, until they were back on the highway, picking up speed.

thirty-six

Rachel gripped the wheel tighter. They were dropping in altitude, heading into Cooma. It had been an oasis, nestled in a rich valley, the river an artery for life. But Cooma had sprawled since Rachel had last seen it. Housing developments spread its edges, pushing up into the hills. New brick and tile thrown together fast. A bigger town meant more people, more obstacles – and the hospital.

At the saleyards they had to slow for the first snarl of cars, spilled vans, goods and bodies scattered over the road. Rachel managed to thread a way through, to keep her eyes above the terrible detail. Still checking every Prius: different plate, no hospital decals, not a woman, not her sister.

They were moving again. But the bridge ahead, over the river, was blocked. They would have to go the back way. 'Okay,' Rachel said. 'I'll try and work my way through all this. But I need you to be my extra eyes. Anything moves, front, back or sides, I want to know.'

Hannah sat up in the seat, held Isaiah closer to her body. 'Got it.'

They crept through back streets, weaving around abandoned cars, bodies, fallen bikes, dead dogs. Here, too, they were in clusters, as if drawn together by some force. If *they* could adapt, influence people through their thoughts, they were going to be very hard to fight.

Bright new shopfronts, fast food outlets and clearance houses, in between stone Federation buildings. The little weatherboard book and music store Rachel had liked to hang out in was still there, untouched. The supermarket was the only structure with lights still blazing.

There were few live dogs, only cats slinking off into alleys, behind spilled bins. It was like the Greek islands, where cats outnumbered people. She was cheered by a glimpse of red fox, just a streak, until she realised what he might be eating.

They turned the corner, the hospital looming ahead. A recent makeover – primary-coloured sails, a roof garden, a wall of half-dead plants – had attempted to make it less institutional. The sight of it still made her sick.

Rachel parked near the entrance, but not too close. Planning each step in minute detail, going over and over it, calmed her.

She scanned the cars, the neighbouring park, and the auxiliary buildings for movement. She checked every mirror, the way Monique had taught her to do, before reversing, before opening the car door. 'Most accidents happen in the car park,' she used to say. It wasn't true anymore but Rachel didn't want anyone sneaking up on them. It took a moment to register that most of the cars were empty. *The people are inside.*

She opened the door. 'So, you and Isaiah should wait here,' Rachel said.

'We work together, remember?' Hannah said, her hand on the door handle.

'We don't know who or what's in there.' Rachel's stomach was warning her: that lurching feeling, its contents pushing up to her throat.

She stared at the hospital entrance, visualised walking inside. That particular smell, the bright light. Tears threatened, nearly as old as the cool metal beneath her hands. The door opening, the end of a hospital bed, an empty chair. The huddle of doctors and nurses, her mother's hands, legs hidden beneath blankets, too many tubes. Monique's shoulders heaving beneath her thin blue blouse. It was her sister's face, when she finally turned around, that had frightened her the most.

Rachel's vision had narrowed, as if from the other end of a long bright tunnel – the hospital corridor. She was so low to the ground, a child again. And afraid. *They* had her this time. In her mouth and throat, like smoke.

I. Can't. Breathe.

'Ray?'

She closed her eyes. Shut the images, feelings down. *No.* Somewhere she heard a currawong calling. Her sister walking along a tree-lined street with Bill. Whether it was real, in the present, or the past, she couldn't tell. *Keep going, Ray.*

Hannah slid across the seat, put her hand on Rachel's.

Rachel wiped her eyes with the back of her hand. 'If I'm not out in thirty minutes, just keep going, okay?' Plans and backup plans, preparing for the worst. It was the new mode of thinking. Children, mothers, in this new world, were important. More important than her.

'We're not going without you.'

'Hopefully not. But, Hannah, if I don't come back, promise you'll keep going? Don't come in after me,' she said.

'We'll be here.'

Rachel took the duffel bag from the back and slung it over her body. Fourteen strides across the car park, exposed to the world, towards the building she hated most in the world. Still, she walked with purpose, not panic. She breathed, filling and emptying her lungs, lengthening her spine. At the entrance, the double glass doors remained closed. No power; no system. She pushed against the single glass emergency exit door to the side, not even hoping, but it swung open.

Rachel leaned against the wall for a moment to steady herself. She placed four drops under her tongue. She had always struggled in hospitals. No one was ever in them for a good reason. Except having a baby or visiting someone who'd had one. And she had never done either of those things. It was the smell. The too-bright fluorescent lighting. That subtle flicker, like lingering spirits.

There were no fluorescents now. Just the glow of emergency track lighting along the floor and green exit signs. It wasn't disinfectant Rachel could smell, as she ran up the hallway, but death. The sickly sweet scent she was getting to know all too well. It was in her nostrils and clothes and hard to scrub off her skin.

There were bodies piled up by the doors, as if they made it so far but could not go on. There were people – corpses – in neat lines along the corridor, backs against the wall, waiting for help that never came.

She stopped at the lift, open and inviting, but for the bodies either side. *Move.* But she couldn't. Lifts scared her at the best of times; the closing metal doors, locked in the enclosed space with others, rushing up and down the bowels of a building. And *that* lift. That very lift had carried them down to the ground floor without their parents, just Mia with a hand on her shoulder, to stop Rachel running when she saw the bright sunlight outside.

There was no one holding her back now. Rachel blocked out the distractions, the horror all around, the questions about what had happened, and the answers that threatened to bubble up, like the panic inside her – and ran. She was good at running, moving over the earth at speed. Long legs, powerful muscles – it was only her mind that was weak.

She took the stairs two at a time, stepping over bodies and bags. Here and there the blue scrubs of a nurse or orderly and the white coat of a doctor. This death didn't discriminate.

Every corridor was the same, like the one they had waited in, on cold hard chairs. Every room was like the one they had been shut out of. The room where their parents had died.

All these years later, Monique had still visited the building every week. And now Rachel had come back, too – when she had sworn she never would. *Keep moving.* She followed the signs hanging overhead, turned left.

The reception desk was unattended, bodies fanned out around it. The waiting room was full – of the dead. Had they come here, from all around, when it started? Or was it just where they happened to be, for all the usual reasons people ended up in hospital? It was the faces that undid her. A father and child, turned towards each other, in orange plastic chairs. Rachel stared a moment too long. Their features were similar, mirroring each other's fear, but he had gone first. The child's distress, at being left alone with *them*, was more than grief, more than fear, it had torn her in two.

Rachel hadn't yet seen or heard a single sign of life. But the alarm in her body, the hair on her arms standing up, the nausea, made her slow down, pause at the corner to listen. There were bodies on the ground, more recent. She stepped her way through limbs, hands, shoes, her own boots silent on the blue carpet.

The medical supplies room had already been raided. Morphine, pethidine, codeine and methadone cleared from the shelves. Anything for pain, oblivion. One man had done himself in on the spot, needle still in his arm. His face, unlike the others, was peaceful.

The remaining supplies were a jumble of boxes and packets. Rachel stood tall, the dead man's legs between hers, and worked methodically from the top down, turning the packets to the front and scanning the labels. It was tempting to sweep the lot into the bag and run, but she pulled down only what they needed: more amoxicillin, half a dozen spare boxes of penicillin, just in case. Her eye kept returning to the single box at the back of the shelf, right in front of her: a nasal spray, *Pitocin*. The label said oxytocin, the same as was in her drops. She had seen it before. In Mon's surgery probably – it reminded her of something, but there wasn't time. She added it to the bag. Then the basics: Panadol, bandages, dressings, antiseptic, tape, burn gel, antihistamine, Stingose, butterfly clips. Trying to anticipate everything that might go wrong.

A noise came from the corridor, a low moaning. Rachel threw in surgical glue, sutures, scalpels and disinfectant wipes for good measure and turned without closing the bag.

One of the corpses she had stepped over was not a corpse. Not yet. The man was sitting upright in the doorway, struggling to wake from whatever dream he had been hiding in. She saw now the spent needles, the empty packets of hospital food. He had been there a while, and had probably thought himself alone. The last man on earth.

'Hey,' Rachel said. 'Are you okay?'

'What are you doing with my stuff?'

'I'm not taking anything you need.' She stepped around his stockpile of hospital food from the kitchens; barely food at all. But he lunged for her ankle, and gripped it, like death itself.

And then *they* were there. They had been all along, just waiting. In the rooms, the corridor, the lift – softening the corners, blurring the edges. Her vision narrowed. She couldn't shake him free. She was stuck inside the hospital, her childhood, with all her memories and fears. And another room, pinned to her own bed.

With a strength she hadn't anticipated in such puny arms, he yanked her leg, bringing her down, face first into the carpet. This time she did not wait to see what he would do next. Rachel turned, and kicked, boot connecting with jawbone – a sickening crunch.

It was enough to make him let go. Rachel leapt to her feet, gathered up the spilled items – and ran for the stairwell. She zipped up the bag and slung it over her shoulder, leaned hard on the railing and used it to slide down, leaping over bodies and an upturned trolley, all the way to the ground floor.

Natural light streamed in through the entrance. She squinted to make out the Beast, Hannah's outline, still in the passenger seat. She ran for the doors, without looking back, without thinking, shoulder charging the emergency exit, side-stepping through, and sprinting across the car park.

They were going for Hannah and Isaiah. The shadows were harder to see in the full light of day, but they were closing in on the Beast.

'Hannah!' Rachel ran towards the car, swinging the bag over her shoulder. *They* seemed to disperse, fade from focus. She threw the bag in the back and secured the tarp.

Hannah leaned over to unlock the driver's door. 'Thank goodness. I thought something terrible was happening to you.'

Rachel slid into the red leather seat and took what felt like the first breath for hours. When she turned the key, the engine rumbled to life. There were few things in life that had never let her down. The ute was one of them. Rachel reversed without checking behind her and roared out of the car park.

thirty-seven

Hannah lifted Isaiah to fasten her seatbelt. 'Okay?'

Rachel shook her head. 'But I got the antibiotics. The sound of her boot connecting with the man's head, the impact, was on repeat. His tight grip on her ankle. *Them* waiting for her to fall.

'People? *Them?*'

'Someone alive. An addict, I think.'

'You talked to him?'

'He wasn't making much sense.'

They navigated their way around cars, trucks, vans, caravans, motorbikes, bodies. Twice they had to back up, find another way. Rachel focused on the path through, the space between obstacles, not the obstacles themselves – or the horrors they contained. The horrors in her own mind. She had felt desperate to get away, but would the man have actually hurt her? And what state had she left him in?

The cars, people, chaos thinned and then they were climbing out of the valley again, away from the town, passing the Snowy Mountains Hydro visitor centre – another monument to man's triumph over nature. Driving along the empty road, it seemed a hollow victory. The golden church on the hill sat silent, looking back over the valley in judgement.

The Monaro Highway curved away, taking them towards Canberra. It was dry, as dry as she had ever seen it. A wide brown land. Sheep straggled single file along dusty tracks, dams low, water troughs were empty. Tumbleweeds blew across the road. The air was heavy with smoke. She hadn't realised how much her little valley had sheltered her.

She took the water bottle Hannah handed her and drank, her throat parched, her body dehydrated from the wine, adrenaline.

'Is it oxytocin that's in your system after childbirth?'

'Like a hormone?'

'Yeah.'

'Maybe,' Hannah said. 'Why?'

'Mon made a point of me taking the drops. They have that in them. Other things, too, but —'

'You think that's why I'm alive?'

'Maybe. I think it suppresses fear.'

'There was that other mother, back home.'

'You're more sure you saw her now?'

Hannah nodded. 'Your sister would know.'

'She will.'

Rachel had to slow for a mob of cattle over the road, Angus–Hereford crosses. They had knocked down a fence to access the long grass along the roadside. It was what drovers had done, back in the day, taking stock along roads and lanes during drought, to take advantage of any remaining feed. Not so much to fatten their cattle for market, but to keep them alive.

The cattle moved out of the way, but in no particular hurry. Calves meandered, loose-limbed, in sight of their mothers.

Once they were clear of the steers at the back of the pack, Rachel accelerated away. A signpost listed the destinations ahead: Canberra, Queanbeyan, Sydney. If what they had found in Nimmitabel was what they would find everywhere, they weren't really towns and cities anymore. Just locations.

Hannah pulled the bottle from her bag to feed Isaiah tepid milk. Breast milk. Life. Her hands were shaking. Rachel stared a moment before focusing on the road. They had seen enough horrors, enough for a lifetime. They passed another signpost, counting down the distance remaining between them and the city in 25-kilometre increments.

'Is Kyle staying near the Defence precinct?'

'A flat in Ainslie.'

'Okay.' Rachel was still trying to figure the best way to approach the city, where there would be least traffic, more ways through.

'You lived in Canberra?'

'While I was at art school.' And on and off for a decade after that.

'Anywhere else?'

'Sydney, Adelaide, Venice, Berlin.' All a lifetime ago.

Hannah turned. Trying to imagine Rachel, perhaps, in a big city. On the other side of the world. She could no longer imagine it herself. 'Why Berlin?'

'A residency. It was only a year.'

'You speak German?'

Rachel shook her head, though Hans had taught them plenty

198

– all the expletives and superlatives, at least. 'In the studio, English was the common language.'

'How did you go working with other artists?'

'I was used to that then,' she said. In truth she had not produced much for the first few months. There had been too much testosterone and ego, jostling for position. Too many alcohol-charged evenings. She spent the time wandering the streets, hanging out in museums and galleries. Lingering over the old glass – Greek, Roman, Byzantine – in opaque blues and greens. Two-thousand-year-old bowls, platters and goblets that had somehow survived the fall of their civilisations.

'All those galleries and museums – it must have been amazing.'

'What about you?' Rachel said. 'Have you travelled?'

Hannah stared out at the denuded brown hills. 'I've never even been to Tasmania,' she said.

thirty-eight

The road wound through a treed gully and dry creek, its sparse gums close enough together to almost form a canopy. The smoke haze was heavier, lower, casting an otherworldly light, the sun veiled and weak. She had seen it like that before, during the fires. They'd had to come up with a new weather symbol for the smoke that obscured the sun for months, even in the cities. It had gone on so long she had thought it would never end, that she would never see the horizon again. That fires were the future.

When they saw the woman standing by the guardrail, they just stared at first, as if she might be an apparition. Rachel took her foot off the accelerator, worried the woman might step out in front of the car.

'Is that a child?' She was holding something tight against her body.

'I can't tell,' Hannah said.

'Should I stop?' They were still decelerating.

'Let's go past slowly. We can always pull over up ahead.'

The woman was dressed in grey cotton, layers of similar

colours. Too late Rachel saw it was a bundle, not a baby. And the woman was a man, with a scarf tied around his close-cropped head. He lunged for Hannah's door. Rachel was only moments ahead of him, banging her elbow down on the interior lock as the man grabbed the handle.

Hannah screamed, wrapped her arms around Isaiah. Then Rachel saw the others, through her window, coming out of the trees, running downhill towards them. The man was just a decoy, banging on the window now, running beside the ute.

Hannah was staring straight ahead, tilting her shoulders forwards so that Isaiah couldn't look around, couldn't see the man, couldn't see out. Her chest was his world. She was humming that damn pop song again. Rachel hadn't been able to get it out of her head for days after the walk. But it had worked then, and they needed it now.

'Drive. Drive! *Drive!*'

Rachel pushed her foot to the floor. *Fuck!* It was such an obvious trap. She struggled to wind up the manual window, her fingers slipping from the handle. There were four more, running after them, throwing stones, yelling. What they wanted, she didn't know. Their wheels, Isaiah, Hannah . . . It didn't seem real, let alone make sense. Why here, in this place?

They were all dressed much the same, outfits pulled together from old blankets, or a roll of cheap material. She had never been so glad to be locked inside a vehicle.

The ute didn't have the best pickup, but they were away. Or so she thought, until she saw the top of his head in her rear-vision mirror. One of the youths had grabbed hold of the tailgate and climbed onto the tray. He monkeyed across the tarp, banging on the window behind them. It was toughened glass, but he had some sort of weapon or tool – doing damage. Hannah hummed louder, keeping Isaiah calm, but all the noise and movement was beginning to blur together. Then he was on the roof, working at the edge of the skylight. The speedometer was climbing but still he clung on somehow.

Rachel braked. Hard. The tyres screeched on the road, smoked. He flew off the roof of the cab and onto the road in front of them. She dropped the stick shift back into first, pushed the accelerator flat to the floor. He rolled out of the way, just in time. Then he was up and after them again, but limping now, and they were away. Speeding down the highway. *Flying*. There was just the engine, and their breathing, slowing now. The black and white of the road, guideposts ticking past.

Hannah touched Rachel's arm. 'You did good, Ray.'

'I really didn't see that coming.'

'There's a prison near here. Maybe they escaped.'

'So many?'

'I'm starting to wonder about the sort of people who've survived this,' Hannah said.

'Like us?'

'*Not* like us. Junkies, prisoners, looters. People who aren't scared of *them* – aren't scared of anything.'

When Rachel had just been trying to survive, get away, with adrenaline in her system, she hadn't been afraid, either. 'What about Mon?'

'Maybe because she's a doctor, used to controlling her emotions or something.'

'A prison would have a hospital, right?'

'You're thinking of the drugs?'

'There was only one box of oxytocin left at the hospital.'

'But how would they find out about that?'

'I don't know.'

Rachel gripped the wheel, scanning the road. From now on they needed to take more notice of what they were travelling past. The human landmarks on the map, not just the terrain, the distances between towns. If they were to survive, they would have to adapt more quickly.

thirty-nine

They had shifted into farming land, speeding through a once-fertile valley. The Murrumbidgee River curved close to the road, strong and broad, then swept away. Rachel couldn't stop herself checking the rear-vision mirror, still seeing those people running in rags. As if they would always be there, chasing them. Like the people on the river, the bodies beneath the liquidambar.

Isaiah had started coughing again. And blinking his eyes, as if they hurt. Hannah closed off the air vents and rubbed his chest. 'So much smoke.'

'Fires somewhere.' There would be no one to stop them this time.

Hannah was expressing milk, the sucking sound of the pump a little unnerving in the car. 'Tell me something about Berlin.'

'Did you see *Wings of Desire*?'

'Is that the one in black and white?'

'Partly. That's how the angels see our world,' Rachel said. 'When I needed some peace and quiet, I'd hang out in the library in that film – where the angels used to go, listening in on people's thoughts.' It had been the architecture that had taken her there. Spiral staircases, floors of books, rows of futuristic lights, all angles and shadows.

'I remember those scenes. They'd pass each other on the stairs, and no one spoke, but they were thinking all these terrible thoughts. So lonely.'

'I guess they were worried that anything they said or did would end up in a Stasi file. Reported by their neighbour or uncle or whatever,' Rachel said. 'But the angels would put a hand on someone's shoulder when they were suffering. They never knew, but they'd feel lighter.'

'Didn't one of them choose to become human?'

'For love,' Rachel said. 'Anyway, you remember the giant golden angel that they sit on? That's real. It's called the Victory Column, in the middle of Tiergarten, near the zoo: miles and miles of trees that turn all colours in autumn. You can climb up inside her and look down on the city. I'd been working in the library for weeks before I noticed that you could see the angel from most of the desks. When the sun shines on her . . . it's like magic beams. Then, when I walked up the stairs, inside the angel, they sparkled with gold. As if I'd been shown a secret. Let into the city.'

'Maybe you were.'

That same day, in the timber-lined library cafe with its port-hole window, a man had walked in barefoot and sat opposite a woman crying, without saying a word, almost like a scene from the film. And on Rachel's way out, a stranger had given her a ticket to a concert at the Berlin Philharmonic, over the road.

The library and concert hall were twin buildings, dressed in the same yellow scales, speaking to each other across Potsdamer Strasse. When she went – dressed in a men's dinner jacket from the Flohmarkt – she found the same staircases, the same Sputnik lights hanging from high ceilings. The orchestra's golden harp had glowed, like the angel, and within the storm of Sibelius's Seventh Symphony.

'Did you do any actual work?'

It had all come in a rush at the end. 'A series of decanters and beakers. Aqua glass – like Roman glass – but with bubbles and specks of gold.'

'Like your glasses at Monique's?'

'Yeah.'

'We saw that film at uni. But it never occurred to me that it was a real library or that I could go there,' Hannah said.

'Did you always want to be a librarian?'

Hannah shook her head. 'I wanted to study art history, but I let my mother talk me into taking a safe option.'

Isaiah's coughing was getting worse again. Rachel closed off the air vents.

'Hopefully it's just the smoke,' Hannah said. 'You know, in that film there was all this secrecy, government control. Fast forward fifty years, and we're sharing all our information with the whole world. But we're even more lonely.'

'And it's big companies keeping the files. Using information to identify our vulnerabilities.'

Hannah turned. 'That reminds me of *them*. It's as if they know everything I'm afraid of, everything bad that's happened to me.'

'It's like that for me, too. All the things you'd never talk about.'

'Maybe we should,' Hannah said. 'Maybe it would help.'

forty

The next village was nestled where the highway crossed the river, a ribbon of green. A truck had stopped in front of the service station, cars jammed up around it, drivers' doors open, bodies in and out of cars.

Rachel reversed and turned off, taking the street running parallel to the main road. People had gathered in a dusty park, as if warned of an emergency, and died together there, cross-legged, in a half-circle, holding hands, like some sort of offering.

They worked together, watching for threats, aiming to keep moving, keep their distance from any concentration of bodies. There was nothing they could do for the dead. If the drive had taught them anything, it was that it was as urgent to avoid the living.

She turned back onto the highway at the edge of town. The old inn, dating back to Cobb and Co. stagecoach days, was dark, its big open fires out, cars still parked at a neat angle on the street front, a line of motorbikes. It was better not to imagine the scenes inside, people stopped mid-beer, halfway to the bar.

The shadows moving near the railway line thinned and dispersed as soon as she tried to focus on them. But her body was telling her *they* were all around. The noise in her head, the difficulty keeping a clear mind.

The road out of town was blocked by an ambulance and two silver sedans. There was something about the emergency vehicle that had her hoping for help, a friendly survivor. She took her foot from the accelerator. But there was no driver, and the passenger's dead white face was pushed up against the window in awful, bloated detail. It was hard to imagine ever being able to forget the eyes of the dead – fear reduced humans to the animals they were.

One of the silver sedans was an early model Prius with Cooma hospital decals. Rachel slowed, her stomach pitching. But it was a young man driving, not Monique. His door was open, as if he had tried to get out, in a hurry, but his seatbelt was still on over his dark suit, shirt and tie. Dressed for work, on duty, until the very end. Just like her sister.

'Ray.'

'Sorry.' *They* were trying to pull her in again.

She drove up onto the footpath to avoid the tangle. The collision made no sense, the way the vehicles were arranged. She couldn't tell which way they had been going or who had been in the wrong. Like the larger disaster, she wasn't able to quite get her head around the puzzle, as if there were pieces missing.

To squeeze between a street sign and the veranda post of the pub, she had to drive over a dead dog. Hannah winced at the resistance under the tyres, something giving way.

Rachel had to hope that Monique was ahead of them. Hannah

cleared her throat. Rachel could smell and taste the smoke, raising a primal alarm in her body, taking her back to the fires. Isaiah's coughing was more and more frequent, deeper in his little lungs, so new and tender. As they had found out after the fires, those particles could kill.

It was frightening, being responsible for such a tiny being, who could not tell them what was wrong but relied on them to make good decisions, act in his best interests.

'When you see somewhere to pull over, I need to change him,' Hannah said.

Rachel parked in the rest stop. There were no other vehicles. Just a closed-up coffee van, its roof busy with solar panels, aerials and a mini satellite dish. It was almost too quiet, no vehicles passing, no one pulling in. There was clean tank water and a composting toilet, which Rachel used while Hannah was changing Isaiah. An old Telstra exchange sat silent, camouflaged by fading graffiti.

The smoke was sharper outside the car, hurting Rachel's lungs. She washed her hands and set out their lunch: green apples, cheese, lettuce and chutney sandwiches. *Monique's chutney.* But she wasn't hungry. It was hot. Much hotter than it should be, the air so dry it was electric. And the wind was picking up.

With the smoke, fire nearby, it wasn't good. Rachel went back to the ute for the face masks. There was a minibus she hadn't seen on the way in, in the culvert, overturned. The windows were so dirty she couldn't see in. Hopefully it had happened *before*.

Rachel sat the masks on the table.

'I think I've stopped here,' Hannah said. 'When I was a kid.'

'With your mum?'

'Dad. Some road trip. He'd taken us to the snow for the day. When he lived in Canberra.'

'What did he do?'

'Drove trucks for a while. Had a mowing business on the side.'

'Practical.'

Hannah pulled a face. 'In some ways. But you should have seen him ski.' She swished her hand back and forwards in an elegant line. 'I thought he was Superman when I was little,' she said. 'My brother was never fooled – saw right through him.' Hannah sighed. 'Could you hold Isaiah while I wash my hands?'

'Sure,' Rachel said.

Isaiah wriggled and grabbed at her ponytail. She flicked it out of the way and tickled his hands to distract him, running her forefinger around his palm. He giggled then coughed, his face crumpling into a frown. It was just how she felt when she was sick.

Hannah cleaned up, packed his things away and took Isaiah from her.

Rachel reached over to hold his socked foot, so small. 'He's a little fighter, isn't he?'

'Takes after Daddy, not me.'

'What does Kyle do for Defence?'

'He's in IT.'

'How long has he been doing that?'

'Since he graduated, really. He used to work for them full time.'

'And now it's just contracts?'

'He was at Jervis Bay after Canberra. That wasn't too bad, the commuting, but then his position was made redundant. And he took a package.' Jervis Bay was on the coast but notionally part of the Australian Capital Territory – a kind of outpost.

'That's why he took the job?'

'The twelve months was up. That you can't work for government again. We'd renovated the house and put some money away. He was doing some freelancing. But then we found out Isaiah was coming. He thought we'd need more. That it would be better for him to get back in the system. With paid leave, healthcare and all that.'

'And where's all that money now?'

'Exactly. It means nothing.'

Rachel spread the map over the table, searching for potential pitfalls between them and the city. But the map wasn't particularly recent, and buildings, shopping centres and prisons weren't marked.

'Can you think of anything we need to worry about on the way?'

'The roads into the city are going to be bad.' Hannah chewed her thumbnail. 'And there's that new detention centre at the airport.'

They could avoid the airport, for now. 'What's he like? Your Kyle.'

'He makes me laugh. And he questions things, doesn't just accept what you see on the news or whatever. He's really smart. He loves his mountain bike. Triathlons, all that. Typical fitness junkie. Adrenaline junkie, too. He used to fly planes, ultralights. But I put a stop to that.'

'Why?'

'Once I knew about Isaiah. I thought it was only a matter of time till something went wrong. I told him I didn't want to be a widow, a single mother.'

'Fair enough.'

'Bit dramatic. I wish I hadn't said anything. He loved it so much. And what does it matter now? I'm a single mother anyway.'

'We don't know yet.'

Rachel set up the coffee press but the coffee wasn't in her pack or the ute. 'I was sure I put it in,' she said.

'I don't mind,' Hannah said.

'I'll need something to stay awake,' Rachel said. She jogged around the back of the coffee van.

'Ray.'

'There might be something,' she said.

The door of the van was unlocked. Rachel could almost smell freshly ground coffee. But when she opened the door, it was the stench of dead bodies that poured out. And *them*, rushing from inside that small space, in a black *whoosh* over her head, nearly knocking her down.

A trap.

She was alone. Black trunks, white earth, grey sky, no horizon. The hard truths of the world she had been left. Dehydrated, depleted, without hope, *they* had her surrounded. It was *them* – not real – but she couldn't swallow, take a breath. Even when she visualised the river, *her river*, home, it took all her strength to open her mouth, to move her lips and tongue. 'Run!'

Rachel grabbed their things from the table and sprinted for

the Beast. She opened the door and flung herself in, turned the key. The Beast rumbled to life, cutting out *their* noise. She took off while Hannah was still closing the door, clinging to Isaiah.

'Ray!'

There were more and more of *them*, pouring out of the minivan. They moved as one, joining with the others. *Like a swarm*. Rachel fishtailed out of the car park and onto the highway.

Hannah turned to look through the back window. 'I can see them – sort of. They're coming after us.'

Seeing wasn't quite the right word, it was as much their other senses. In her side mirror, all Rachel could be sure of was that they were darker than the smoke.

'They can fly.' There were tears in Hannah's voice. Fear.

'Hum that song?' Rachel said. 'And tell me when you can't see them anymore.'

forty-one

They were struggling to breathe, the smoke thick even inside the car, their face masks damp from their breath. Hannah had Isaiah tucked up under her chin, holding a mask over his face. They were descending, coming down from the escarpment. The dense trees and undergrowth, after the bare slopes of the Monaro, was uncanny. The edge of Namadgi National Park rose sharply on one side, circling Canberra to the south. Out of Rachel's window the sheer rock faces of the Great Dividing Range – the country they had worked so hard to climb and cross – reared above the treeline. The pass between was narrow, walling them in, funnelling the smoke.

When the road swung around, the verge dropping away beneath them, Hannah gasped. Rachel pulled up in the middle of the road.

Namadgi was on fire. Thick smoke plumed behind an advancing storm of flame, angry red at its front. Another mushroom-bomb of pink cloud rose from behind the range. There were two fires ahead of them. The sun, in comparison, was a weak red disc.

'Shit.'

'We've got to turn around,' Hannah said.

It was a natural instinct to turn and run. To get as far away as possible. But *they* were behind them – in greater force than they had seen so far. Rachel gauged the wind, the sky, the temperature, the lack of moisture in the air, the inversion effect locking the smoke in the valley. There were no turnoffs on the road behind. A car wasn't a good place to be in a fire.

'We can't go back. *They*'ll be waiting. And then we'd have to outrun it,' Rachel said. 'Those fires are going to join together.' Once they did that, it wasn't a force they could stop or escape.

They had already come this far. And it hadn't been easy. There were no choices left, only forwards or back on the highway.

Then the sky split open, galahs, parrots, black cockatoos wheeling ahead of the smoke, screaming warning. Kangaroos, hundreds of them, bounding through the valley, fleeing the fire.

Not again. Whatever they were going to do, they needed to do it now. Rachel opened her door, ran to the back of the ute. She pulled out the blankets, a towel, extra facecloths, a water container. Her fingers fumbled the fastenings, trying to tie down the tarp again. The wind was strengthening, starting to gust. She took a moment to assess the distances: between them and the first fire, between the two fires, and the likely point at which they would join. She threw the blankets on the seat, handed the water to Hannah, jumped in and slammed the door.

Hannah had taken the keys from the ignition.

Rachel put out her hand. 'Hannah! We need to go *now*.'

'It's suicide. We have an infant in the car!'

'The fire's not as close to the road as it looks. We can get to

215

the other side. Into the city. But it's going to take these ranges.' She gestured around them. 'And we can't go back. *They*'re too strong.'

Hannah closed her eyes, held out the keys.

Rachel started the ute and drove on, down the centre of the road, accelerating steadily. Hannah blew on Isaiah's head to soothe him, as if to give him her own air, keep the smoke from his lungs.

'You could wet the facecloths. Stuff them in the vents, to keep the smoke out.' Just the smoke, the heat, could kill. 'Then, when we get close, put a blanket over you. Just in case.' She said it as calmly as she could manage, without looking away from the road. Without looking at Isaiah.

Day had turned to night. The sky shifting from orange to red, deeper than the richest sunset. It would be beautiful – if it wasn't so horrific. Thick smoke filled the valley. Rachel could only see a few hundred metres ahead. Then a hundred metres, eighty, fifty. Kangaroos and wallabies were still bounding out of the smoke, veering in front of the car at all angles. Other animals, too, creatures with no choice but to run. She was forced to slow. If they hit a big kangaroo it would smash in the bonnet, stop the ute, leave them stranded in front of the oncoming fire.

The smoke was sharp with burning eucalyptus oil. Blackened, blistered leaves rained down over the ute, thwacking into the windscreen, over the road, the dry grass all around them. Some were still alight.

Then the burning eyes, like the spirits of fire itself, live embers landing on the bonnet, in the dry grass, sparking spot fires all around them, melting into the rubber around the windscreen, rolling along the road towards them, under the car, splaying out behind them. It was why it was called an ember attack – the strike force flying ahead of the front, wanting to spread the fire.

The only turnoff was coming up, one of the entrances to the national park. But it was already burning. Heading down a narrower road, surrounded by dry forest, was more risky. They had no choice but to stick to the highway. It was too late to turn around, go back.

Hannah was crying, Isaiah was coughing, they were struggling to breathe. Rachel could no longer hear her sister's voice, or fill her lungs. She had done it before, faced worse. But that was the problem; part of her mind was back there, her body remembering, shutting down.

Ahead, the mountains pushed towards the road again, forming a tunnel into the valley that held the capital. It wasn't far to where they were going. Rachel had read it on the map, driven it years ago, could visualise it still. But the smoke was so thick, she couldn't see the way forward. It cleared only long enough to see the flames, a wide wall of fire, moving fast downhill, towards the road, towards them, too hot to even look at, hotter than the sun.

It was gusting and swirling, driving forwards, gathering force as it went. The fire was generating its own wind, its own weather. She knew how it would appear on the radar, as if there was a tropical low over the mountains. But it was fire. The only precipitation was burning leaves and embers.

The other fire was already over the ridge, tearing downhill. It was almost more than her senses could take in.

Mistake.

'Ray, this is scary.'

It had all changed so quickly. 'I know. Hang on.'

Isaiah started crying. Hannah was making animal sounds in her throat, her hands clenched. 'They're. Going. To. Burn. Us.'

Think. Breathe. But breathing was the hardest thing to do. And keeping *them* from her mind, images of being trapped inside the ute, inside the fire. She had one job: to keep these people alive.

The fronts were going to merge sooner than she thought. Even if the Beast did not stall, did not catch fire, even if she did not pass out, it was going to be a tight race. Then the smoke thinned. Rachel saw an opening between the fires, to the other side, past the mountains. But the window was small.

'I'm going for it,' Rachel said.

She put her foot to the floor, weaving around stationary cars, wallabies, dark against the flames, still bounding away. Black cockatoos and bats wheeled in the same sky. Rachel's cheeks were hot, the car heating up.

'Hannah. Wet him down. Cover his face.'

Hannah fished around in the bag at her feet, pulled out another facecloth, a spare nappy. She poured water over Isaiah, wet her own top. She reached for Rachel's water bottle, offered it to her.

Rachel shook her head, kept her eyes on the fire. 'Hang on.'

Hannah draped the wet nappy around Rachel's head and neck. The grass either side of them was in flames. Larger cinders rained down, bouncing over the road, burning into the grass, driven by the breath of the fire.

They sped down the middle of the road, towards the narrowest point. Rachel could no longer see ahead, only react to what was immediately in front of her. There were no sirens, no flashing lights, no roadblocks, no emergency ABC announcements to guide them, no helicopters whoofing overhead. No one was coming.

It was too hot for the blanket, but Hannah pulled it over them all the same. Rachel's face and hands were hot, the backs of her legs sweaty. Smoke crept in under the dash. She would have worried about the Beast if she wasn't so worried for their lives.

The sound she had thought was wind against the speeding car was the fire itself – roaring. Burning sticks and bits of timber flew through the air, meteors crashed onto the bonnet, the roof of the cabin. Trees were exploding. Fire was tearing the forest apart. Something landed on the tarp, they smelled burning rubber. But she could not stop.

The sky went black. Cars, animals, debris appeared out of the smoke. Rachel swerved, overcorrected, regained control.

The speedometer crept towards a hundred miles an hour. The engine was too hot. The warning gauge well past red. Still-burning cinders rained down all around them. Black and red was all she saw and thought. The road turned soft, melting, shifting beneath the wheels. The tyres had to melt, too, or blow. Her eyes were streaming, her mind shutting down. She pulled the wet cloth around her face, sucked a little liquid from it.

We're probably not going to make it.

Hannah put her hand on Rachel's leg, squeezed, and did not let go.

The steering wheel was hot beneath Rachel's hands. Smoke filled the cabin, sneaking in around old seals, edges, through flimsy cloths. They couldn't breathe or see. There was a moment of terrible silence.

Then the roar, louder than before, like something from the underworld, something they shouldn't ever hear. *Whoomph, whoomph, whoomph.* It was as if they were screaming but their mouths were closed. Fire was all around them, heat pressing against the car, against their fragile bodies. The side window cracked.

They were inside the fire. They were fire, and the fire was them. They had survived the end of the world, only to burn alive in a car. A situation she had chosen to place them in. Rachel kept control only by remembering the studio, heating glass, where fire was her friend.

And then they were out.

Rachel caught glimpses of the white centreline, torched earth, blackened trunks, burning branches. She dodged fallen trees, flaming branches, sticks. She no longer cared about the car, what they hit. She was alive. Hannah's hand was still on her leg. She could hear Isaiah coughing. If the tyres held, they might make it. They might make it after all.

Rachel kept both hands on the wheel, afraid to slow down, too afraid to look at Hannah and Isaiah.

the capital

forty-two

They were through the fire. At some point they had crossed the border, leaving New South Wales behind and entering the Australian Capital Territory. Isaiah was struggling to breathe in the smoke-filled cab. Rachel's eyes were stinging, her throat raw. The front of her head ached, a sharp line running up from her sinuses. They wound down the windows but the air outside wasn't any better. The tree trunks were burned black, the scorch line high up into the canopy. All the undergrowth had burned away, white ash covered blackened ground. Trees, logs, stumps smouldered, here and there bursting into orange flame, running along the ground, searching for more. A branch crashed down. Everything radiated heat. Rachel's cheeks were tight, as if she had been working in front of the furnace all day.

The road was a mess of charred animals, cars, bodies, sticks and limbs. Thick smoke shrouded the valley, spot fires spread into the surrounding mountains. The sun was pale, as if robbed of its strength.

Hannah handed Rachel her water, their fingers touching for a moment. At last she drank, emptying the flask.

'I thought we were going to die.' Hannah coughed again, trying to clear her throat.

'Me too,' Rachel said.

Isaiah's eyes were closed, coughs wracking his little body. Hannah wet him down, blew on his skin. What would he remember of what they had passed through, what they had to pass through yet? It was not a world to bring a child into.

For now, they were beyond the reach of the fire. The paddocks, though flat, brown and dry, were unburned. It was still the 'country capital', built on sheep grazing land along the Molonglo River. Rachel's eyes seized on anything green: pines, wattles, casuarinas, clumps of native grasses.

They passed row after row of gleaming black angled panels – the solar farms now powering the outer southern suburbs. Rubbish fluttered over the broad hill ahead, the landfill station left untended. It wasn't the most auspicious entry to the nation's capital.

Traffic on the road was building, like the clogged arteries of peak hour, only it wasn't moving. It probably wasn't ever going to move. In larger numbers, the uniformity of models, makes and colours was more obvious: white, grey, silver.

While inside the fire, she had forgotten the world outside, all that had happened. Everything had been pared back to survival. And surviving seemed a miracle, something to be thankful for. Some part of her had hoped that passing through the fire and out the other side would erase what had happened, kill *them* somehow, cauterise the infection. Or take them backwards through time.

But it wasn't over. The towns had been bad, but Canberra was so much worse. The scale of it threatened to overwhelm her. *They* were everywhere, somehow, through the roads, streets and centres, part of the city.

'We survived that fire. We can survive anything,' Hannah said.

Rachel nodded. She had only to drive, to steer them through it. They numbed themselves to what was inside each car, the smell, the misshapen horrors. To their own feelings, to any desire to break down. They had to. The Beast's tray cover was shredded, flapping behind them.

When they finally reached the first two-lane roundabout, it was solid with car bodies in all directions. Trucks and four-wheel drives had tried to ram their way through, pushing cars up the embankments, into culverts. There was no way forward.

Rachel pulled up. Two boys, twins, stared out of the back of the station wagon in front them, hands against the glass, their identical screams swollen and sliding. The stench was over-whelming. Crows lined the road, feral dogs didn't flinch at the sound of the car. The flies were thick.

Something else moved. Shadows, sweeping low through the cars. More solid than before, more real, moving as one. *Looking for survivors?* Rachel rubbed her stinging eyes, unsure if she could trust them. There were so many, even more than at the road stop. But they seemed intent on their task, whatever it was.

'I see them, too,' Hannah said. 'What sort of animals are they?'

'Animals?'

'What do you see?'

'Shadows, like ghosts of people, but they move differently.'

Hannah let out all her breath, and sucked in another. 'Let's take this turnoff. There's a back way. You come out on Long Gully Road. Maybe that will be . . . easier.'

They edged around a silver people mover slewed over the exit, each seat now occupied by a gruesome face of death. The driver was wedged halfway out of the window, trying to flee what was inside.

'Turn right here,' Hannah said.

'Are you sure?' The hills ahead were still smouldering. They had entered an area of the city Rachel had never been in. The sort of ordinary suburb that had always made her claustrophobic. Where normal families lived normal lives, went to and fro from ordinary jobs and mowed the lawn on weekends. The houses were all dark 1970s brick, too close together. Their neat little gardens, car ports and driveways so planned, like a government architect's model.

'I had a boyfriend who lived out here,' Hannah said. 'When I was at uni. Before Kyle. I used to take this way home on Sunday afternoons to avoid the traffic coming back from the coast. Or the snow, in winter.'

Rachel nodded, eyes flicking from one side of the road to the other.

'He was a drummer in a rock band I saw play on campus. How clichéd is that?'

Rachel glanced across, to judge whether she was teasing. She couldn't imagine Hannah wasting her time on anyone flaky. Or a drummer living out in the burbs in some brick and tile.

'Was that fun?'

'He was fun,' Hannah said. 'And I loved going to gigs. Free drinks and all that. A lot of wild nights.'

They passed empty houses, garage doors, front doors, car doors all wide open. A policewoman lay trapped beneath her motorbike, phone in one hand, the other on her pistol holster. Her face was beginning to leak from her helmet.

Worst was the school yard, its uniformed children huddled in groups, as if playing statues. Except for one boy sitting out on his own, excluded to the end. Hannah placed her hand on the back of Isaiah's head. She had her own way of breathing, trying to calm herself and him.

The road rose, passing through a steep nature reserve, away from the houses, bodies – but back into the fire zone. Fallen trunks and branches still smouldered, orange flames licking to life, taking any remaining grass. Rachel slowed to veer around a tradesman's utility, gutted by fire, blackened bodies inside. The fire front still raged in the mountains, balls of flame exploding from the ridgeline, smoke pluming upwards, joining the black cloud shrouding the sky.

'And right here,' Hannah said. 'This joins up with Mugga Lane.'

It was the road passing the waste-processing centre and industrial area, connecting two arterials in and out of the city. The pine plantation either side of the road was razed, a black Marsscape. Where the fire started, perhaps. All that oil, those close-planted resinous trunks, would have gone up like a box of oversized matches.

There were fewer cars, more trucks and vans, people with business on the road. But somehow two SUVs had skidded and swerved across the road, forming a blockade. One was packed with people and belongings. The other was empty, without a driver.

Rachel pulled over. There wasn't room on the steep verge to drive around them. Her hands were sweaty on the wheel. When she closed her eyes, the road was still moving, the white centre-line flashing by, flames at the edges of her vision.

She reached for her drops, emptied the last of the bottle beneath her tongue. There were dints in the bonnet, the Beast's duco blistered. When she got out, her legs unsteady on the unmoving ground, she saw the melted radiator grille, the paint stripped from the number plate, its letters and numbers unreadable. But the steel wheels and heavy-duty tyres had held. The Beast had got them through what a new car never would have.

'I'll try to push it off the road,' Rachel said. 'Like before.'

Hannah stood behind her open door. 'I'll be right here.'

Six steps to the first vehicle. Left hand on the door handle, lift. Locked. As if they had thought they could keep the threat out, when it was inside their own heads the whole time. The other SUV was also locked. Its floor and seats were covered with shopping bags. Rachel searched the ground for a stone, something to break a window with. There was a red house brick in the dry grass, fallen from the back of a truck on its way to or from the recycling centre.

Four steps to the brick. When she bent to pick it up, the pressure in her sinuses made her unsteady on her feet. She was still thirsty. Navigating this new world, keeping control of her thoughts, was so very draining. Much more draining than before.

'Ray.'

Rachel spun around, gripping the brick. There was a woman standing beside the empty SUV. *Where did she come from?*

'This is a toll point,' the woman said. 'If you want to pass, you have to pay.' Her voice was singsong, her facial expressions and body language loose.

Rachel searched the long grass for a sign of someone else. A rusty shipping container the other side of the culvert, door open, could contain anyone, anything.

One moment of weakness and she would bring *them*, in a great wave. They were pressing, waiting for her to fail, to find her breaking point, for Hannah and Isaiah to be left alone. But Rachel was too tired, too numb. Let them come. She had been through fire.

'Lady, we don't have *anything*,' Hannah was saying. 'We've walked halfway across the country. What good is —'

Rachel held up her hand. 'I have money.' She unbuttoned her pocket and removed the wad of notes. 'Move the car.'

'Money first,' the woman said. Her hair was matted and dirty, her head constantly moving, eyes never quite settling on Rachel.

She split off half the cash and threw it at the woman. 'The rest when we're through.'

The woman squatted to pick up the notes, counted them, and slipped them inside her bra. She unlocked the empty SUV and climbed in. The vehicle swerved backwards, towards the culvert. The woman braked hard, sending up a cloud of dust.

Rachel dropped the brick and ran to the Beast. Hannah was already back in the passenger seat, Isaiah held tight to her chest.

'Is she nuts?'

'I think so. Don't engage.'

Rachel drove through, scanning in all directions, the mirrors, for an accomplice, *them*.

The woman was out of the vehicle and running towards them.

Rachel wound down the window a few inches, threw out the rest of the cash, and pushed the accelerator to the floor.

'Where did you even get that money?'

'Mon left it,' Rachel said. 'You okay?'

Hannah nodded. 'You did good, Ray.'

'There might be more people,' Rachel said. 'Like her.'

forty-three

They re-entered the arterial road in the city's inner south. Rachel worked around a snarl of vehicles at the intersection. Chaos within the chaos. The road's wide shoulders were clear; as if drivers had been trying to stick to the road rules, to normality, right up until the very end.

Canberra drivers had always been a particular breed, driving 20 kilometres above the speed limit on city roads. Until it rained, when they dropped back to 20 kilometres below the limit, as if they had never seen rain before. Some of the younger drivers probably hadn't. Rachel used the open space to roar past the cars, pile-ups, bodies, all the way to the next round-about.

Parliament House rose, tomb-like, out of the smoke haze, part of the hill itself. Rachel drove around the roundabout counter-clockwise, weaving through the spilt cargo of a delivery van. Washing machines or dishwashers, judging by the size of the square cardboard boxes, the brand printed on the side. They were as much use now as all the other human aspirations: wealth, status, beauty. Now there were only those who had survived and those who had not.

She cut between the two upmarket shopping centres, passing the European cafe where, for a time, she had made a habit of stopping for a croissant and flat white on her way to the Glassworks, sitting at the window bench, watching people go by – a habit that seemed so indulgent now. She drove down the street planted with redwoods, where she had always parked, so as to touch their furrowed trunks and stare up at their spoked crowns.

'You're a Southsider?' Hannah asked.

'Not really. I worked over here for a while.'

She took the curving road past Manuka Oval, its great lights staring down over an empty field. People packing into grounds, paying to see live sporting contests, seemed a practice of the past, like walking through the Colosseum, the empty amphitheatres of Europe.

'You know how to get to Ainslie, right?' Hannah sat up higher in the seat, scanning the streets. 'I was thinking we should go there first.'

Rachel kept her eyes on the road. Finding Isaiah's father, Hannah's husband, probably did trump finding Rachel's sister. But she had assumed they'd look for Monique and Bill first.

The parliamentary precinct was strangely vacant. No bodies, fewer cars. It always had been a world of its own. Canberra Avenue was almost empty, as if the traffic had been cut off before the crisis hit. For a moment the old stone Presbyterian church was juxtaposed against the giant silver masthead squatting atop Parliament House. The flag, at half-mast, fluttered in the breeze.

The normally immaculate green lawns running up and over the hill, between the two sides of the house, were shaggy and brown.

Rachel hesitated at the intersection, where the three-laned avenue crossed the ring roads circling the House. There was power. The traffic lights were flashing red and orange.

'What is it?' Hannah asked.

How to explain the colours she was seeing, moving through her, images and sensations from the past. *Breathe, Ray.* Her sister's voice. Closer now. Monique was alive, and in the city.

Rachel leaned her head out of the window, but the smells only added to the overwhelm: the sharpness of imported pines, burned eucalyptus leaves, smoke. And underneath, the pervading sweetness of death.

'I need to make a quick stop,' Rachel said.

Hannah frowned. '*Now?* We're almost there.'

Rachel turned at the sharpness in Hannah's voice. Her hands were clenched, knuckles white, preparing herself for the worst, daring to hope, as they worked closer to Kyle.

'It won't take long,' she said. 'And I'll have a view over the city from up there. Before we try crossing the lake.'

Hannah opened her mouth to speak but closed it again, turning to stare out the window.

Rachel crossed State Circle the wrong way, mounting the kerb to avoid another empty orange Action bus. It gave her a perverse sense of pleasure, going against the flow, rejecting the imposed order of the city.

From the ground, they could no longer see the House. The ironbarks, box and wattles planted around its base had grown into a significant woodland. Rachel turned off, heading for the shaded open car park but found it blocked by heavy white boom gates.

She parked in the shade of a gnarled yellow box.

'Where are we?' Hannah said.

'Just below the staff entrance,' Rachel said. 'I can walk up from here.'

forty-four

Rachel leaned over Hannah's legs to open the glove box, her arm touching Isaiah's warm back. She shuffled through the pile of old membership cards and passes until she found the blank cream rectangle she had never got around to returning. It was a long shot. But, as Hans always said, 'You'll never know if you never try.' He meant with the glass, but it was as true for life. He had toughened them, until they were brave in the hot shop, risking everything for the chance to create something special.

She opened her door and swung herself out. 'I won't be long,' she said.

'We're coming,' Hannah said, releasing her seatbelt.

'Look, I probably won't even be able to get in. I'll get the lie of the land and come back.'

'I'm sorry for snapping,' Hannah said. 'I just need to know, you know? I'm scared.'

Rachel nodded.

'Anyway, I'm not staying down here. It's creepy.'

It *was* creepy. Too quiet, too empty. *Who'd emptied it?* Rachel touched Isaiah's cheek. 'How is he?'

'Tired,' Hannah said. 'I need to give him more antibiotics. But he doesn't like the cold milk much.'

'Bring it with you. If we can get in, we might be able to heat it.'

When Rachel slammed her door, the side mirror swung loose and fell onto the ground. There would be no repairing the Beast now, no greasy panel-beating shop, detailing or courtesy car. No old-timers exclaiming about the excellent nick the vehicle was in. None of that mattered anymore. Only finding Kyle, Mon, and then home.

They made their way up the hill, dry leaves crunching beneath their feet. The trees' sparse crowns cast no shade in the haze. The smoke caught in Rachel's throat. Her nasal passages, whole respiratory system, was raw and sore. Their clothes reeked of smoke. Everything did.

Whether it was breathing through the smoke or what they had been through, walking was more taxing than it should have been. They trudged across Parliament Drive and climbed the cement steps up to the entrance, where white Commonwealth cars had once queued when Parliament was sitting.

There were no cars, no bodies on the road or the approaches, as if there had been some sort of clean-up. It would have taken a team of people and vehicles – but where were they now? The great doors of bronze and glass were intact. Parliament House had its own solar power grid, a backup generator, and probably a backup for the backup. There was, it had always been whispered, a self-contained bunker-city underneath, with tunnels linking up to Defence and Intelligence buildings. For emergencies only imagined until now.

The bullet-proof glass guard booth was unmanned. Rachel swiped the pass against the old reader. Nothing happened. But then the locks released with a heavy click.

She gripped the cool brass handle and held open the door.

Hannah lifted her face to the ceiling. Even now, it was hard not to be moved by the space, so much timber, glass and light. The way the building brought the landscape in.

'First time?'

Hannah nodded. 'Why do you have a pass to Parliament House?'

'Long story,' Rachel said. She took a moment to get her bearings. 'This way.'

It was cool inside. She could no longer smell smoke. She could breathe. The fires, and even *them*, seemed far away. Her shoulders relaxed. Rachel was filled with a sudden energy, breaking into a jog. Hannah followed, holding Isaiah against the bumping of her body. It was so absurd, running through the empty corridors of power, over the polished timber floorboards, when the world outside was broken and burning, that they erupted into laughter.

Rachel skidded to a stop outside the side entrance to the Great Hall. She took a deep breath and opened the tall timber door just a crack. It was still there; another miracle. *Thank you.* She pulled the door fully open and stood aside, so as to watch Hannah. To see that magic moment when her face changed. Despite the smoke, enough sun streamed into the linked hearts of claret glass, their chambers carrying light instead of blood. Together, they formed a larger heart, hanging from the ceiling, which seemed for a moment to shift and swell, as if beating.

Hannah read the brass plate on the wall. 'You did this?'

'With a couple of helpers.' Tom – on one of the rare occasions he had been a part of one of her projects – and an honours graduate had worked with her for a fortnight straight in the Glassworks hot shop at the height of summer. They all shed a couple of kilos in the process. The graduate – Nora or Nina, her name had been, far too sweet to be a glass maker – had carried each finished heart reverently to the annealer.

'They're anatomically correct.' Rachel had had to visit a university lab, to dissect the human heart, study it in pieces. Like Parliament, it had its chambers, each reliant on the others. 'There was one for every person in detention.' Numbers had only gone up after that. Where all those displaced people should live, and who was responsible for them, no longer mattered.

'It's beautiful.'

They were standing side by side, shoulders touching. Isaiah twisted around, as if trying to see where the light and colour was coming from. Without having to struggle for breath, he was already brighter, giggling and grabbing at the red beams. He turned to look at Rachel, as if knowing she was responsible for the show. For the first time, she felt that he saw her, as a being, that they were making eye contact. He grinned, all gums. And, for a moment, her heart – the fleshy still-beating one inside her – went out to him.

'Did it help?' Hannah said.

Rachel shrugged. 'It was more political than they wanted.' She rubbed at her face, her hands still coming away smeared with black. 'You can imagine the dinners and fancy international events they had in here. The media drummed up a lot of vitriol. I didn't get another big commission after that.'

She had gone into hiding, to be fair. Gone off social media, and then offline altogether.

'What about your peers?'

'The men were hyper-critical, but I'd expected that,' she said. The harshest insult had been that the piece was too obvious. And that had come from Tom. 'Women glass makers were the worst. One of them actually said that I blow glass like a man. Social media trolls had a field day.'

'What does that even mean?' Hannah said.

'I know.'

'We should go,' Hannah said.

Rachel glanced back, before closing the door. That had been her once. She had made big things, taken risks, been someone.

Emptied of people, of purpose, the corridors were out of scale. Even when she and Tom had finished the installation, at four in the morning, the House had not been so quiet. So quiet she could hear the subtle shift of the air-conditioning cycle. The building was still running on full power.

Isaiah had resumed a tired whimper, loud in that silence. Like their footsteps.

'The kitchen is through here,' Rachel said.

She led the way to the cafe, once the gossip and lobbying centre of the House, a meeting point for press, staffers and politicians. The doors were open, the lights on, but the tables and chairs vacant, the coffee machine silent. Neat piles of face masks and newspapers were stacked by the counter. Rachel scanned the headlines: it had started in the US, two days before Hannah had knocked on her door. In less than a week, the world had changed completely.

Rachel took three orange sports drinks from the still-bright fridge and drained one bottle on the spot. It didn't quite wash away the taste and smell of smoke. Her stomach growled. It was hours since they had left Nimmitabel, and their lunch had been left unfinished at the rest stop.

She sat the drinks on the stainless-steel counter and walked around the bench, into the kitchen. It was empty. There was no mess, no dishes in the sink.

Hannah unpacked her kit and the last of the milk she had expressed, rocking Isaiah as she opened the microwave.

'How is there power?'

'The House has its own isolated grid, supposedly threat-proof.'

Rachel slid open the cool-room door, still stocked full of cheeses, meats, eggs, milk, bread, great glass jars of sun-dried tomatoes, olives, artichokes and pickled aubergine. All the ingredients for a late breakfast or the toasted sandwiches that had kept her and Tom going through the installation.

'We should eat, too. While we can.'

She switched on the sandwich grill and ferried ingredients to the counter, making up two fat sandwiches, packed with cheese and vegetables. If the formal dining room was as fully stocked, they could live inside the House for months if they had to: use the gym, pool, spa, read books from the library, walk around the grand building like queens, and pretend nothing terrible had happened. Much like politicians had done for years.

When the cheese started to sizzle and ooze, she switched off the machine and lifted out the sandwiches. She cut them in half and placed them on takeaway plates. The smell was making her mouth water. Only then did she notice the one item out of place: a silver men's watch on the shelf above the sink.

She tucked the bottles under her arm and carried the plates to Hannah, already feeding Isaiah by the windows. Outside, white wire chairs gathered around empty timber tables in the courtyard garden. The plane trees, even the Budget Tree – an elegant Japanese maple – were taller than she remembered.

They wolfed down the hot food, thankful for power, melted cheese and a smoke-free, air-conditioned environment. Isaiah drank half-heartedly, taking a little milk, then stopping. Hannah didn't rush or push him, coaxing him to drink again from the bottle before switching to her breast.

'Why aren't there any bodies?' Hannah said.

'Maybe Parliament wasn't sitting when it happened?'

'But what about the staff, media?'

'Evacuated, maybe. There's some sort of bunker space underground.'

'For how many people?'

'Parliamentarians, plus essential staff, I guess.'

'People can't live underground for ever.'

'True.'

Too late, Rachel registered the tiny buzz, the movement. The camera above them was still working inside its black glass dome.

Hannah turned, following Rachel's gaze. 'Someone's watching us?'

'Maybe.'

241

'It's all too weird. Let's go.'

Rachel stuffed the last of her sandwich in her mouth and wiped her hands on the napkin. She dumped their rubbish in the bin by the counter, stuffed her pockets full of chocolate bars and cough lozenges, and grabbed a handful of fresh face masks. A picture on the front page of the *Canberra Times* caught her attention: a mother and baby, mountains on fire behind them. The by-line suggested that the 'love hormone' offered hope for humanity. Rachel skimmed the text: there were reports of new mothers surviving, a scientist suggesting that oxytocin was the answer.

'Ray!'

'Coming.' She tucked the paper under her arm and ran to catch up with Hannah.

They took the same sweeping corridor back to the entrance, past the library, all the serious portraits of once-important men and women staring out from the walls. The shaded courtyard gardens where so many interviews had been conducted, cigarettes smoked, secrets shared, betrayals planned.

They passed three more security cameras, each emitting a little whirr, as if awakened by the movement and following their progress. They walked more quickly but resisted the urge to run.

When Rachel stopped to release the doors, she thought for a moment she heard footsteps echoing over the polished floor-boards. But when she turned, there was no one. She followed Hannah and Isaiah outside.

After the air conditioning, the thick smoke was a shock, sharp in their throats, stinging their eyes. Hannah and Isaiah coughed in unison. Rachel unwrapped a lozenge and offered the packet to Hannah. There were cameras outside, too, peering down from silver poles. Rachel's senses were on high alert, waiting for a shout, an approaching car, someone to appear.

They hurried along the footpath, around to the gravelled forecourt, the columned main entrance of the building. The water feature was still, the detail of the grand mosaic no longer obscured by tourists. They turned their backs on the building and crossed the road.

The city was laid out beneath them. Straight wide roads intersected arcs and roundabouts, the spaces filled with European trees in fading blossom. Old Parliament House was directly below, aligned with the grand avenue leading up to the War Memorial across the lake. The instruments of governance, law and order all still in place. But the grim haze and muted red sun heralded a new era, a changed world. The chances of finding Kyle alive were slim. Hannah's brother, *Monique*.

Rachel put her hand on Hannah's shoulder. 'Hannah, have you considered —'

'Is that a car moving down there?'

'Where?'

Hannah pointed. 'At the base of the mountain.'

Rachel lifted the binoculars. It was a white station wagon, pulling up behind one of the new Defence office buildings in the defence and intelligence precinct across the lake. Even with the smoke, it was all too easy to spot a moving vehicle from any high point. She scanned for people, bikes, other cars, but saw no one else.

'What are they doing?'

'I don't know. But we'd better leave the Beast, walk from here,' Rachel said. They would be just as obvious in a vehicle.

Hannah nodded. 'Look, the bridge is blocked anyway.'

Rachel shifted her focus. Both bridges and their sweeping approaches were solid with vehicles at all angles, spilled in a series of pile-ups – disorder unprecedented in the carefully designed capital. Black Mountain *was* black, its forests already burned, the old telecommunications tower on top was dark, the glass burned out, metal twisted. The fires in the surrounding mountains were spreading fast, the wind picking up. If the direction changed, it would threaten the city again.

'Describe where we need to go,' Rachel said.

'Past the car. Between the shops and Mount Ainslie.'

'Right.' Imagining moving through those streets, entering houses, passing bars and shops sparked a jumble of uncomfortable half-memories. Something moved on the mountain, shapes shifting across the ground – just kangaroos, probably. But the hair on Rachel's forearms stood up, her stomach lurched. They had been standing there too long.

Inside the House, she had lost focus. She pulled back, into herself, opening her awareness to the sky, the mountains, the trees, the birds calling. The landscape was bigger, so much more than the city, Parliament. And she was part of it, attuned to the breeze on her skin, smoke in her lungs, the fires building behind them. *Them*, too. A shadow gathering.

She felt a vibration beneath her feet, a humming. One of the car park doors opening.

'There's another vehicle coming,' Rachel said.

Hannah followed Rachel into the trees. They hurried downhill, their footsteps too loud on the dry leaves. When Rachel looked back, a black van with darkened windows crept along the road above. She ducked, slipped and dropped her drink bottle. When she leaned down to pick it up, she lost her footing completely, landing on her backside. The binoculars crashed on to her collar bone.

She thought she heard someone shout, 'Wait.' But the voice could have been inside her head.

Hannah stopped, shrugged Isaiah onto one shoulder to help Rachel up. 'Okay?'

Rachel nodded. But she could hear the vehicle, coming down the ramp behind them. *Who are they?* And she could feel *them*, moving through the city centre. Exactly where they were headed.

When they reached the car park, she had the key to the Beast out, ready, unlocking and opening the door all in one movement. The van would soon circle back. They only had a few minutes.

Rachel and Hannah emptied out the cab, throwing whatever they could reach into the pack: food for a few days, water, flares, a fresh bottle of drops, the first aid kit, and the oxytocin spray she had lifted from the hospital. Rachel patted her hands against her sides.

'What's wrong?' Hannah said.

'The newspaper, I must have dropped it. There was something in it about mothers surviving.'

The sound of an engine was unmistakable in the silence. One van in a city that had once hosted thousands now somehow terrifying.

'We've got to go,' Rachel said. '*Now.*'

forty-five

They avoided the roads and footpaths, sticking to the nature strips and parklands. Rachel adjusted her pace to Hannah's, a steady jog that allowed her to breathe easily and stay aware of the details. The smoke made everything harder, hurting their lungs, stinging their eyes, weighing on their limbs. They passed the Foreign Affairs buildings, topped with terracotta pyramids, then Prime Minister and Cabinet, Finance, Treasury – a procession of empty instruments of power on empty streets.

'They must have evacuated the Parliamentary Triangle *before*,' Hannah said.

'That means they knew it was coming.'

'*Who* knew?'

'Exactly.'

'The government? Maybe they're friendly?' Hannah's face was hopeful.

'Then why are they chasing us?'

They ran on, through the Aboriginal Tent Embassy in the gardens in front of old Parliament House. Sovereignty was still spelled out in white letters beneath the red, black and yellow flag. Rachel paused in front of the still-burning campfire, hoping for life, but saw no one. *Sorry.* So much could easily have been different.

She heard the van, only a block or two away. It was eerie, crossing the shrouded parks, buildings only appearing when they were almost upon them. But they were hidden, too.

Rachel lengthened her stride to catch up with Hannah and Isaiah. They kept to the trees as best they could while making a line for the lake. The van would have to work its way around by road, hopefully searching in a methodical grid rather than heading them off at the bridge.

They were on the move, too, sparking memories of Rachel's younger self, cruising Canberra's roads in the Beast, windows down, elbow on the window ledge, Van Morrison blaring. The person she used to be. She coughed and spat, her phlegm black with soot.

They were in sight of the water when Hannah stopped. She stared up at the pale columns and copper lintel of the National Library. Leonard French's mosaic windows glowed in the strange red light. The cafe's bright umbrellas had tumbled over the deck, where Rachel and Monique had so often met for lunch.

'Okay?'

'I had a placement there while I was at uni,' Hannah said.

'How was that?'

'The best six weeks of my life! It was like a gallery. Every project was a box of treasures. They offered me a job afterwards. But I just didn't want to live in the city. Or that's what I told myself.'

Rachel nodded. Looking back, reconsidering their choices,

was easier than facing what lay ahead. The black van turned in at the National Gallery, its headlights creeping towards them. 'Come on,' she said, tugging at Hannah's sleeve. 'We need to get across that bridge.'

Isaiah's face was peaceful in sleep. Rachel hoped he stayed that way. They cut across the unmown lawns, past the Henry Moore sculpture, to the neat rows of Manchurian pears, their red and orange leaves reflected in the still lake.

The flags of the world fluttered at half-mast. There must have been people left to lower them, wanting to believe it was important, that life would go on as it had.

At the water's edge they returned to chaos. Blackened leaves and ash littered the bike path. Ducks and swans patrolled the lake, as if still hopeful for a crust or fallen sandwich. And then they saw the bodies – bloated and floating. People had jumped from the bridge, still suited up for work. So much death in the city where it had been possible to count the number of murders on one hand.

Rachel turned at the sound of a car door. The van had pulled up at the end of the road, below the library. Two men got out. They would have to come after them on foot or circle back around the library.

Hannah and Rachel ran along the path to the bridge, a low white arch reflected in the water. They climbed the spiral ramp, threading through bodies, spilled satchels, handbags, bikes. Every step held a new horror. A woman and two young children, still holding hands, was the hardest. Rachel took Isaiah while Hannah threw up, over the rail. The movement woke him, blinking against the sting of smoke.

Shielding his eyes from what they saw was a full-time job. He probably couldn't see, probably wouldn't remember – but their instincts were to protect him from what they would never unsee.

'Sorry.' Hannah took Isaiah from Rachel and stowed him back in the sling.

The bridge was worse. Cars, trucks, taxis, motorbikes, bikes, all in a compacted tangle. Rachel couldn't help but think of other bridges, other cities. She reached into her pocket for her drops. Something to fortify herself with. Beanies, phones, bags lay abandoned by the railing. Car doors flung open – more bodies inside. The smell was unbearable, so close, in such concentration. All those faces frozen in fear.

Rachel had a flash of *them* swarming, sweeping through the city streets and avenues, like fire circling back on itself to burn what it had missed.

They were vulnerable, in the middle of the bridge. There was water, far beneath them; the river dammed to make the lake. Her own river still flowed, in Rachel's mind, but she had begun to worry that she may not see home again. That even if she made it back, everything would be burned to the ground. Images of crumpled buildings, twisted corrugated iron in the ashes, blackened trunks as far as she could see, flickered like a slide show.

They were coming. Surging over the bridge, through the cars, through the bodies.

'Get down,' Rachel said.

Hannah kneeled behind a taxi, holding Isaiah. Rachel held them both, sheltering them with her pack and body.

'I'm not afraid,' Hannah said. 'They're not stopping me.' She hummed softly, rocking Isaiah.

Rachel focused on the sound, the vibration, the warmth of Hannah and Isaiah's bodies against hers. There were more of *them* than ever before, moving fast, closer and closer. She knew that if she opened her eyes, they would be the airborne creatures of before the fire, who Hannah had seen as winged. But Rachel did not want to see.

They were all around them, rushing forwards as one, feeding off lingering traces of fear. There was a pause in the flow, like the river passing around a fallen tree or an outcrop of boulders. Isaiah tensed. *They* were aware of the three of them huddled there on the bridge, as one being – as *they* were one being.

Rachel felt them trying to take her back inside the Beast, inside the fire, driving Hannah and Isaiah to their deaths. But she was already there, speeding down that highway, through the flames. Part of her would always be there. She was real, of the earth, and *they* were not. She trusted Hannah, humming to protect Isaiah, to keep *them* out. *They* were moving too fast, driven by some unstoppable purpose, to stop or break apart. And then they were gone.

Rachel was left bilious, a metallic taste in her mouth. The terrible taint remained, somehow, as if they had passed *through* her body, altering her molecular construction, taking something from her. Her limbs had been stripped of strength, her core drained of energy, her mind flattened, her senses dulled, as if she had aged a decade in those few moments.

forty-six

They stood to watch the dark wave sweep along the avenue, veering around City Hill and on to one of the satellite city centres. The air shimmered in some sort of violent displacement. *They* were adapting, like a virus. Isaiah squinted into the smoke, and whimpered, as if feeling the residue of what had passed. Rachel pointed at the black van, creeping back up the ramp to Parliament House. Hannah nodded and opened her mouth but seemed to lack the strength to speak. Her face had matured, the soft flesh of youth falling away to reveal high cheekbones and a strong jaw.

They trudged on, through the horrors, until they were almost to the other side of the bridge. The smoke masked the stench, dimmed their vision. Rachel focused on the bright orange ribbon unfurling from the museum across the water.

When the local government decided to demolish the old hospital buildings to make way for the museum, a huge crowd had turned out to see the implosion, like the annual fireworks display, families lining the lake with picnic blankets and summer wine.

Only the explosion had gone wrong, sending bricks flying across the lake into the crowd. A girl was killed, others injured. It had been the first tragic incident in the city's memory. Until the fire storm that swept through pine plantations, into the suburbs. Until now.

The fountain was still pumping lake water high into the air. Rachel lifted her head to the cool of its spray on her face. Her cheeks were radiating heat. Hannah's face was red, too, Isaiah's nose pink.

They took the bike ramp off the bridge, to the city side of the lake, working around another terrible tangle of people and bikes. Rachel was starting to see the patterns: those who had pushed forwards, and those who had tried to turn back.

Willows wept beneath the bridge. There were fewer cars, fewer bodies, but the same horror. A skinny dog made a run for it, down to the water to drink. They passed a car parked in a picnic area. It was almost possible to believe that the two people were just sitting peacefully inside, holding hands. Whether they had chosen the spot deliberately, to have a view of the spectacle of the mountains on fire, or it was just where they happened to be, at least they had been together.

Hannah didn't look that way, but kept her eyes, body, facing forward. They were only two suburbs away from finding out what had happened to her other half.

They avoided the three-lane avenues leading in and out of the city, solid with stationary cars. Instead, they walked up and over City Hill, the grassy knoll inside the giant roundabout. Another flagpole, another flag, the Australian Capital Territory this time: blue and yellow, still fluttering.

The hill had been part of the Burley Griffin's original design, major avenues radiating outwards, like arteries from the city's heart. The cypress and pine trees had grown tall, making the hill seem grander than it was. Now shaggy with cape weed and dandelions, rabbits and hares didn't bother hopping away. There were bodies among the trees, inside sleeping bags or sprawled on flattened cardboard boxes. The city's homeless, driven out of bus shelters and shopfronts, out of sight, huddled together, forgotten.

Her first-year class had set up next to the flower beds during orientation week, lobbing hand-painted rainbows of toilet paper across the road during the brief after-work rush hour. A few of them had partied on, spending a night beneath the pines, where Rachel had finally lost her virginity in a drunken fumble. Not that she had let on that it was any big deal. Boyd was just a surfer from the far south coast then but would go on to be a leading ceramicist. The best thing that could be said for the experience was that it happened outside.

She'd spent a few nights on the hill after that, mostly on her own. It had always been peaceful, looking out over the city, headlights circling like fireflies, passing over the lake.

The city centre was laid out below, rendered sepia by the smoke. There were more high rises than Rachel remembered, a larger central business district, with metallic, highly designed shapes suggestive of a real city. And yet, the original white 1920s Melbourne and Sydney buildings, with their stately arches, still defined its character.

Rachel sensed *them*, in twos and threes, outliers left behind by the pack, searching out the back lanes and spaces. If she allowed her peripheral vision to dominate, she could see a shape, a shifting form, darker than smoke, more fluid. A kind of *creature*. Creatures that could roam the empty streets singly or in groups and, together, move through the air. What they lacked in substance they made up for with the power of suggestion.

Rachel and Hannah hesitated beside the garden beds at the base of the hill. The pink petunias were losing their flowers, the leaves turning brown. There was no denying what had happened, the scale of it. This city was every city – the future.

forty-seven

At street level, the smoke crept lower, closer, reducing visibility
to one block in any direction. Rachel sucked on another cough
lozenge, her throat rough, her lungs tight and sore. She fitted a
mask, handed two to Hannah. Isaiah's almost covered his face.
It was hard to tell if it was helping or hindering his breathing.
They had only to get past the city centre, through one suburb
into the next. But distance and time seemed to have stretched.

Any signs of normality, king parrots chattering in the trees or
a pair of fluttering orange butterflies, were dwarfed by stationary
cars, bodies slumped where they had emptied. The apocalyptic
sun.

They hurried along the footpath, Rachel half a step in front.
She cut between office buildings on the southern edge of the city.
Nothing larger than a crow moved. Canberra always had been
called a ghost town. Now it really was.

'The university campus is just there,' Rachel said. 'Five
minutes. The medical research centre, hospital. They could help
us.'

'We'll come back,' Hannah said. 'We need to find Kyle first.'

Rachel blinked. Her own need was pulling her in a different direction. Northbourne Avenue, the main thoroughfare through the city, was the usual blockage of cars, taxis, vans, bikes. So many bikes. Hannah cut between three lanes of vehicles without looking back. Rachel followed. There wasn't really a choice.

'Why are all the buttons, screens, covered off?'

'Surfaces – from the pandemics. People don't even really touch each other anymore, outside the family unit,' Hannah said. 'Not so much back home, but in the city . . .'

When they reached the wide centre strip, Rachel stopped in front of a bright red carriage. 'What the . . .'

Hannah's voice was fuzzy though her mask. 'The tram.'

The door was sealed shut, two men in suits, two older women and two school children locked inside with the female driver. The girl and boy, in the same private school uniform, had been trying to open the doors.

Rachel's eye followed the shiny tracks through a great space where the avenue of mature peppermint gums, growing since the city's creation, had been.

'They just cut them all down?'

Hannah nodded.

The straggling replacements were dead inside their metal guards. They stepped over the tracks, ignoring warning signs and barriers. Rachel could sense movement beneath them, a vibration. A stainless-steel manhole as big as her furnace scarred the grass. 'What's that?'

Hannah shrugged.

They were aligned with City Hill, and Parliament House

beyond. Rachel felt the emptiness branching out beneath, Canberra's underground. The windows of the surrounding buildings glinted, tilting in towards them, as if the city itself would tumble over. An image of her sister, in white, behind glass. A long corridor. They were going the wrong way. Monique was behind them.

'Ray?'

Lines and shapes spun, blurred. *Just breathe.*

'Ray!' Hannah squeezed her hand.

Rachel blinked into the glare. The city, the smoke, the past, the strange fatigue in her bones, were slowing her down.

Rachel gave up screening every car for movement, danger; there were too many. They passed a hotel, blocks of apartments. The city's profile had risen, property values too. All that development, investment, negative-gearing, jobs and growth – now they were paying the price.

They cut through the service station, past a woman slumped against her vehicle, nozzle still in the petrol tank. At the rainbow roundabout, they crossed the road and an empty car park until, at last, they were out of the city, into parkland – the narrow ribbon of pines and other exotics linking Black Mountain and Mount Ainslie. Sulphur-crested cockatoos, bright white against the fading lawn, fed on fallen pine kernels, their yellow combs bobbing.

They stuck to the park, the solidity of the trunks either side steadying Rachel's thoughts. They were well into Ainslie when Hannah led them out of the trees, along a cracked and uneven footpath. Her back was straight, body tense, holding Isaiah close.

The original brick houses were on big blocks, dwarfed by

gardens, mature trees, orchards and vegetable beds. Magpies watched them pass, strung out along the power lines. A pair of speckled juveniles played on an old clothes line, one swinging upside down on the wires, the other nestled inside a bra cup. Rachel couldn't help smiling – until she saw the woman crumpled beneath the line, a white T-shirt dropped in the dirt, the basket of washing, never hung out, still beside her.

There were more people ahead, by a car in a driveway. The sun was low in the sky, the light so strange, the city so full of death. Why had they survived, only to endure all this?

Hannah looked back over her shoulder. 'Ray?'

She tried to get her breath, the smoke pressing on her hair, her skin, her lungs, the mask wet. Hannah was right in front of her, her eyes large. Isaiah had that worried little expression he got, wanting her to smile.

'It's too much,' Rachel said.

'It's our duty, as survivors. To find our loved ones. To witness this.'

Hans always said that a real artist can't afford to look away. She had been looking away for a long time.

'Ray, *please*. We're nearly there.'

Hannah led Rachel by the hand, past the family half in, half out of their Prius, and up a liquidambar-lined cul-de-sac. The trees would always remind her of carrying the bodies from the surgery back at Nimmitabel. It already seemed like months ago, when that was the worst they had done.

She brought herself back to her breath, her steps, putting one boot in front of the other. Hannah stopped in front of a row of single-storey flats, one of the early waves of subdivisions to provide additional inner-city housing. A wisteria snaked over the timber pergola, its spent purple flowers rotting on the ground.

People – families, couples, singles – had lived in every one of these houses. She scanned windows, doors, gardens, car ports. The smoke made it hard to tell the time of day, her vision clouded by shadows at the end of the street, the corners of the buildings.

It wasn't just smoke. The creatures were gathering again. But whenever Rachel looked directly at them, they slunk back into the shadows.

'Do you want me to go first?'

'We'll go together,' Hannah said. It was the last flat in the row. The path led to a black timber door. A bike lock hung from the railing but there was no bike. For a moment Hannah just stood on the steps, holding Isaiah. Then she knocked, twice. It already seemed a strange thing to do.

The door did not open. The curtains did not shift, there was no sound. Even the birds seemed to have been silenced. Rachel watched as Hannah kneeled, holding Isaiah to her, to dig a dirty ziplock bag from beneath a mossy buddha in the shaded front garden. She stood, removed a silver key, and placed it in the lock, turned the key and opened the door. Rachel closed her eyes for a moment, then followed her inside.

forty-eight

The screen door slammed behind them. The flat was small, with low ceilings and little natural light. Rachel stopped in the middle of the kitchen while Hannah rushed from room to room. The dishes were washed in the sink. There was rubbish in the bin but no smell. No signs of violence. She counted her steps to the dining-room table, covered by laptop, modem, speakers, screens, cables – all dark.

The windows were obscured by heavy security screens. The front door was the only way in or out. The confined space was closing in on her, the smell of the leather couch, dish cloth, cheap woollen carpet, making her nauseous. And that particular slant of smoke-muted light through the vertical blinds.

'He's not here,' Hannah said. 'But his phone is missing. And his bike.'

Isaiah started to cry, as if picking up his father's absence, his mother's distress. Hannah rubbed his back, still moving from room to room.

Rachel slid one arm and then the other out of the pack. She

needed to be strong, for Hannah, but it wasn't a safe space. *They* were all around, forcing her back to another flat, another city. When she had woken in the middle of the night to find someone standing over her bed, the streetlight casting shadow lines through the blinds, his face slowly coming into focus. Rachel had not been strong or brave but froze, unable to move her arms or legs or even cry out. Only sinking deeper into the mattress. *No.*

She could hear Hannah speaking but it was far away, muted.

Isaiah's crying escalated, the higher pitch bringing Rachel back. Hannah was flicking through papers on the table, talking too fast. Rachel poured a glass of water from the tap, but when she saw the colour of what came out, she left it on the sink. The fires had impacted the city's water supply again. It explained the slab of water on the floor. She pulled two plastic bottles from their packaging, handing one to Hannah.

'Drink,' she said.

There were framed pictures of Hannah, Kyle and newborn Isaiah at the hospital. Another of Kyle with his mountain bike, victorious in some sort of competition.

Rachel examined the snarl of electronics on the dining table more closely. It looked like someone had been trying to rig up some sort of communications system. 'What area of Defence did you say?'

'Yeah, Intelligence.'

'Would there be some sort of watch office?'

Hannah tapped a laptop key again and again but the screen remained blank. 'Maybe. He didn't tell me much.'

'What would he do?'

'He'd go into work,' she said. 'They would think it their duty.

They were brainwashed like that, for exactly this sort of crisis. I couldn't shift that thinking even after he left. And then he went back . . .'

'Maybe he thought that was his best chance of finding you, getting information?'

'Maybe.' Hannah looked down at Isaiah, as if he had the answers. 'I need to feed and change him. Then we can start searching.'

'It's nearly dark,' Rachel said.

'I can't just do nothing!'

Rachel sat on the edge of the black couch, her face in her hands. What she wanted most was to get outside. But the creatures were waiting, and neither of them was thinking straight. 'Hannah, we're exhausted.'

Rachel opened the bottle of red wine still in its brown paper bag on the bench, a Cabernet Merlot from Margaret River. The west coast was now beyond reach, let alone crossing the oceans to other islands, continents. She poured Hannah half a glass. By the time she came back from settling Isaiah, Rachel was already on her second. She would be sorry in the morning, but she needed to numb her senses to stay in the city, in such a small space.

The electric stove was no use, and Rachel had left her cooker in the Beast. They lit candles and set them around the kitchen and lounge. Hannah put together a platter of cheeses past their best, olives, pickled vegetables and thin slices of the Nimmitabel bread, and set it out on the coffee table. Rachel ate to soak up the wine.

Hannah dropped her phone on the couch. 'I can't even look at his photographs, his emails.' Everything was on screens, devices, stored in the cloud. Without power, that world had evaporated. 'Why didn't he leave me a note?'

Rachel frowned. He couldn't have known what would happen, that Hannah would end up in Canberra.

'How did you meet?'

'In my final year he came to a concert on campus. He went to ADFA, which was like a whole different world. Different social circle. Anyway, I wasn't getting served at the bar – and he stepped in.'

'You liked that?'

'And he was interesting. Had travelled. Most of the guys on my course, not that there were many, were pretty one-dimensional.'

'You'd ditched the hot drummer by then?'

'He moved to California. Joined a band that was big for a while.'

Rachel nodded. They were talking but only half-listening to each other. On edge, listening for a step, a key in the door. With the windows closed and the blinds drawn, the room was even smaller. The smoke crept in, somehow. There wasn't enough air.

Hannah rummaged through drawers, until she found a box of photos. She spread them over the coffee table, poring over images of faces the way people only did after someone was gone.

The creatures were moving in. Rachel had been trying to quash the feeling of them streaming over the bridge, passing *through* her body, but it was back, dredging up long-buried memories. 'Everything you resist returns.' Another of Hans's wisdom-bites.

Living in the flat on her own and staying at Tom's at weekends had worked for a while. But then he was preparing for the big Opera House show, getting home at all hours, the same old pulling away she was used to but growing tired of. He spoke of them as equals, but his actions made clear whose work was more important.

She hadn't thought much of the card left in her mailbox, without a stamp. Somehow they had found out where she lived and got inside the building. Even back then, she'd had her routines. Walking the same way to and from the studio every day, having her lunch in the same spot, shopping at the same store. As the police would later imply, it made her an easy target.

Rachel always left the balcony door ajar at night, even in winter, so she could breathe. That day, she'd had a bad feeling, a premonition. It took ages to get to sleep. When she woke in the dark, to see him standing there, she thought her heart had stopped. It wasn't the first time she had experienced that sort of paralysis, just the first time it had really mattered.

'Ray?' Hannah was holding out a photograph. 'What's happening?'

Rachel was balled up in the corner of the couch. She blinked, tried to focus on Hannah's face. It really had felt like her own mind, voluntarily bringing up those old memories. She unfolded her arms from around her legs. 'I had a bad experience in a place like this,' she said.

'Somebody hurt you?'

'Sort of,' Rachel said.

'Someone you knew?'

'We met at an exhibition opening, apparently. He stalked me online, followed me around the city, building all these elaborate fantasies.' For fourteen hours Rachel had been a hostage in her own apartment. She still couldn't really remember most of it. But the feeling was still in her body.

Hannah put the photos down. 'What did you do?'

'When he finally went to the bathroom, I called the police. They took for ever. And he was convincing . . . made out there was some history. I couldn't speak. I didn't think they were ever going to get him out.'

'That sounds terrifying,' Hannah said. 'Was he charged?'

'Trespassing.'

'That's it? It's assault, even if he didn't physically harm you.'

But he had. Holding her down, his full body weight on top of her. She could still feel him. And her inability to resist.

Isaiah's whimpers built to a wail, waking up alone in a room he didn't recognise.

'Sorry. I'd better feed him,' Hannah said.

'We should probably go to bed, anyway,' Rachel said.

'I'm not sure I'll sleep. I just keep imagining Kyle walking in the door, you know?'

'I know.'

Rachel unlaced her boots and slipped them off. 'Try to rest. I'll be right out here.' She stretched out her tired body on the too-soft couch and closed her eyes, trying to settle on an image of the river, molten glass, a flow that could still her.

forty-nine

The smoke woke Rachel in the early hours. It crept in through the gaps, under doorways, around window frames, a lot like *them*, still working their way into her mind. Her throat was rough, her lungs tight, her head ached. The space had become even smaller in the dark.

There was no moonlight, no streetlight. She heard only two cats fighting. And then the screams started, a street or two away. In some ways, it was worse when they stopped.

Why hadn't the creatures just come for them? She searched the bare walls, cornices, surfaces, the cable-clogged table, in the gloom, as if they might hold the answers.

Hannah was up again, lifting a crying Isaiah from the crib. Rachel had come to recognise the shift in sound as he went from horizontal to vertical. The peace and quiet of the trees, Rachel's river, seemed a lifetime ago. She counted the nights she had been away from her own bed. Much longer than she had planned.

At the birds' first stirrings, she lifted herself off the couch and opened the blinds. She stretched her shoulders across the bathroom doorway, three or four vertebrae cracking into place. She stripped off and stepped into the shower, washing herself down as best she could with brown tepid water, mouth firmly closed. More awake, alert, she put on clean clothes and tied back her hair. Her head was wooden, heavy behind the eyes, from the wine. She searched for her tablets in the jumble of items in her pack, emptying everything out onto the floor, separating things into piles. They weren't there. Somehow, in the scramble back at the Beast, she had dropped them, or left them in the tray.

'Crap.' Of all the times to go cold turkey.

In the kitchen, Hannah was expressing milk, measuring Isaiah's antibiotics dose. Her hair was wild, her movements less definite than they had been.

'Morning.'

'Hey,' Hannah said. 'I remembered the barbecue in the shed.'

She had set it up on the kitchen bench, a saucepan of water heating on top. Rachel stared out into the yard, a thin strip of unmown grass and bare fence palings backing onto a park. They didn't talk about what they had heard. What it might mean. Hannah's face had settled into something flat.

'I was thinking Kyle must have ridden up the mountain. It was Tuesday when it happened. When I saw those first reports. He rode up there every Tuesday and Friday morning at dawn. Always a picture, a selfie of him with the city behind. The sunrise. That morning it didn't come. We need to walk up there, retrace his steps.'

'But Hannah. If he hasn't come back . . . ?'

'Maybe he went straight into work from there. Maybe they can help us.'

She wasn't making any sense. 'Who?'

'The Defence people in the car.'

'Did you get any sleep?'

'Not really,' she said. 'If I just find his bike. At least then I'll *know*.'

Rachel needed to know what had happened to her sister, too. But even if Hannah found the bike, they still wouldn't know anything. And if they found his body, Hannah might lose it altogether.

'But we don't know what or who is out there, on that mountain.'

'I can go on my own. It'll be quicker,' Hannah said. 'You could mind Isaiah.'

'Hannah.' Rachel leaned against the kitchen bench. It was as if whatever had been keeping Hannah calm and sensible had run out. Rachel's whole body screamed that it was the wrong thing to do. But she couldn't let Hannah go up there on her own. Or separate from Isaiah; it might be all there was keeping them alive. 'We stick together, remember.'

fifty

They were walking uphill again. Rachel's feet were sore, her whole body. Her head was dull, from the hangover, from starting the day without coffee or breakfast, and the beginnings of withdrawal from the medication. She had only her drops to rely on. Smoke shrouded the city, fine white ash rained down. She couldn't breathe beneath the mask. Her stomach was uneasy, flip-flopping. She had a bad feeling about the mountain. Whatever they found was not going to be good.

They hurried away from the houses, from two sad, small bodies in a backyard treehouse, straight uphill and then following the track around, towards the city. A family of grey kangaroos lounged beneath the gnarled limbs of yellow box. A galah was digging out a tree hollow, renovating a new home, while her mate watched on, in pink and grey, squawking advice.

They passed a round structure of woven branches, shelter for more than one person judging by the bedding inside, and signs of a fire. Rachel kept one ear out, between their footsteps and the few words they exchanged, for the inhabitants.

There were too many tyre tracks to follow. Footprints, too. Rachel could picture, as if on a time-lapse recording, all those people riding, exercising their bodies, breathing in fresh air, striving to live good lives. And in the end, it had made no difference.

Without the pack, Rachel was striding ahead, her limbs loosening. The dog bite had almost healed, and she was walking-fit from the journey. Away from the city, from all the bodies, she did not feel *them* as intensely. Something in her body started to let go.

But Hannah still had Isaiah's weight to carry. She was pink about the face and throat, fatigued from the lack of sleep, all they had been through, facing the reality about Kyle, worrying about Isaiah. He, at least, was getting better – or he would be without the smoke. His temperature was back to normal. Colour had returned to his face, the occasional smile. It was only the cough that lingered.

He was changing every day, getting bigger and heavier, but also more alert and engaged, and less satisfied being strapped to his mother. He wriggled and squirmed, and made frustrated noises, as if keen to explore the world on his own.

'He's growing so fast,' Rachel said.

'If we *don't* find his bike,' Hannah said, 'then maybe he's okay, maybe he did go into work.'

Was it *them* talking? Or her hormones changing already? Hannah had been so practical and rational until they got to the flat. And there wasn't much hope of her getting good news to bring her out of it. When they got back, she would suggest Hannah take the oxytocin. Just in case.

Rachel strode ahead, spotting another of the woven wooden shelters. People were living on the mountain, or they had been. Hannah scanned the undergrowth for a bike or a body, while Rachel worried about the sort of people who would hole up in the bush so close to the city – and why. Trauma changed people. The need to survive did something to people, too. Made them desperate. She and Hannah had already done desperate things. But disruption, upheaval, created a particular space for those who had already lived outside society, outside of its rules. It was those people who worried her most. People without fear. The young men in Nimmitabel, the prisoners, the roadblock woman. The van up at Parliament House. Too many people.

She waited beside a water tank, bright with layer upon layer of graffiti, for Hannah to catch up. A willy wagtail flicked its tail from side to side in the middle of the track, a black and white signal.

Hannah pulled down her mask to drink from her water bottle. 'Do you think they're aliens?'

Rachel couldn't read Hannah's expression; it hadn't appeared on her face before. 'Why do you say that?'

'Well, what else *could* they be?'

'Something we made?'

'What do you mean?'

Rachel shrugged. The knowledge came from her body. 'They seem to work a lot like we do.'

'That makes me feel sick,' Hannah said.

The threats to human existence had always been imagined as

coming from the outside: beings from outer space, asteroids, a contagion loosed from the jungle.

'What if we did this to ourselves?'

In the open space beneath power lines, they stopped again. Through the smoke, Rachel recognised the city planned from the start rather than evolving, with its five satellite centres. There was something comforting about the circles, the green, the patterns, houses nestled between mountains and hills. Even now, there was more bush than sprawl, which was probably why she had managed to live there so long.

Rachel trained the binoculars on the closer landscape, where the mountain met the city. There were no cars moving, the roads blocked with pile-ups and abandoned vehicles. Bodies inside. But it was the Defence precinct that she was most interested in. Vehicles were parked outside in an orderly fashion, bikes locked to bike racks. The windows were impossible to see into, as they were designed to be. Still, she had the sense that there was something going on inside.

'Which is his building?'

'The one with slots for windows.'

It shimmered, as if releasing heat.

'There's that white wagon again,' Rachel said. It was threading its way along the narrow access road.

'Can I see?' Hannah put her hand out for the binoculars.

Rachel lifted the strap over her head, passed them over.

'Two men inside,' Hannah said. 'Not Kyle.'

The car pulled up in front of one of the other buildings.

For a moment Hannah seemed torn between objectives. Rachel shut her eyes, hoping they could turn around.

'Let's keep going,' Hannah said. 'We can look there on the way back.'

The trail they were on continued around the base of the mountain, descending behind the War Memorial. Instead, they worked their way upwards, following the track that Hannah said Kyle cycled.

It was steep at first. And then they were traversing again, past a forest of ghostly brittle gums, and beneath the twisting bough of a yellow box as old as the city. Rachel spotted the occasional kurrajong, with their itchy seed pods. An understorey of younger wattles had sprung up. Twice she stopped, certain she had heard a twig snap or a rock roll. But when she looked back, she saw only trees. She was trying to walk with fox feet, to remember what Uncle Leon had taught her, but her boots were big and clumsy. Hannah was crashing forwards, looking from one side of the track to the other.

At last the path crossed the summit trail. Hannah led them straight up the back of the mountain. It was paved but much steeper than the way they had come. Only a sadist would ride it. Rachel had checked her pace, but Hannah was red in the face, her throat blotchy.

'I can take him for a while,' Rachel said.

'Would you? I'm really struggling today.'

'Sure.'

Hannah unfastened the papoose and wrapped it around Rachel's torso. Isaiah reached out with both hands for his mother. For a moment his face was distressed, and then, when Rachel pulled a stupid face, he grinned and settled into her much larger, firmer body.

The weight wasn't much extra to carry, but it was a strange thing, to have another living creature attached to her. The responsibility of a dependant was not something she had ever known. That was probably the biggest difference between her and her sister. More than education and training, career. Monique had always had to be responsible.

Crimson rosellas called all around, their blues and reds bright against the pale trunks of the higher ground: mature brittle gums, snow gums and scribbly gums. Some of the scribbles were almost writing, signs to follow, clues carved by moth larvae. If only they could read them.

Hannah led on, watching the ground in front of her, the bush either side. Isaiah had fallen asleep, Rachel's walking was rhythmic enough to settle him, no matter the difference in her gait and smell.

Again, Rachel felt eyes on them, half-heard noises that were not wild animal. But whenever they stopped, the noises stopped too.

They had reached the stone steps, the final approach to the summit. There were tyre tracks either side of the path, riders having to work their way around the steps.

'Need a minute,' Hannah said. 'Hard to breathe.'

They sat in the shade to drink a few mouthfuls of water. Rachel opened a protein bar and offered one end to Hannah.

'I'm sorry about the assault,' Hannah said. 'You should have said.'

Rachel shrugged. 'It was a long time ago.'

Hannah broke off a piece of the bar. 'There's a picture of you with someone, at Monique's. In Venice, maybe.'

'Tom,' she said. 'He was a glassworker, too.'

'What happened?'

'He let me down. Distanced himself during all the noise about the heart piece,' Rachel said. 'Then he was busy with a big exhibition. And weird about the assault. Jealous, kind of. Blamed *me*. He didn't even visit me in hospital.'

'Hospital?'

'Ah – more of a mental breakdown.'

'That's when you went to live with Monique?'

Rachel looked up. 'Yeah.' Monique and Bill had packed up her flat and studio. Relocated everything to Nimmitabel. 'I guess I ended it by default. I didn't contact him when I got out.'

'Do you want to try and find him?'

'He died – before all this.'

'How?'

'Took his own life.' She had come across the obituary in *GlassWorld*. Just turned the page to see him staring out, with an end date by his name. Pictures of his wife and children.

'That's so sad,' Hannah said.

Tom's creative process had always been manic – working around the clock, pushing out the deadlines. They were such major pieces, massive undertakings for public institutions. And then he'd crash when it was done – for weeks. She had heard that there were financial pressures. And those big pieces would have been harder, physically, as he got older. He, too, would have felt what was happening to the world, all the ways it was being torn apart, breaking down.

Hannah stood, put her hand on Rachel's shoulder. 'Can we push on?' Her voice was raspy.

'Okay.' But Rachel's body was tired.

The breeze had thinned the smoke. They powered up the last rise, with fresh energy, knowing it was almost over. Their laboured breathing, boots on the pavers, inside the tunnel of trees was, for those fifteen minutes, their whole world.

From the summit, they could see the true extent of the fires. The skyline was aglow. It had all but taken the Brindabellas, with blazes raging out of control to the north, east and west. They were surrounded. Canberra was a bowl in the landscape, filling with smoke. It was only a matter of time until wind brought fire back on the city, pushing into the bushland and through the suburbs. Maybe that would be for the best, to cleanse the city of its dead. The only way Canberra could be reborn, the world remade.

Hannah put her hands to her face, smothering a sound in her throat. A men's mountain bike had been thrown off the edge of the path. A bike Hannah recognised.

Rachel felt eyes on them, movement nearby. Someone *was* following them. And they were out in the open. Too late, she saw the glint of glass, smelled metal.

By the time the first shot rang out, Rachel was turning, diving, sheltering Isaiah with her body and bringing Hannah down all in one movement. Something crunched under her hip, piercing the skin. The second shot hit her shoulder blade, knocking all the breath out of her.

Hannah screamed. 'Isaiah!'

Rachel ripped the mask from her face. 'I've got him.' She

crawled forwards, sheltering behind a bench seat, sucking in air. 'Hannah? Are you hurt?'

There was no answer.

'Hannah?' Rachel reached out to touch Hannah's ankle, shook her leg. 'Oh, no.'

She was gone.

fifty-one

Rachel shut her eyes and turned away, putting her body between Isaiah and his mother. 'Oh, Hannah.' Of all the possibilities, scenarios she had worried about, being shot hadn't been one of them. Hannah had been so much tougher than Rachel had imagined. Tougher than she had ever given her credit for. And kind. A sob rushed into her throat before she could stop it.

And then Isaiah started to cry.

'No, no, no. Not now.' Blood seeped from her shoulder, already soaking her shirt. It hurt. But when she touched her hand to the wound, it was only shallow. The bullet must have glanced off something first, or hit the one buckle on the papoose.

Rachel pulled back, into her body, visualising what she had seen the moments before diving, the direction of the footsteps, the trajectory of the bullets.

There was no time for ceremony or sentiment. Rachel had to leave Hannah where she had fallen and get Isaiah off the mountain. It was instinct, and not entirely her own. She dragged the mountain bike from the scrub and mounted it. It was a little small, but its tyres were, miraculously, still more or less full.

She didn't head back the way they had come, but straight down a narrow bike track. It took a moment to adjust to the additional weight on the front of her body. She shifted her balance back, sitting out of the saddle, legs and arms absorbing the bends and bumps. Her back arched to stabilise Isaiah, swinging in front of her in the papoose.

The back tyre skidded and spun out in loose gravel. They were moving faster than was comfortable, faster than anyone should ride with a baby on board, but the sooner they were off the mountain the better.

Isaiah's heat against her was comfort and incentive. To protect, to survive; it was primal. As if her mind had relinquished control, handed over to her body. It was difficult to judge distance and direction, over crunching leaves and sticks, the whirring of the wheels, her own blood thumping in her ears. But there was something crashing after them. She loosened her grip on the brakes, hurtling down the track, gathering her body around Isaiah, half-expecting another shot. A moving target was harder to hit, and they were moving, too. She could only try, and hope.

There was no choice but to jump the log across the track, and land as best she could. She had never been a mountain biker, despite the time she'd lived in Canberra. Only now did she see the point, maybe even understand the pleasure of it. If you weren't carrying a small child, afraid for two lives, and hadn't just lost someone. But she couldn't think about Hannah now. She couldn't afford to feel.

Trunks flashed past, birds startled and flew off, smoke and

eucalyptus filled her nostrils. She focused on the mountain as a whole, becoming one with it rather than fighting against the obstacles.

Just as she relaxed into the seat, hunched down low over Isaiah, gunshots split the forest. Something hit a rock and pinged away. But she and Isaiah were intact, still moving. *What do they want?*

Rachel crossed a gravel four-wheel drive access road but stuck to the single track. It was no longer as steep; she had to peddle. Isaiah was wriggling, whimpering. The start of what would be a terrible longing for his mother, her milk. All of that would be the next problem to solve but she still needed to get away and back into the flat – without being followed.

She accelerated into a dip and out the other side. The track narrowed between two trees – just wide enough for the handle-bars – and dropped again. A stone gave way, shifted under the front tyre. Rachel raised her shoulder and managed to get her hand around Isaiah's head, her arm along his body – to protect him from the fall. She hit the ground hard, something cracked, winding her. Isaiah started to howl – and who could blame him. She rolled, got to her feet. Felt his soft skull, and limbs, afraid of what she would find. But he seemed unbroken.

'Sshh, kid.'

She ran downhill, towards the Defence buildings. There was something moving, fast – too fast – in her peripheral vision. She turned for a moment, took in the two dark shapes on dark mountain bikes. They were carrying something across their backs, maybe guns.

'Fuck.'

She – they – crashed through the undergrowth, straggling

You're wounded. And we need to have the child assessed.' His chest and shoulders strained at his shirt. A gym-built body, rather than lean muscles made through hard work.

'I need to get back to where we're staying, get his things.'

'What's your name, Ma'am?'

'Rachel,' she said. Anything was better than Ma'am.

'Rachel, you're injured. It's not safe out there on your own. These are dangerous people.'

She did not like the way McNeal was looking at Isaiah, his eyes glassy.

'What do they want?'

'The child,' he said. 'They think babies are immune.'

'Are they?'

'We're not sure. But if you want to start a new society . . .'

His boots were loud in the tunnel. Rachel registered a breeze on her face, some sort of exit ahead. They reached another set of lift doors. There was no signage, just the letter D on the wall. And again, an empty trolley by the lift, alongside a dozen empty containers. Something had been delivered and unloaded into the buildings. There *were* other people inside. There was truth to what he was saying. But there was something he wasn't telling her, too.

When she did not follow, McNeal turned. 'Rachel, please. Let us patch you up. Check the child over. You'll be safe here,' he said.

'I have to get back.'

'Look, we have an antidote. It will protect you against the creatures.'

'*Antidote?*'

'A team over at the university developed it. There are top scientists there, and a doctor. We were the guinea pigs, of course.' His smile softened his face, seemed genuine.

'A doctor?'

'It was her idea, apparently. Travelled here from out past Cooma.'

Mon. Rachel's legs threatened to give way. 'The university's medical research centre?'

'Correct,' McNeal said.

She leaned against the crates and shut her eyes. If they had gone straight there, none of this would have happened. Hannah would still be alive.

McNeal stepped towards her, arm extended. 'Are you okay?'

Rachel moved away.

'Rachel, I'm trying to help you.'

Isaiah started to wail, the sound echoing around that vast space. 'I need to feed him. He's been sick.' Rachel put her fingers to the top button of her shirt. 'Give me a few minutes?'

'Of course,' McNeal said. 'What if I fetch the medic? Bring him here?'

'Okay,' she said. 'Thanks.'

McNeal hesitated at the lift, as if sensing her intention, but didn't turn around. He couldn't – it would be inappropriate to do so when a mother was breastfeeding her child.

But Rachel was not Isaiah's mother. And never would be. The minute the lift doors closed, she ran.

fifty-two

Rachel hurried down the empty tunnel, Isaiah swinging in front of her. Her shoulder was throbbing, every breath hurt. The landscape had changed again. Too much information. Information she wasn't sure she could trust. She reached into her pocket, for her drops, wincing at the sharp pain across her fingertip. The bottle was smashed in her pocket, empty. Her boxers and cargoes were soaked through with blood.

'Hang on, Isaiah.' He needed changing. The smell was real, at least. Should she have got medical treatment instead of taking Isaiah back into danger? Was she making another bad decision?

She needed to get to Monique. Rachel could trust her. Only her.

The tunnel ended abruptly at a concrete wall, blank but for a series of numbers. Coordinates, perhaps. A steel ladder led up to a manhole. She stopped at the bottom. Her legs were jelly; she couldn't seem to get her breath. Her shoulder and hip throbbed.

She climbed hand over hand, the rungs cold under her sweaty

palms. The round tap-like handle turned easily. When she placed her hands under the lid, and pushed upwards, it opened, coming down on dirt with a thud. She squinted into the smoke and glare, then climbed out.

It took a moment to get her bearings, to believe that it wasn't a trap, that they weren't going to be set upon by soldiers or militia on mountain bikes. But she could feel the creatures, aware of her again. Isaiah was whimpering, hungry and uncomfortable in a dirty nappy. His mother was dead. *Hannah is dead.* All the realities rushed back in, amplifying her doubts about how she was going to look after a baby. Whether she was fit to care for another human being.

She jogged around the base of the mountain. Houses once full of people, families, life. The bodies were passing beyond being bodies. The number of flies had multiplied exponentially. Her side was hurting, her lungs burning, and her legs threatening to give way. She had just started to think she was going to make it when she heard a shout, a bike tyre skidding on gravel.

Fuck. They had found her. She cut between houses, a cycle path leading down to the park behind Kyle's. The hip-high bars staggered across the path would slow their pursuers, but only for a moment. Rachel had one trick left.

She headed not for the front of the flats but the back. She swung on the low branch of the blue gum and flung her legs out, over the fence, but landed awkwardly, the palings cutting into her backside. She slid off into a crouch, hand over Isaiah's mouth, biting down on the pain, which had her seeing only white, until she heard the particular whir of mountain bike tyres at speed grow louder and then fade away.

She squeezed down the side of the flat to the front door, almost blind with pain, fumbling in the papoose pocket for the key. For a terrible moment she thought it had fallen out, somewhere on the mountain, or in the tunnel. It was enough to bring her close to panic – locked out, with *them* moving in again. Creatures with a growing purpose.

But then she felt cool metal against her fingertips. The key slid easily into the lock, the door opened. She closed it behind them, locked the deadlock from the inside, put the chain across. She leaned against the thin timber and slid down to the floor. Isaiah looked at her with a worried expression, a tentative smile. It was enough to bring tears. Tears that built into great wracking sobs that shook both their bodies.

Isaiah was mewling like a kitten, hands kneading her breasts. He was hungry and filthy and she was just sitting there, crying. Rachel forced herself to her feet, to the bathroom. She peed with Isaiah still strapped to her. His face was covered with dirt, his clothes smeared with her blood. And he stank. She sat him on top of the washing machine and undid all of the tiny buttons, removed his jumpsuit, singlet and putrid nappy and threw the lot in the laundry tub. *Yuk.* Was it normal for a little human to produce such a sticky, stinking paste? It was everywhere. She filled the bathroom basin with bottled water and a squeeze of baby body wash, sponged him down with a clean facecloth. He whimpered and shivered.

'Sorry. It's cold, I know.' She tried to go more slowly, be more gentle, examining every inch of him for injury or damage. His skin was so fine, so soft, her sore shoulder making her hands clumsy. Hands used to glass, not babies. He had already been put through way too much in his short life. But he seemed physically intact, his limbs, torso, face, hands, feet, unmarked and moving.

She towelled him dry and did her best putting his chubby little legs in a fresh nappy. The result was untidy but she managed to fit him into a clean jumpsuit, and he looked and smelled more like a cared-for baby.

Rachel swallowed three painkillers and an antibiotic with a few mouthfuls of bottled water. She searched everywhere for Isaiah's antibiotics: in the bedroom, kitchen, lounge, bathroom, Hannah's bag. But she couldn't find them. Hannah must have had them on her, somewhere. And Rachel couldn't go back to get them.

She lit the barbecue and filled a saucepan with water, placing it over the hottest area of flame. It took for ever for a single bubble to appear but eventually came to the boil. She washed out the bottle and teat and sterilised them, warming half the milk Hannah had expressed, testing it with her little finger the way she had seen Hannah do. It was impossible not to think of Hannah, with her breast milk on her fingers, Isaiah in front of her. Hannah's last gift to her child.

The only child Rachel had seen alive.

She broke open her last antibiotic capsule and added a little to the milk, shaking the bottle to mix it in. Isaiah gripped the warm plastic with both hands and started to drink, gurgling happily. Then he stopped, dropped the bottle on the floor. Rachel picked it up, washed the teat, but couldn't get him to start again. 'C'mon. You can't waste this.'

Was it the wrong temperature? Could he taste the antibiotic? She walked around the room with him against her chest, rubbing his back. Rocking him the way Hannah had. She tried again with the milk, but he rejected the bottle and started to cry.

'Shhh. *Please.*' Nothing she did made him stop. Did he know that his mother was gone? Was he in pain? Injured inside, somehow? *God.* She was the last person who should be left alone in charge of a baby.

fifty-three

Isaiah was still crying. He had been crying for hours. His face was splotchy and red, angry even. And it seemed there was no stopping the noise. He had worked himself up into some sort of hysteria. His body was missing Hannah's. It was more than hunger, more than physical need, more than discomfort. It was pain.

'I know. I miss her, too.' She couldn't stop her own mind playing and replaying that moment. Why had she chosen then to take Isaiah? If she hadn't, maybe Hannah would still be alive. But maybe Isaiah wouldn't. It was hard to tell right from wrong, better from worse. Every part of her body ached. She rubbed his back, tried to soothe him.

'Shh.' Rachel said. 'Please, kid. *Please stop*.'

She needed to wash herself, tend to her wounds, but she felt unable to leave him. Even going to the toilet, as quickly as she could manage, had set him off afresh. He was only expressing the same fear inside every person. No one wanted to be left alone. He was just a baby. But the noise was making her crazy.

It reverberated and magnified in that small space, already airless and starting to stink. Anyone from miles away could hear. Men on bikes, uniformed men inside buildings. *Them.* Waiting outside, growing in strength, as if knowing she had a new vulnerability, wanting to take control of her head, what was left of her energy, her life.

How could anyone think, make decisions, with all that noise? His crying was placing them in danger, putting her at risk.

She put Isaiah down in the crib, raised the side. Still he screamed, his face ugly and swollen. She closed the bedroom door on his suffering, but she could still hear him in the lounge, the kitchen. Even with her hands over her ears, a pillow over her head, there was no end to it.

She reached again for her drops. But they were gone, too. The bottle smashed. She peeled down the top of her cargoes, to examine the spot that hurt, on her hip flexor. It was a mess of cuts, open and bleeding. Maybe glass inside. Her shoulder had settled into a dull throb. The pain in her ribs pinched. She couldn't take a proper deep breath, fill her lungs, even after calming herself.

Isaiah was screaming even louder now. It was inside her head, her body – unbearable, as if she were screaming herself. A better human, a better woman – a mother – could stand it. But Rachel could not. She dragged her pack into the bathroom and shut the door, turned on the shower full-stream, and peeled off her bloody clothes. She washed herself down in cold murky water, shivering, watching blood and dirt swirl down the drain. The cold, the sting of her wounds, cleared her head a little. But as soon as she shut off the taps, she could hear Isaiah again, his screaming.

She stepped out onto the bathmat, dried herself and examined her shoulder in the mirror. It was still bleeding, needed stitching. She patted it dry, slopped antiseptic in the wound, and bit down on the pain. She applied the largest bandage in her kit as best she could with her left hand, using the mirror. Every movement burned in her side. She could not take a proper breath.

She raised her left arm and felt gingerly along her ribs. There was already purple bruising, excruciating to touch. One, maybe two, ribs broken. There was nothing she could do, except strap them. And strapping them properly was not possible without help. *Monique.* More tears threatened, but she shut them down.

She struggled into clean underwear and a T-shirt and sat on the toilet seat with the torch in her mouth to examine her hip. She picked out the glass shards she could see with tweezers, and washed the wound as best she could. She applied antiseptic, used a suture to close the worst cut, and placed a padded bandage over the site.

Still Isaiah screamed. Surely he had to run out of energy eventually? Rachel pulled on a clean pair of cargoes. She transferred the ingots from the pockets of those clothes she was discarding – ripped and filthy, blood-soaked.

She was clean, patched up, dressed. And still Isaiah cried. It was desperate now, working up into a crescendo and down again, in a repeating cycle.

Stop.

Everything that had happened was piling up, accumulating as a noise inside her head. She couldn't follow a single thought right through to any resolution, let alone make a plan or decision. She needed to get Isaiah to her sister, but the city was vast and overwhelming, the threats too great: the outliers, the military, surrounded by fire, *them* closing in. It was too much.

I can't do this.

She opened the bathroom door and gathered up her gear, separating it from Hannah's and Isaiah's, throwing things in her pack in no proper order. Isaiah screamed, as if he could read her mind.

She opened the front door, placed the pack outside, and bent to lace her boots. Isaiah screamed all the louder.

I'm sorry. She shut the door behind her, struggled into the pack, and ran up the middle of the street in the dark to the park at the base of the mountain, to quiet, to safety. She leaned her forehead on the trunk of an old blue gum – still, calm, just the evening rush of sap. The ground was solid, unmoving, eucalyptus oil sharp in her nostrils, clearing her sinuses, despite the smoke.

For a moment, she breathed. Blocked out the pain and drifted with the night sounds: crickets, the slow wing beats of an owl, the heavy thump of a wallaby. She sank down on her bootheels, at the base of the tree, and let herself cry. Silent sobs that hurt her body. Nothing was as she had planned or what she had wanted. Nothing was fair. There were no answers or solutions. She had failed.

The time after the heart installation and the assault had been dark, a blank and barren landscape without energy or hope. And what was a person, without the will to move, to live, to imagine another day? She had felt so alone. But Monique had found her and put her back together.

Those selfish, first-world concerns seemed like nothing now. And there was no big sister to help. Something screamed, long and thin. Maybe a powerful owl, but it had sounded half-human. Nowhere was quiet, nowhere was safe. She couldn't escape what had happened – or herself. It was only a matter of time. Why fight?

Isaiah.

fifty-four

Rachel sat up, alert. Hannah had made sure Isaiah was never afraid, never alone. Even in the middle of the fire, she had been there, holding him, singing that stupid pop song. And Rachel had just abandoned him. He was afraid.

Rachel forced herself up. Her body had cooled, stiffened. The temperature had dropped and the breeze was picking up. A southerly change was coming. She steadied herself against the tree's rough bark. The smell of smoke, soot, intensified. Shapes came into focus in the dark. She couldn't remember if she had shut the window, the blinds. She sprinted down the middle of the road, along the broken white line, back to the flat. Car bodies glinted in the moonlight.

Isaiah had stopped crying. The empty streets were silent. *They* were nowhere to be seen. *How long was I gone?*

The bedroom window was open two inches. Rachel struggled out of the pack, digging in the side pocket for the torch, emergency flare and oxytocin spray. It was half an idea at best, but the only flammable item she had. She took a moment to visualise what she knew she would find, and coiled her body into a weapon.

Rachel turned the key in the lock and flung herself through the door into the dark flat. She burst into the bedroom, holding the torch above her head – shining the light on Isaiah. He was still in the crib, eyes open. Alive. But breathing fast. It was him they wanted.

Mother?

They were all around Isaiah, filling the room. She could see them, not quite faces, but turning towards her, shrinking from the light. They were pretending to be Hannah, what he wanted most, offering comfort in the dark. But they *were* the dark.

'Isaiah.'

His eyes shifted to Rachel, recognising her voice.

'I'm here.'

She held the torch in her mouth to light the flare. It fizzed and flamed. The creatures shrank back from the heat and light, the pluming orange smoke, into the corners of the room, smaller, less unified. Then she lifted the spray. It wasn't an aerosol, like they'd used for party tricks at art school, but it would burn. Rachel spat out the torch, pressed the nozzle and roared all at once. The *whoof* of flame filled the top third of the room. Rachel held the flare high and scooped up Isaiah with her free hand, clutching him to her chest. He gripped her overshirt and pushed into her neck.

She swung the dying flare around in a circle. Plastic dripped down, burning her hand. There was something pathetic about *them* in the light, their shifting outlines, feeding on fear, needing so much.

When she spoke, it was from somewhere deep in her body. 'You can't have him,' she said.

There was a rush of air, *them* leaving the room, and then the flat. They were gone. She dropped the spent flare on the floor and picked up the torch, slamming shut the window. She closed the door and locked it.

'I won't do that again, Isaiah,' she said. 'I promise.'

She lit a candle and lay down on the couch, boots still on, with Isaiah on her chest, hoping her heartbeat, her warmth, would calm him. He gripped her thumb in his fist. Eventually his breathing slowed. She watched his face change and settle, the rise and fall of his back. There was a rightness to it. His little body had left an imprint on her somehow. Like glass, her cells had a memory, and kept returning to the same shape.

Rachel caught a whiff of wet dust. At first, she didn't recognise the smell or the sound – a few drops, then steadier, drumming on the roof, splattering on the pavement, the earth. Like rain. It *was* raining. Real, set-in rain.

Rachel closed her eyes, imagining the water soaking into dry ground, dampening the fires, slowing them down.

fifty-five

Rachel woke with Isaiah squirming on her chest. It was still raining, the smell of wet soot sharp in her sinuses. She struggled to her feet, stiff and sore. She changed Isaiah on a towel on the dining table. All her neatness, routines, rules, out the window. The practice she had spent years developing had melted away. She still dreamed of gathering glass, the pipe, the bubble swelling with her first breath. But for now, they just had to survive.

She folded the dirty nappy and held it out in front of her, dropping it in the laundry tub with the others.

Rachel held her breath as she wiped Isaiah down. It was amazing how much crap one little baby made. Just from milk. She patted him dry with a clean towel and fastened the last fresh nappy as best she could. Isaiah was patient, though they were not the hands, the face he was used to.

'Not as neat as your mother, I'm afraid,' she said. 'Total newbie.'

Isaiah grabbed at her fingers, rolled and wriggled. She had to coax his arms and legs into a fresh jumpsuit. She lit the barbecue to warm the last of Hannah's milk, the last of her. While he drank, more hungrily this time, she poured the hot water over a tea bag in a white Defence cup.

She was slicing the last of the bread to toast when the barbecue spluttered out. She ate a bowl of dry muesli from the cupboard instead, staring at the bike in the photo of Kyle, almost certain it was the one she had ridden off the mountain. She could only guess what had happened to him – or his body.

She lay Isaiah in the crib, humming Hannah's song to settle him. 'We'll be on our way soon.'

She rinsed the bowl and spoon, placed them upside down to drain, cleaned her teeth with bottled water, and sealed up the toiletries bag. Then she emptied out her pack and started again, with Isaiah's clothes, bottle, sanitary wipes, tissues, a clean face-cloth, water, first aid kit, torch, compass, protein bars, face masks. The express kit was no use. She would have to find milk powder. And nappies.

Rachel slipped an extra bottle of water in one outside pocket of the pack, and the last emergency flare in the other. She knew some things about *them* now. They could get inside her head, pass through human bodies, but they couldn't move through walls, buildings. And they didn't like fire. Or oxytocin.

'Time to go, Isaiah.'

She tickled him until he giggled, then tucked him into the papoose. She fitted it over her body, hand against his back, and strapped him to her. Then she squatted, to slip the straps of the pack over her shoulders, and stood. She was balanced, at least, but the strap cut into her wound and her side burned whenever she bent, turned or breathed.

The rain had petered out. Somehow there was still smoke in the air. But they wouldn't need the masks for now. Rachel returned the key to its hiding place. Crickets, frogs trilled from somewhere damp, gardens returning to wild.

The supermarket's lights were out, the front doors shattered. She listened for footsteps, the whir of a bike's tyres.

The shelves had already been picked over, and she was in unfamiliar aisles, but she found a tin of formula and two packs of disposable nappies. She leaned the pack against the shelf, stowed the nappies and formula and added a box of tampons from the next aisle, the ache in her lower back telling her what was coming. The shift of hormones, too. And forty-eight hours without her medication – no wonder she'd had a meltdown.

For a moment, she felt the old anxiety coming on, her body starting to freeze. She couldn't tell if the footsteps outside were real or imagined, human or animal. Then they passed, taking the fear with them.

A soft toy by the counter caught her eye – a fluffy-tailed orange fox. She picked it up and tucked it into the papoose.

'He's a survivor, Isaiah. Like us.'

A few plumes of grey smoke still coiled upwards from the mountains, black and scarred but no longer alight. A little more rain and perhaps some sort of renewal could start. She settled into a jog, trying to minimise the sound of her boots hitting the footpath, the pack creaking with the impact. Every step hurt her ribs, she couldn't get enough breath, and her rhythm was off, more of a swinging lurch.

Somehow, Isaiah slept. He had adjusted to her body, her movements. Perhaps, later in life, he would need to keep moving to feel calm, to sleep, and never know why.

She could no longer remember the last time she had slept peacefully, the comfort of the forest around her, the river flowing by, infiltrating her dreams, her work. Waking rested, with that sense of excitement for the day: birds stirring, and her plans for what she would do in the studio. She wiped her face on her sleeve. Her old life was becoming more and more distant. But it was something to hold onto, the hope of return.

This time the park was all trunks, bodies and shadows. Some of the shadows moved. Rachel ran on, the sharpness of pine sap keeping her alert, grounded.

She stopped at the edge of the road, opposite the university campus, the six-lane artery heading west, to another satellite centre. When it was still just a big country town, she had held up the traffic in the same spot, to allow a mother duck and her brood to cross safely. And, while still living on campus, she had driven home so drunk that the streetlights, traffic lights, headlights all blurred together, like something in the furnace. Somehow she had made it back to her single bed in the small room with the small window, and smaller sink. The brick college residence had been her first home out on her own, without her big sister. It was long gone, making way for some grand multi-purpose centre that now had no purpose.

Isaiah woke, as if sensing her emotions moving inside her like water.

'Hey, kid.'

He grabbed at her sore breasts, moving his lips – shadow

drinking. She placed her hand on the back of his neck until he settled. 'We're going to find my sister. She'll be able to look after you better.'

Rachel took a breath and ran across the road, between a new shopping complex and multi-storey car park, heading for the more familiar vine-covered buildings on the original campus.

When she reached the art-deco façade of the Film and Sound Archive Rachel slowed to catch her breath. Beyond it were the old weatherboard residences among the gums, for old white male professors. Academics like Bill.

Her memories of Bill's place were all of dinner parties with interesting people – thinkers and artists, academics from the sciences and humanities – laughter and wine. Big brains and big ideas, raging against the problems of the world, governments of the day.

She had been young then, too absorbed with her own world to really appreciate it, but she had recognised that Monique was happiest there.

She hadn't intended to go but her feet would not take her past.

She crossed the road to stand in front of the low white buildings of the art school. Her breath caught in her throat, and not just from running, the broken rib.

It was where it all started. Where she had become an artist, an adult. She was frozen by the sudden rush of mixed feelings. Feelings that had been working their way to the surface. Embarrassment, at the naïve young person she had been. Nostalgia, too, for that time as part of a creative community, the excitement of finding her path, working towards her first exhibition, her life ahead. A life of glass. And, mixed up with it all,

Hans, the man who made Canberra a hotspot for glass. The man who had driven her, too hard – who drove her still. But for a time, she had *belonged*, passed for normal among other creatives.

Rachel followed the curving wall around to the treed courtyard, ghostly birch trunks encircled by timber benches. She put her hands on the glass, to peer through the windows. The fish tank, they had called it.

For a moment it flared, fully lit, furnace blazing, someone gathering glass, someone flashing a work in progress in the glory hole, someone placing a finished piece in the annealer, someone sketching out a design in chalk on the floor. Students working in groups of two and three, conscious of each other's movements, like a dance. The maestro at the centre, conducting his orchestra. It had been her creation place. The heat, not just fire and molten glass, but of bodies, companionship. Glass making, more than any other art form, was a team effort. In her own studio, she had constructed her work-arounds, hoses and pullies, to manage alone. But it wasn't the same.

She felt *them*, moving into the courtyard. *Another trap*. And she had walked right into it. They just didn't give up. Dredging up every old feeling, until it paralysed her: humiliation, shame, inadequacy, failure . . .. Rachel braced her hands against the glass. Its strength, cool against her hot cheek, calmed the rush in her blood. She let it come – the pain. For that's all it was: grief, loss, loneliness – all the things she was clinging to, had been clinging to for years. Rachel gave it voice, a full-bodied yell from the deepest part of herself, until there was no air left and she was sure she would bring down the building.

The walls stood, unmoved. Rachel let the feelings pass through her body and away, until it had all emptied out. She was still alive, still strong. It was a gift. Everything had become so very simple. There was a precious life wriggling against her chest, whimpering, confused, and far more vulnerable than she was. Her one job was to protect him.

She sucked in three painful breaths and visualised herself striding through the low-rise city for the last time, all-powerful, a giant – without fear.

fifty-six

The university campus had been transformed, from leafy court-yards around daggy, low-slung concrete buildings to a new megaplex technology hub. When public funding had been cut, it had rebuilt its business around overseas students. But that market had evaporated during the pandemics. The dead were local students, many of them mature – retraining, upskilling. There was a pattern to the way the bodies fanned out from the lecture halls towards their cars, buses, the tram. As if they had all been released at once, fleeing the campus in terror, never to reach home.

Rachel skirted around Union Court, and the building that had once housed the cafe-bar where she had spent too many evenings. It was a gym now, and there wasn't a band poster, empty bottle or dive bar in sight. The signs for the medical research centre and hospital took her to the new part of campus. It was all glass and steel, some designer's vision for the future that had never quite come.

A timber boardwalk curved through native gardens just

beginning to mature. Branches bent under the weight of rosellas and king parrots, feeding.

The idea of reaching her destination had given her body room to speak. Her shoulder was hurting; she could barely move her right arm. Her ribs were on fire. She had started to visualise taking her pack off for good, handing over Isaiah. Hugging Monique. Sleeping for a very long time.

She paused for a moment in front of the timber and steel sign, to be certain it was real, before climbing the wide steps to the medical centre. The sun reflecting on glass was too bright. Her heart hammered in her chest, waking Isaiah.

Rachel stood in front of the entrance doors, turned her face towards the security camera and raised her left arm.

Currawongs called, the breeze carried eucalyptus oils and wattle resin over the smoke. Nothing moved inside the building or out; even the camera made no sound. Was she too late?

An older woman appeared, in a long white lab coat. It was only when she smiled and shook her head, at that particular angle, that Rachel knew it really was Monique.

The interior doors slid open. Monique stepped through and waited for them to close again before opening the external doors. She had always said labs were like submarines. They stood staring at each other through the thick glass, the extra fifteen seconds of separation unbearable after all those moments, the long journey across the landscape. Monique's face was thinner, more lined. Her hair had turned grey. But her eyes, smile, were just the same.

At last, the doors opened. Rachel staggered inside. They embraced in the void as the doors closed again, Isaiah between them. All that had happened no longer mattered. They were safe.

'Ray,' her sister said. 'How . . .' Her arms were as strong as ever, but her voice broke in her throat.

Rachel bent to rest her head on her sister's shoulder. 'I knew you were alive. I heard your voice in my head.' All the tension she had been holding in her body flowed out, dissolving into tears.

'I waited but . . .'

Rachel swallowed, wiped her face on her sleeve. 'We got there later that same day.'

'Oh, no. I'm so sorry.' Monique leaned back, hands still tight on Rachel's arms. Tears streamed down her cheeks. 'You came on the highway? Through the fires?'

Rachel nodded.

'God. I was so worried. But I was imagining you safe, on the river.'

Isaiah was awake, looking from Monique's face to Rachel's.

'And who is this?'

'His name is Isaiah.'

'But . . . ?'

'It's a long story.' Rachel swayed.

'You're hurt,' Monique said. 'Let me take him.' She loosened the papoose and lifted Isaiah free with expert hands. She rested him on her hip to release the doors, and they stepped inside.

'Come and see Bill. So you don't have to repeat yourself. And then we'll get you fixed up.'

Rachel followed Monique across a light-filled foyer, and through more double glass doors, into a lab looking across the lake. Bill and two young staff in the same white coats as her sister were leaning over a bench.

Bill looked up. 'Ray?! As I live and breathe. Is that really you?'

'I think so,' Rachel said.

He strode over, arms out wide, older and heavier than she remembered but still the same enveloping hug. 'How the hell?'

Rachel grunted as he squeezed her ribs. Bill took in her torn, blood-stained clothes hanging from her shoulders and hips. 'Looks like it's been a standard-issue Ray adventure then.'

Rachel would have laughed but it hurt too much. And there were two strangers in the room – a youngish woman with a sharp bob, and a compact man with a shaven head and black-rimmed glasses.

'Nam, Sharma, this is my sister-in-law.'

Monique rolled her eyes. 'You'll have to marry me before you get Ray as *your* sister.'

'Well, we're all family now,' Bill said.

'You've come from Nimmitabel, too?' Nam asked. His eyelashes were long and dark, magnified behind thick lenses.

The room was cool and light, all silver and white, the surfaces clear of clutter. They had power, operating screens and readouts. 'Down the coast,' Rachel said. 'You were all here when it happened?'

'We just assumed it was another virus,' Sharma said. 'That we'd be safe as long as we stayed in the lab.'

'So you weren't afraid,' Rachel said.

Bill nodded. 'Exactly. Saved by stupidity. It was only later, talking to our sister lab in Singapore, that we started to understand,' he said. 'But what about you?'

'I didn't know anything,' Rachel said. 'Then this woman turned up with a sick baby.'

Bill held Isaiah's foot in his hand. 'Another one,' he said.

'There were quite a few new mothers who survived initially,' Monique said.

'Initially?' Rachel said.

Bill glanced at Monique. 'What happened to his mother?'

'The militia,' Rachel said. 'We were out looking for her partner.'

'Oh, God,' Monique said.

'What did you mean *initially*?' Rachel said.

Nam cleared his throat. 'Some mothers survived but then their . . . immunity seems to wear off.'

'Once they stop breastfeeding,' Monique said. 'Sometimes before. We think it's the hormones.'

'Hannah *was* starting to act differently,' Rachel said. 'She'd been so strong.'

Nam's forehead creased. 'Wait, if he's not your child, how did *you* survive?'

'Hannah and I worked together, to kind of keep the creatures out of our heads,' Rachel said.

'Ray is on anti-anxiety medication,' Monique said. 'And you've been taking the drops?'

They were all staring at her.

'I haven't actually taken either for days. I was able to fight them off on my own last night.'

Monique shifted Isaiah to the other hip. 'How?'

'An emergency flare and oxytocin spray. Like a little explosion. I don't know if it was the fire or the oxytocin – or both. But now that I can see them, I'm just not scared.'

The corners of Bill's mouth twitched. 'You can *see* the creatures?'

'Hannah could, too. In the end,' she said.

Nam pushed his glasses back up onto the bridge of his nose, as if to look at Rachel more closely.

Isaiah was squirming, reaching for Rachel.

'I can take him,' Rachel said. 'Some army guy said you're developing an antidote?'

'We're trialling something. A synthetic version of oxytocin,' Bill said. 'With some other things thrown in.'

'We tested it on ourselves first,' Nam said. 'Made some tweaks for Defence personnel. Ideally, we'd have a proper trial. We don't really know how long it lasts. But we figure we need to get it out to survivors.'

Sharma nodded. 'The idea is to administer it to as many as possible within a short window. Give us a chance to eradicate the creatures.'

Rachel took in the pile of boxes by the door. 'How many people are we talking about?'

'Forty-three in the Parliament House mob,' Bill said. 'Forty-four counting you. Now we've got communications up again, reports are starting to come in of more across the country. We'll establish the hospital as a recovery centre first. And then set up others.'

Rachel leaned against the bench. 'Are you including these militia?'

Nam and Sharma exchanged a look.

Bill shook his head. 'Not at this stage.'

'Do they know about the serum?'

'We don't think so,' Sharma said.

fifty-seven

Monique examined Isaiah first, running her hands over his entire body, taking his temperature and listening to his heart, and somehow keeping him giggling and smiling at the same time.

'How long since his mother died?'

'Hannah.' Rachel struggled to calculate hours, dark and light. 'Yesterday morning.'

'How have you been feeding him?'

'Hannah was expressing milk so we could mix in the antibiotics,' Rachel said. 'But I've used all that.'

Monique made a noise in her throat. 'He had an infection?'

'Pneumonia maybe. That's why Hannah came to me, and why we walked to yours.'

'He's recovering well. But we'll need to get some formula and nappies.'

'I've got all that,' Rachel said. She watched Monique quarter fill the sink with warm water and baby soap and sit Isaiah among the suds, sponging down his whole body. 'Who are these militia people? Why aren't we working together?'

'They pre-date all this. They were behind the protests, disruptions. Even in Nimmitabel they effectively had us under siege for months. One of the leaders had just had a child. She used their immunity to rally people, set herself up as some sort of saviour. Other survivors are coming in to join them: refugees, escapees, the homeless.'

'Outliers,' Rachel said.

'They're anti-Defence, anti-government. So they won't co-operate with us. Some Defence personnel have defected. And, we think, supplied them with weapons.'

'Why would they do that?'

'They want to start a different sort of society – not just resurrect the old one.'

'About time.'

'I knew you'd say that,' Monique said. 'Except that many of these people have mental health issues. It's not a cohesive or progressive movement. They shut down our First Nations primary school, the abortion clinic in Cooma. I can't tell you how many times a brick was thrown through the surgery windows when my single mothers group met. The militia have accessed oxytocin from chemists and medical suppliers. In its raw form, oxytocin can exaggerate those conditions, and cause aggression, social separation.'

Rachel clicked her fingers. 'You're thinking that the defecting Defence personnel have told them about the serum. This place.'

Monique nodded. 'Existing oxytocin supplies will be dwindling. And our tailored version is much safer. I'm *more* worried that they want the children. Thinking they'll protect them. To build this new society.'

Monique knocked on the door. 'Ready for me to strap those ribs?'

'Just a sec.'

Monique stood behind her, watching her work. 'Is that Hannah?'

'Yeah.'

'She's beautiful,' Monique said.

Rachel nodded. 'It's for Isaiah.'

'I'm so proud of you.'

Rachel sniffed back tears. 'I made a lot of mistakes.'

'Oh, Ray.' Monique put her hands on Rachel's shoulders, and bent to kiss the top of her head.

Mon helped her slip her shirt back on over the strapping, a little tighter than was comfortable.

'Are you ready for something to eat? You picked a good day. Nam is cooking.'

Rachel's stomach was growling, responding to the rich spices wafting from the kitchen. She followed her sister down the pale corridor. 'Solar?'

'When they built the hospital, they made the whole centre self-sufficient.'

The dining area was just a staff lunchroom. But a pleasant one, with timber panelling, bookshelves, a wall of indoor plants, and floor-to-ceiling windows looking over the gardens and the sky, blood red over the Brindabellas.

'Will you stay here?'

Sharma looked up from setting the table. 'They want us to

move up to the House after inoculation. Where they can guarantee our safety, but . . .'

'We prefer life above ground,' Nam said from the stove.

'They'll let everyone upstairs once they've been protected,' Monique said, giving Rachel a stern look. She wasn't going to give up on the needle.

'Did the army clean up the Triangle before or after?' Rachel said.

'They evacuated parts of the city early on, barricaded them off,' Sharma said.

'What about the militia?' Rachel said.

'That's the next problem,' Bill said. He set the rice steamer on the table with a serving spoon and went back for the curry.

'The vegetables are from the campus garden,' Nam said.

Rachel's mouth was watering. 'And the rest?'

'Pilfered from the restaurant next door,' Sharma said. 'We mounted a raid.'

'We have enough fresh food to live well for months,' Bill said.

Sharma spooned rice into round white bowls. 'They won't really force us out, will they?'

'Never!' Bill tucked his serviette into his collar.

Monique put her hand on Bill's. 'We'll go voluntarily if that's what they advise, won't we?'

Bill gave an exaggerated shrug. 'Let's hope it doesn't come to that. In the meantime, let's eat.'

fifty-nine

The black van backed up to the rear entrance of the medical centre right on nine. The driver stayed behind the wheel. Two uniforms got out. The woman opened the van doors. The man walking towards them was McNeal.

'Morning everyone,' McNeal said. 'Big day today, huh?'

Bill shook his outstretched hand. 'Colonel McNeal, this is Dr Monique Sanders, Dr Nam Trang, and Dr Sanders' sister, Rachel,' Bill said. 'Dr Rumbachs is on the loading dock.'

'Rachel, why didn't you just say so?' McNeal said.

'Sorry,' Rachel said. 'I didn't know what to think. And I don't think very well underground.'

McNeal nodded. 'Well, I'm glad you're okay.'

Sharma trolleyed the boxes three at a time from the lab to the door, Nam took them to the top of the ramp and Bill, Monique, Rachel and McNeal passed them by hand, a human conveyor belt, to Lawson, the officer at the van. The boxes were only light, and Rachel's position involved the least lifting and turning but, even so, the movement caused her pain.

Monique shook her head and would have berated her, but they needed all hands to move the load as quickly as possible. With almost the entire stock of the serum out in the open, the centre's doors unsecured, they were vulnerable.

Bill was whistling, ever the optimist. And maybe he was right. The sky was the clearest it had been since they arrived, birds were feeding all around them. It was almost possible to think of returning to some sort of normal. A path to recovery.

'Your child's all right?' McNeal said, handing a box to Rachel.

'He's fine,' Rachel said. 'Thank you, for rescuing us.'

The van was still only half full when the rosellas and parrots took flight all at once. A vibration came up through the ground, through Rachel's boots, into her legs. All the hair on her body stood on end. A vehicle. And then human feet, running.

Nam shouted from the loading dock. 'Militia! Everybody inside!'

They were under attack. Two shots passed close enough for Rachel to feel the displacement of air. She threw, rather than placed, boxes in the van. McNeal slammed the doors after Lawson and banged his hand on the rear of the vehicle. 'Go. Go. Go.'

The driver was already going. The van screeched out of the cul-de-sac and onto the road, Lawson firing from her window. McNeal did his best to cover them, spraying shots in an arc as he retreated to the ramp. Rachel saw a line of bullet holes appear on the side of the van, and then it was gone.

One of the militia fell, clutching her leg. That left at least a dozen surging towards the back of the medical centre. There were more streaming in from the oval and gardens. There was so much noise, movement, that Rachel could no longer make sense of what was happening. They were badly outnumbered, probably surrounded.

She ran for the doors. Bill and Monique were ahead of her, trying to push boxes back inside.

'Leave them!'

Rachel saw the impact of the shot before she heard it, as if in slow motion. *Thlunk*, right in the middle of Bill's back, pushing his chest out, his arms back. He fell full length, hitting the concrete just short of the entrance. Sharma was screaming. Rachel and Monique dragged Bill through the doors, a trail of bright blood behind them. McNeal was still shooting from the dock.

Everyone was shouting at once. The noise was closing down Rachel's thoughts. And she could hear Isaiah crying.

'Help me,' her sister said.

McNeal locked the fire doors behind them, shutting out some of the sound. Together, they carried Bill into the infirmary and laid him out on the bed. He was breathing but his eyes were closed, his face white. He had already lost a lot of blood. The bullet had gone right through, the wound in his chest bleeding, too.

Monique was moving fast, gathering equipment, washing her hands up to the elbows. 'Nam, I'll need you,' she said. 'Ray, you get Isaiah. Sharma, can you let them know what's happened up at the House? Find out if they got the serum.'

Rachel stared at Bill's unmoving face, her sister's steady hands. 'Is he going to make it?'

Monique cut through Bill's shirt with surgical scissors. 'I don't know.'

Isaiah reached for her. 'Hey,' Rachel said. 'We're on the move again, kid.'

She changed and dressed him in record time. Monique had shown her how to rig the papoose so that she could carry Isaiah on her back, which was much more comfortable. She threw their things in the pack, dragging it into the lab.

Designed for medical emergencies, the accidental release of chemical or organic contagions, it could be sealed off from the inside. Whether it could withstand a military attack was another question.

McNeal barked into the satellite phone, frowning at the security cameras. 'I've got nineteen here. Three down. Only twelve are armed. But it looks like the others are carrying some sort of explosives.'

The militia were concentrating their gunfire on one of the outer doors – high-powered rifles and some form of semi-automatic.

Rachel watched over McNeal's shoulder as the outer door cracked and then shattered. Two women and one man, all in black, stepped inside the void and started stacking something against the inner doors. Their faces were covered, but from the way they moved, Rachel was sure they were only young.

'Tell them everything you see,' McNeal said, handing her the phone. 'I'm going up on the roof. To try to stop them using that.'

'Wait,' Rachel said, grabbing his arm. She was watching something else on the screen. The darkness flooding the oval, as big as the smoke cloud had been over the fires. 'The creatures are here, too.'

sixty

Rachel watched a thin stream twist down from the black cloud to pick off the militia on the outer perimeter. A young woman looked up as the shadow passed between her and the sun. When her mouth opened in a scream, they funnelled in, tamping the noise with themselves, pouring into her body. The militia did not break formation but fell where they were, one by one, knowing what was coming but unable to stop it.

The swarm seemed to grow in strength and unite more fully, such that Rachel could no longer see individual shapes. They shifted and moved in mesmerising patterns, like the flocks of birds flying as one that she used to see at dusk. Then they passed out of sight of the cameras.

They were massing above the research building. The three militia by the doors were intent on setting up the explosives, carrying in their gear. It wasn't the militia *they* were after, but what was inside.

McNeal reached for the satellite phone. 'Where's our backup? We've got creatures here. Big time.'

They were surrounded. Under attack from above and behind, human and non-human. Bill was badly injured. There was so much stacked against them, they couldn't fight everything. They had to work with it, somehow.

Rachel watched the young man outside fumbling with the wiring. 'What if we let the militia blow up the lab?' she said. 'But we lure *them* inside first?'

McNeal nodded. 'Could work. We open the front doors, leave those guys to their thing at the back. Get everyone out the fire exit at the side. Lock them in. And *boom!*'

Nam spoke from the doorway. 'But we'll lose the rest of the serum.'

Sharma was on the satellite phone. She nodded, held up her hand. 'The others got through with the boxes we had packed.'

'When I sprayed the oxy on the flare, it ignited. And reduced the creatures. Maybe the canisters will, too. If they're part of the explosion? Kill them, even.'

'Maybe,' Nam said.

'How do we get them inside?' McNeal asked.

'Oh, they'll come,' Rachel said.

Nam dropped his hands from his head. 'But someone will have to shut the front doors after them.'

'I'll do that,' Rachel said. 'Just get everyone to the fire exit.'

It would all come down to timing. Rachel skidded along the hall to the infirmary, Isaiah bouncing on her back, hanging on to her hair.

Monique was still working on Bill, closing up the wound.

'How is he?'

Monique shook her head. 'Punctured lung. Some internal damage. Too soon to tell.'

'We've got to get out. Now. The creatures are here. All of them, it looks like. We're going to draw them into the building and seal them in. Hopefully just before the militia blow the back doors.'

'Ray, I can't move Bill,' Monique said.

'We have to.' Rachel pushed the gurney alongside the operating table with a clash and stood behind Bill's head.

Monique stared at Rachel a moment before moving around to grab Bill's feet. 'One, two, three.'

Together they heaved him onto the trolley. Monique winced at the impact, but unhooked the drip bag and dropped it between Bill's legs. They manoeuvred the bed through the door and into the hallway. One of the wheels had a wobble, squeaking all the way.

'I just need to grab some supplies,' Monique said.

'See you outside,' Rachel said.

'I can take Isaiah.'

Rachel shook her head. 'I need him.'

She ran back to the main doors. She opened the interior door and stepped through. The sky was black with creatures, swirling around the building, searching for a way in.

Rachel unhooked the papoose, feeling more than Isaiah's warmth leaving her – a physical pain.

'I'm sorry, kid.'

She placed him on the ground and stepped away. Knowing that he felt the separation as she did, that he would be afraid, that he would start to cry. His eyes hadn't left her face.

Then she pressed the green button on the wall to release the outer doors.

The glass slid open. Isaiah started to wail. The dark cloud paused, swung around, and spiralled downwards. They streamed inside, circling around Isaiah, until they formed a solid black dome, as if it was exactly what they had been waiting for. As if they had read her mind – or pushed her, somehow, to do precisely this.

I'm right here, Isaiah.

Rachel forced herself to be still until they were all inside, almost filling the foyer, lab and hallways. They couldn't see. Not the way she did. They felt their way by fear. Without it, she was invisible. With the slightest movement, she rocked back on the button to close the doors with her hip.

Then she walked forwards, right into the midst of the thick darkness that was them. They recoiled, as if recognising her.

'We're not afraid of you. And this child – is *mine*.' She lit the last flare.

It wasn't quite a sound they made, more an intake of air. Before rushing down, as one, a shape with a head, limbs, in one last grab for Isaiah.

But Rachel was faster. She scooped up Isaiah, clutching him to her chest, her body flooding with warmth. His face relaxed; trust strong between them. She waved the flare in a wide circle above her head and then threw it up in the air, into their centre.

And ran. Rachel grabbed her pack, slinging it over one arm. The way ahead was brighter. They were diminished – but not gone. There was still fear somewhere in that space. *Mon.* Afraid of losing Bill. The only option was to keep the creatures inside, hoping that the explosion, the oxy, would be enough. She juggled Isaiah, managed to get her other arm through the strap of the pack without breaking her stride.

She made it to the end of the corridor to see the others, waiting by the exit: Nam, McNeal, Sharma. But no Monique, no gurney. Maybe they were already outside. They could not afford to wait. McNeal opened the door. Rachel signalled for them to go. They blurred and disappeared into the square of bright sunlight.

Rachel turned at the sound of the squeaking wheel. Monique was behind them, pushing Bill, his head flopped to the side, a sealed canister of serum propped on the end of the gurney, between Bill's legs. And, darkening the corridor, rushing up behind her sister, what was left of the creatures.

Rachel's boots were stuck to the grey linoleum floor. She needed to hold the creatures off somehow, get between them and her sister, just for thirty seconds. Or close the door, and lock them all in. Finish the job. But she had Isaiah now.

Monique read it all on Rachel's face. She half-smiled. 'Go.'

Her sister reached for the canister and turned to face them, still pushing the gurney backwards, towards the door.

Isaiah whimpered, sensing the creatures close again. Rachel's body took over, turning and leaping in one movement, propelling her body along the shrinking corridor. Towards the light. Somehow her legs kept going, she kept her grip on Isaiah, and she was out through the door into open space, fresh air, sunshine.

She heard the fire door slam shut behind her. And then it was all noise, heat and light. The ground came up fast. She couldn't tell what was *them* and what was the explosion. There was so much *pressure*. Until the second noise, the *whoomph*, when something let go. They were no longer creeping into her mind, no longer clouding her vision.

Dust and debris rained down, like the soot and ash of only days ago. Her ears were ringing, the noise a blade inside her head. Something warm was running down her face. She could make out McNeal crouched behind a hospital minibus, hands over his face, Nam and Sharma beside him, holding each other.

Rachel checked on Isaiah, in the cave beneath her body. His eyes were wide, a little glazed, and there was a graze on his nose, but he was alive. She struggled to her knees. Bits of rubble tumbled from her pack. It had shielded her from the blast. She took a shuddering breath and turned to face the emptiness she could already feel.

There was no one there. No one between her and what was left of the building, a tangle of upended shapes and angles, smoking, steaming and burning. Just ash-covered gravel and a gentle rain of debris.

'No!' Rachel slumped forward. Isaiah moved against her, his face scrunched with discomfort, maybe pain, but she had nothing left. Had Monique not made it to the door? Or had she closed it on purpose? *It should have been me.*

And then Nam was there, helping her to her feet. His lips were moving but no sound came out. Everything was far away, as if in a dream. A nightmare. He touched her cheek, showed her the blood, bright against so much grey. Rachel wiped her face on her sleeve, touched the cut on her eyebrow with her fingertips.

She moved towards the wreckage but Nam grabbed hold of

her pack and held her back. There was no building to search. Nothing whole to find. He guided her towards the bus. The gravel shifted beneath her boots but made no sound. Isaiah clung to her neck so tight it hurt.

Nam helped her up the steps, his face perfectly still but for the tears tracking through the dust on his cheeks. McNeal threw two serum cannisters onto the passenger seat and climbed in, strong arms on the steering wheel, jaw tight. Sharma was struggling to close the door, shoulders heaving. And then they were moving.

Rachel stared back at the smoking remains of the medical centre. 'But they were right behind me.'

sixty-one

Rachel hummed Hannah's song as they raced through the empty streets. The vibration distracted her from the ringing in her ears. Nam produced a medical field kit from a bag under the seat, cleaned the cut on her eye. It was nothing compared to the great hole torn in her. Mon had been there Rachel's whole life, and now she was not.

Sharma was still sobbing, though she made no sound.

Across the lake, Parliament House seemed to have grown, filling the foreground. Now that she knew there were people inside, other children, it seemed a warmer place. A city within the city.

Just as she was wondering how they would cross the bridge, McNeal sped into a car park, winding down and down, opened a grilled door with a pass, and swept into the concrete tunnel under the lake everyone had whispered about without really believing. Rachel focused on the line of orange lights along the walls, the numbers working backwards from five.

She could no longer hear Mon's voice in her head. Although

she knew what her sister would say, and the love was still there, would always be there, it was not the same. Rachel was on her own.

But not alone. Isaiah gripped her arm, strong enough now to leave a bruise. There was a lot she didn't know. But she would figure it out. They would figure it out together. She lost time, beneath the weight of water pressing down. Something had ended. So many things. And something else had begun.

They emerged in a broad, open space. McNeal stopped in front of a concrete stairwell and wide lift, guard booths either side. *The Bunker.* They were beneath Parliament House.

The door opened, Sharma and Nam climbed out, still coated in dust from the explosion. Nam took Rachel's pack, offered his hand to help her out.

McNeal turned, leaned over the seats, gesturing that she should follow the others. They were all waiting for her and Isaiah.

Rachel shook her head. 'We're going home.' She could barely hear her own words, but she could feel them in her chest.

Nam leaned in. 'Rachel. You're in shock.'

They all were. But without Monique she wasn't staying another minute. Recovery couldn't really begin until she was home, back on the river.

'Enough,' she said.

McNeal glanced at the others. 'Okay. Take one of our vehicles. Anything else you need.'

'I have a car.'

Nam placed her pack on the floor of the bus. 'Let me examine Isaiah, at least.' Nam felt him all over, checking his ears and eyes, clicking his fingers, first where Isaiah could see and then out of sight, below him.

'He's lost his hearing,' Nam said, squeezing Isaiah's foot. 'Probably only temporary. But there may be some damage to his eardrums.'

If that were the only mark left on him, she would be grateful.

Sharma leaned in to hug Rachel. 'I'm so sorry,' she said. 'They were like parents to us.'

McNeal took the ring road around the base of the hill, back to the car park. It seemed like weeks since she and Hannah had parked there. Yet everything had happened so quickly she had never quite been able to catch her breath.

McNeal pulled up in front of the Beast, which was just as she had left it.

'Are you sure you won't stay a few days?' he said, glancing again at Isaiah.

Her ears were ringing, sounds approaching and retreating in waves. Rachel still had to read his lips to be certain of what he was saying. The Beast was battered by fire, no longer perfect, but hers. 'I'm sure.' Rachel stepped out of the bus, into fresh air, onto solid ground.

'Well, you know where we are,' McNeal said. 'Stay safe. And take good care of him. These children, they're our future.' His voice cracked.

Rachel saw him properly for the first time. 'You lost your family.'

'I did,' he said. 'My wife and two little boys.'

332

'I'm sorry.'

'Take one of these. Just in case,' he said. 'There are four doses inside.'

She took the cannister, the handle cool in her hand.

Then the door was closing. McNeal saluted. Rachel raised her hand in farewell.

What was left of the Beast's tarp was coated with a layer of white ash, blackened leaves. Their gear was still underneath, though damp from the rain. The two sleeping bags pulled her up for a moment. *Hannah.*

Monique. Bill. Rachel dropped in the pack and leaned against the tray. She hadn't even told Monique that she loved her. Let alone thanked her for everything that she had done for her over the years. So much left unsaid.

Isaiah gripped the pocket of her shirt, pushing at the button with his tiny fingers.

'Hey.'

Rachel unlocked the door and slid behind the wheel. 'I don't have a baby seat, kid. You'll have to stay strapped to me,' she said.

She pulled the soft toy from her pack and put it in his clenching and unclenching fists. The engine turned over and caught. There wasn't much room for her to steer or move the stick shift around Isaiah but she could manage. She would have to. Vibration and noise were coming back: birds and cicadas busy in the eucalypts. She wound down her window, rested her elbow on the ledge. The thought of home, the return of her hearing, the pain, had all her senses on a sharp edge. She reversed out, wincing as she turned the ute's heavy wheel, to steer them back onto the road.

She stuck to the shoulder where she could, working her way around the cars. The air was cloying, fading death mixed with eucalyptus and pine needles – a smell she would never forget.

Isaiah threw the fox into the corner of the dash. Then pumped his fists to have it back, pulling the face that meant he was about to cry. Rachel reached for the toy, still watching the road, the approaches either side, and handed it back. Only for him to do it all over again. It was a game she couldn't play while driving.

'Look after Foxy,' she said. 'He needs you.'

Isaiah grabbed hold of the toy with both hands and squeezed.

'Right. Let's get out of this damn city.'

sixty-two

Rachel pulled into the service station just over the border.

The glass doors were open. Empty food packets swirled around the bowsers. She scanned for movement in the stranded cars, inside the building, the bare surrounds, the industrial buildings behind. Would she always have to be so vigilant?

She tried to visualise the journey ahead, the impediments they might face. Through two towns, then the back way, the gravel road down to the valley that was her home. There would be fewer cars, fewer problems than on the Kings Highway, down Clyde Mountain. All those hairpins, clogged with cars. But first, they needed gas.

The single LPG bowser was up the back, behind the recharging points. And, *thank you, universe*, it was working. She sat Isaiah up on the seat, with the door open so he could see her, while she filled up.

Even before Monique had taught her to drive, she had taught her to take care of the Beast. Washing it, checking the oil and tyre pressure, filling it with fuel. Going in to pay at the counter had been excruciating. Everyone knew who she was, who they were. Monique had insisted, as payment for driving lessons, she said. But they both knew it was to force her to socialise, to conduct the transactions she preferred to avoid, so that one day she could be independent.

She had learned to manage. But how was she supposed to go on without her sister in the world?

Rachel wiped her face, only seeing the movement at the last minute, his raised arm reflected in the car window. She dodged – driving back hard with her elbow. Still, he had her around the chest, crushing her ribs against his body. Rachel roared – with pain and rage. She stamped on his foot with all the power she had left in her body.

He let go.

Rachel pivoted. His worn jeans, flannelette shirt and work boots were a long way from the black and khaki Rachel had come to recognise as militia. She backed towards the open door of the car, to shield Isaiah. The man shook his head. Behind her, Isaiah grabbed hold of her pocket.

'What do you want?' She kept her breaths slow and even.

'Have you got this vaccine they're talking about?'

She nodded.

'Show me.'

She had to move to reach the canister.

Isaiah gurgled.

The man's eyes shifted, understood.

She handed over the canister and turned to pick up Isaiah, held him tight.

For a moment, the man's gaze lingered on the Beast, and she

worried that he might take it, too. But there were all the cars in the world to choose from, with more comfort and better performance, without burns and dints. 'You can hear that thing coming a mile off,' he said. 'Just so you know.'

Rachel breathed in through her nose and out through her mouth, but the effort hurt her ribs, made her cough. Isaiah wrinkled his forehead.

'Where you headed?'

'Nimmitabel,' she lied.

'What's there?'

'My big sister.' Rachel's voice quavered.

'Many survivors?'

'Some,' she said.

'Militia?'

Rachel shook her head.

'Army?'

'No.'

The gas nozzle was still in the car's tank. She was holding Isaiah, only one arm left to fight with. Her injured side, at that.

'A boy, eh? Yours?'

Rachel nodded, rubbing Isaiah's back, as much for her benefit as his.

The man whistled. A little girl, four or five, emerged from the service-station shop, eating a chocolate bar.

'My daughter,' he said.

The girl took in Isaiah and Rachel, her eyes no longer those of a child.

'Sorry – thought you were militia. They killed my partner,' the man said. 'Her mother. We'll leave you be.'

Rachel nodded.

'Are they really gone?' the girl said.

'I hope so,' Rachel said.

The man and his daughter walked towards a new RV parked on the street. Rachel unhooked the nozzle, returned it to its cradle and wiped her still-shaking hands with paper towel. For a moment, she thought she saw a shadow, a child-sized shape pulling back behind the toilet block. But then it was gone.

The RV pulled out, headed down the middle of the road, into Queanbeyan. Rachel lowered herself onto the old leather seat, gritting her teeth. She sat a moment, hands on the wheel. She bent to pick the fox from the floor, reinstalled Isaiah in the papoose, and strapped him to her body.

'Not much of a mother so far, am I?'

He only smiled. All gums, and no idea how close they had come, again, to a terrible end. He squashed Foxy in his fists, learning how to use his hands, his body.

She sniffed back tears, took a deep breath and let it out. Then turned the key. The Beast rumbled to life. 'C'mon, kid. To the open road.'

sixty-three

Rachel pulled over at the edge of the escarpment. The fire had burned so hot through the mountains, it was as if a bomb had been dropped. The undergrowth was gone, the canopy; she could see what shouldn't be seen, right through to the next slope and the one after that and the mountain beyond. There was nothing but black trunks and black ground. It still smelled of soot.

She couldn't hear a single animal, bird or insect. Nothing moved. Just dead and empty forest. A graveyard. What had been a rainforested valley on the other side of the road, running through to the Clyde, a Gondwana remnant that had never burned, was gone. Unlike eucalypts, banksias, it could not grow back after fire. It had survived the Jurassic but not the Anthropocene.

The blackened mountains rolled down to the ragged coastline, the white-fringed sea. Her valley lay below them, green and untouched, the river running through it. As it always had, and would for all of time.

She followed the line of the river to where it widened and

slowed, the gorge and cliff behind her place. Her forest. She could just make out the sun glinting on the roof of the studio, between the trees, still there. No fire or tempest had taken it.

She leaned back against the bonnet, hand over her mouth, trying to be still for Isaiah's sake. But she couldn't stop what was coming: relief. Followed by a great wave of grief, for the trees, the wildlife, for everything that had been lost, the sorrow in every blackened leaf. Monique, Hannah, Bill.

And there was gratitude, small and pathetic, that her little place had somehow survived. She knew there was no *why*, no reason. It was not something she deserved. It was more humbling than her own body, still standing, against all that had happened. The life she had been given.

She had woken Isaiah. He placed his hands on her chest, as if to ease the ache there. But that was not his job. She wiped her eyes and drew in a shaky breath.

Rachel set up the little cooker on the tailgate of the ute, heating the formula, sterilising the bottle. She made herself a cup of sweet tea while Isaiah drank, and munched on a chocolate muesli bar, staring out with fresh wonder, taking in every terrible detail, and committing it to memory.

When she looked more closely, she could see grass beginning to shoot. The cycads were green at their centre and would soon send out new leaves. One blackened tree fern was topped with tight spirals, new fronds waiting to uncoil. The forest would not be what it had been, but life would return.

On the drive, she had been daydreaming about glass. Great molten sheets of it. Her hands were itching, in that particular way; needing to make something. She had always meant to do more with the spare room. It was kind of ordinary but got beautiful morning light.

'What about a wall of water? With river stones beneath. Maybe a timber boat.'

Isaiah squirmed against her, grunting and huffing in his own little language.

'Okay, okay.' She unclipped the papoose, lifted him out. She held him, one arm under his arms. '*That* is the ocean. Your mother loved the water.' She pointed with her free arm, an exaggerated movement.

Isaiah grinned, pink-gummed, because she was grinning.

She held him high in the air, on top of the Great Dividing Range, spinning him around and around until he giggled. Her body hurt but it would heal. Soon she would be strong again. Stronger than before.

'See that river, that bend there? That's where we're going. That's home.'

Acknowledgements

Thanks to the teams at Hachette Australia and Little, Brown UK, particularly: Robert Watkins, Lucy Dauman, Ed Wood, Rebecca Saunders, Thalia Proctor, Brigid Mullane, Emma Rafferty, Daniel Pilkington, Lee Moir, Emma Harvey, Andy Hine, Jemma Rowe and Kate Taperell. Thanks also to Charlotte Stroomer and Marco Gonzales.

I'm grateful to Canberra Glassworks and glass artist, Alexandra Chambers, for glassblowing tuition and anecdotes. All mistakes are mine.

Thanks also to John Blay, and his books *Wild Nature*, *Back Country* and *On Track*, which informed Rachel's walk and my own research journeys.

My description of brumbies owes a great deal to a scene featuring musk oxen in Barry Lopez's *Arctic Dreams*.

Hannah's song is 'Getaway Car' by Taylor Swift (for you, Robert).

Rachel is named for two strong women. Rachael Scott, who has been a steadying voice my entire adult life, especially during the writing of this book. And marine biologist, writer and conservationist, Rachel Carson, known by those close to her as Ray. Carson's life is a reminder that one person can always make a difference.